RANGER'S APPRENTICE

BOOK 6: THE SIEGE OF MACINDAW

RANGER'S APPRENTICE

by JOHN FLANAGAN

RANGER'S APPRENTICE

BOOK 6: THE SIEGE OF MACINDAW

JOHN FLANAGAN

PHILOMEL BOOKS
PENGUIN YOUNG READERS GROUP

Published in Australia by Random House Australia Children's Books.
First American Edition published 2009 by
PHILOMEL BOOKS
A division of Penguin Young Readers Group. Published by The Penguin Group.
Penguin Group (USA) Inc., 375 Hudson Street, New York, NY 10014, U.S.A.
Penguin Group (Canada), 90 Eglinton Avenue East, Suite 700, Toronto, Ontario M4P 2Y3, Canada
(a division of Pearson Penguin Canada Inc.).
Penguin Books Ltd, 80 Strand, London WC2R 0RL, England.
Penguin Ireland, 25 St. Stephen's Green, Dublin 2, Ireland (a division of Penguin Books Ltd).
Penguin Group (Australia), 250 Camberwell Road, Camberwell, Victoria 3124, Australia
(a division of Pearson Australia Group Pty Ltd).
Penguin Books India Pvt Ltd, 11 Community Centre, Panchsheel Park, New Delhi - 110 017, India.
Penguin Group (NZ), 67 Apollo Drive, Rosedale, North Shore 0632, New Zealand
(a division of Pearson New Zealand Ltd.)
Penguin Books (South Africa) (Pty) Ltd, 24 Sturdee Avenue, Rosebank, Johannesburg 2196, South Africa.
Penguin Books Ltd, Registered Offices: 80 Strand, London WC2R 0RL, England.

Published simultaneously in Canada. Printed in the United States of America.
Design by Marikka Tamura.
Text set in Adobe Jenson.
Library of Congress Cataloging-in-Publication Data
Flanagan, John (John Anthony)
The siege of Macindaw / John Flanagan. — 1st American ed.
p. cm. — (Ranger's apprentice ; bk. 6)
Summary: Now a full-fledged Ranger, Will must rescue his friend Alyss from a rogue
knight and uncover vital information needed to ward off a Scotti invasion.
[1. Heroes—Fiction. 2. War—Fiction. 3. Fantasy.] I. Title.
PZ7.F598284Si 2009
[Fic]—dc22
2008032630
ISBN 978-0-399-25033-0
1 3 5 7 9 10 8 6 4 2

For my sister Joan:
Publicist, columnist, author.
Pathfinder for the rest of us.

1

Gundar Hardstriker, captain and helmsman of the Skandian ship *Wolfcloud*, chewed disconsolately on a stringy piece of tough smoked beef.

His crew were huddled under rough shelters among the trees, talking quietly, eating and trying to stay warm around the small smoky fires that were all they could manage in this weather. This close to the coast, the snow usually turned to cold sleet in the middle of the day, refreezing as the afternoon wore on. He knew the crew were looking to him for a way out of this. And he knew that soon he would have to tell them he had no answers for them. They were stranded in Araluen, with no hope of escape.

Fifty meters away, *Wolfcloud* lay beached on the riverbank, canted to one side. Even from this distance, his seaman's eye could make out the slight twist a third of the way along her hull, and the sight of it came close to breaking his heart. To a Skandian, his ship was almost a living thing, an extension of himself, an expression of his own being.

Now his ship was ruined, her keel irreparably broken, her hull twisted. She was good for nothing but turning into lumber and fire-wood as the winter weather wrapped its cold hands further around them. So far he had been able to avoid stripping the ship, but he knew he couldn't wait much longer. They would need the wood to build more substantial huts and to burn as firewood. But as long as she still looked like a ship, even with that damnable twist to her hull, he could retain some sense of his pride at being a skirl, or ship's captain.

The voyage had been a disaster from start to finish, he reflected gloomily. They had set out to raid Gallic and Iberian coastal villages, staying well away from Araluen as they did so. Raids on the Araluen coast were few and far between these days, since the Skandian Oberjarl had signed a treaty with the Araluen King. They weren't actually forbidden to raid. But they were discouraged by Oberjarl Erak, and only a very stupid or foolhardy skirl would be keen to face Erak's style of discouragement.

But Gundar and his men had been the last of the raiding fleet to reach the Narrow Sea, and they found the villages either empty—ransacked by earlier ships—or prewarned and ready to take revenge on a single late raider. There had been hard fighting. He had lost several men and was left with nothing to show for it. Finally, as a last resort, he had landed on an island off the southeast coast of Araluen, desperate for provisions to see him and his men through the winter on the long journey back north.

He smiled sadly as he thought of it. If there had been a bright spot in the trip, that had been it. Prepared to fight and lose more lives, desperate to feed themselves, the Skandian crew had been greeted by a young Ranger—the very one who had fought beside Erak in the battle against the Temujai some years back.

Surprisingly, the Ranger had offered to feed them. He'd even invited them to a banquet that night in the castle, along with the lo-cal dignitaries and their wives. Gundar's smile broadened at the memory of that evening as he recalled how his rough-and-tumble sailors had stayed on their best manners, humbly asking their table companions to pass the meat, please, or requesting just a little more ale in their drinking mugs. These were men who were accustomed to cursing heartily, tearing legs off roast boar with their bare hands and occasionally swilling their ale straight from the keg. Their attempts at mingling with polite society would have been the basis of some great stories back in Skandia.

His smile faded. Back in Skandia. He had no idea now how they would get back to Skandia. Or even if they would ever return home. They had left Seacliff Island well fed and provisioned for the long trip. The Ranger had even provided them with the means for a small profit from the trip, in the form of a slave.

The man's name was Buttle. John Buttle. He was a criminal—a thief and a murderer—and his presence in Araluen was a source of potential trouble for the Ranger. As a favor, the young man had asked Gundar to take him as a slave to Skandia. The skirl naturally agreed. The man was strong and fit, and he'd fetch a good price when they got home.

But would they ever see Hallasholm again? They'd sailed slap into a massive storm just short of Point Sentinel and were driven south and west before it.

As they came closer to the Araluen coast, Gundar had ordered Buttle's chains struck off. They were heading for a lee shore, a situation all sailors dread, and there was a good chance that the ship would not survive. The man should have a chance, Gundar thought.

He could still feel the sickening crunch as *Wolfcloud* had smashed down on a hidden rock. At the time, he felt it as if his own spine were breaking, and he could swear he had heard the ship cry out in agony. He knew instantly, from her sluggish response to the rudder and the way she sagged in the peaks and troughs of the waves, that her backbone was fractured. With each successive wave, the wound deepened, and it was only a matter of time before she split in two and went under. But *Wolfcloud* was a tough ship, and she wasn't ready to lie down and die—not just yet.

Then, as if it were some divine reward for the stricken ship's courage and the efforts of her storm-battered crew, Gundar had seen the gap in the rocky coast where a river mouth widened before them. He ran for it, the ship sagging badly downwind, and made it into the sheltered waters of the river. Exhausted, the men fell back on their rowing benches as the wind and wild waves died away.

That was when Buttle seized his chance. He grabbed a knife from one man's belt and slashed it across his throat. Another rower tried to stop him, but he was off balance, and Buttle struck him down as well. Then he was over the rail and swimming for the far bank. There was no way to go after him. Strangely, few Skandians could swim, and the ship itself was on the point of foundering. Cursing, Gundar was forced to let him go and concentrate on finding a point where they could beach the ship.

Around the next bend, they found a narrow strip of shingle that would suit their purpose, and he ran *Wolfcloud* onto it at a shallow angle. That was when he felt the keel finally give way, as if the ship had kept her crew safe until that final moment and then quietly died beneath their feet.

They staggered ashore and set up a camp among the trees. Gundar felt it would be best to retain a low profile in the area. After all, without a ship, they had no means of escape, and he had no idea how the locals might react to their presence, nor how many armed men they might be able to muster. Skandians never shrank from a fight, but it would be foolish to provoke one when they were stranded in this country.

They had food enough, thanks to the Ranger, and he needed

time to think of some way out of this mess. Maybe, when the weather improved, they could build a small boat from *Wolfcloud*'s timbers. He sighed. He just didn't know. He was a helmsman, not a shipwright. He looked around the little camp. On a hillock beyond the clearing where he sat, they had buried the two men Buttle had killed. They couldn't even give them a proper funeral pyre, as was traditional among Skandians. Gundar blamed himself for their deaths. After all, he was the one who had ordered the prisoner set free.

He shook his head and said softly to himself, "Curse John Buttle to hell. I should have dropped him overboard. Chains and all."

"You know, I rather think I agree," said a voice from behind him. Gundar leapt to his feet and spun around, his hand dropping to the sword at his belt.

"Thurak's horns!" he cried. "Where the devil did you spring from?"

There was a strange figure, wrapped in an odd black-and-white-mottled cloak, sitting on a log a few meters behind him. As Gundar said the word *devil*, his hand hesitated, sword half drawn, and he peered more closely at the apparition. This was an ancient forest, dark and forbidding. Maybe this was a spirit or a wraith that protected the area. The patterns on the cloak seemed to shimmer and change form as he watched and he blinked his eyes to stabilize them. A vague memory stirred. He had seen that happen before.

His men, hearing the commotion, had begun to gather around. There was something about the cloaked, hooded figure that worried them too. Gundar noticed that they took care to stay well behind him, looking to him for a lead.

The figure stood, and Gundar involuntarily took a half pace back. Then, angry with himself, he stepped forward a full pace. His voice was firm when he spoke.

"If you're a ghost," he said, "we mean you no disrespect. And if you're not a ghost, tell me who you are—or you soon will be one."

The creature laughed gently. "Well said, Gundar Hardstriker, well said indeed."

Gundar felt the hair on the back of his neck rise. The tone was friendly enough, but somehow this . . . thing . . . knew his name. That could only mean some kind of supernatural power was at work here.

The figure reached up and shoved back the cowl of his cloak.

"Oh, come on, Gundar, don't you recognize me?" he said cheerfully.

Memory stirred. This was no raddled, haggard ghost, certainly. It was a young face, with a shock of tousled brown hair above deep brown eyes and a wide grin. A familiar face. And in a rush, Gundar remembered where he had seen that strange, shifting pattern in a cloak before.

"Will Treaty!" he cried in surprise. "Is that really you?"

"None other," Will replied and stepped forward, holding out his hand in the universal gesture of peace and welcome. Gundar seized it and shook it hard—not the least because he was relieved to find that he wasn't facing some supernatural denizen of the forest. Behind him, he heard his crew exclaiming loudly at this new development. He guessed they were feeling the same sense of relief. Will looked around them and smiled.

"I see some familiar faces here," he said. One or two of the Skandians called out greetings to him. He studied them and then frowned slightly.

"I don't see Ulf Oakbender," he said to Gundar. Ulf had fought in the battle against the Eastern Riders, and he had been the first to recognize Will at Seacliff Island. They had sat together at that famous banquet, talking about the battle. Will saw a moment of pain cross Gundar's face.

"He was murdered by that snake Buttle," he said.

Will's smile faded. "I'm sorry to hear that. He was a good man."

There was a moment of silence between them as they remembered a fallen comrade. Then Gundar gestured to the campsite behind them.

"Won't you join us?" he said. "We have stringy salt beef and some indifferent ale, courtesy of a very generous island to the south."

Will grinned at the jibe and followed as Gundar led his way to the small encampment. As they passed through the members of the crew, a few reached out and shook Will's hand.

The sight of a familiar face, and that face belonging to a Ranger, let them begin to hope that there might be a way out of their present situation after all.

Will sat on a log by one of the fires, underneath a shelter formed by the wolfship's big, square mainsail.

"So, Will Treaty," said Gundar, "what brings you here?"

Will looked around the circle of bearded, craggy faces that surrounded him. He smiled at them.

"I'm looking for fighting men," he said. "I plan to sack a castle, and I hear you people are rather good at that."

2

THE BATTLEHORSE WAS A WELL-FORMED BAY. ITS HOOFBEATS were muffled by the thick carpet of snow on the ground as its rider guided it carefully along the narrow track beside a stream. There was no telling when that thick, soft snow might conceal a patch of slippery ice, which could send them sliding helplessly down the steep bank into the water. The stream itself moved sluggishly, nearly choked with slushy ice, fighting a losing battle against the cold that tried to freeze it over completely. The rider looked at the water and shivered a little. If he went into that wearing a heavy chain-mail shirt and burdened by his weapons, he would have little chance of survival. Even if he didn't drown, the searing cold would be sure to kill him.

It was obvious from his horse and his equipment that he was a warrior. He carried a three-meter ash lance, its butt couched in a socket on his right stirrup. A long sword hung at his left-hand side, and a conical helmet was slung over the saddle bow. The cowl of his chain-mail shirt was pushed back. He had discovered some days previously that in this snow-covered land, there was nothing more uncomfortable than freezing cold chain mail against the skin. Consequently, he now had a woolen scarf wrapped around his neck inside the armor and a fur cap pulled well down on his head. Interestingly, for it was not a normal part of a knight's weaponry, there was a longbow in a leather case slung beside his horse's withers.

But perhaps the most significant part of his equipment was his shield. It was a simple round buckler, slung behind him. Placed that way, it would provide protection against arrows or other missiles fired from behind, yet he could shrug it around into position on his left arm in a matter of seconds. The shield was painted white, and in its center was a blue outline of a clenched fist, the universal symbol in Araluen of a free lance—a knight with no current master, looking for employment.

As the track veered away from the stream and widened out, the rider relaxed a little. He leaned forward and patted his horse gently on the side of the neck.

"Well done, Kicker," Horace said quietly. The horse tossed its head in acknowledgment. He and the rider were old companions. They had depended on each other through several hard campaigns. It was that fact that now led the horse to prick its ears up in warning. Battlehorses were trained to regard any stranger as a potential enemy.

And now there were five strangers visible, riding slowly toward them.

"Company," Horace said. On this lonely ride, he had fallen into the habit of talking to the horse. Naturally, the horse made no reply. Horace glanced around, looking to see if there were any favorable defensive positions close by. He too was trained to regard strangers as potential enemies. But at this point, the tree line was well back from the road on either side, with only low gorse bushes growing between the road and forest. He shrugged. He would have preferred somewhere he could put a solid tree to his back. But there was nothing available, and he had learned years ago not to waste time complaining about things that couldn't be changed.

He checked the horse with slight pressure from his knees, and shrugged the shield around onto his left arm. The small movement was an indication that, despite his youth, he was more than familiar with the tools of his trade.

For he was young. His face was open and guileless, strong-jawed, clean-shaven and handsome. The eyes were a brilliant blue. There was a thin scar, high on the right cheek—where an Arridi tribesman's belt dagger had opened it more than a year previously. The scar, being relatively new, was still livid. As years passed, it would whiten and become less prominent. His nose was also slightly crooked, the result of an accident when an overeager warrior apprentice had refused to accept that a training bout was over. The student had struck one more time with his wooden sword. He had several weeks of punishment details to think over his mistake.

Far from detracting from his looks, the crooked nose gave the young man a certain swashbuckling air. There were quite a few young ladies of the kingdom who felt it enhanced his appearance, rather than the opposite.

Horace nudged Kicker once more, and the horse moved so that he was turned forty-five degrees to the oncoming riders, presenting the shield on his arm to them, both for protection and identification. He kept the lance upright. To level it would be an unnecessarily provocative gesture.

He studied the five men approaching him. Four of them were obviously men-at-arms. They carried swords and shields but no lances, the sign of a knight. And they all wore surcoats emblazoned with the same symbol, an ornate gold key on a quartered blue-and-white field. That meant they were all employed by the same lord, and Horace recognized the livery as belonging to Macindaw.

The fifth man, who rode a meter in front of the others, was something of a puzzle. He carried a shield and wore a leather breast-plate studded with iron. He had greaves of the same material protecting his legs, but apart from that, he wore woolen clothing and leggings. He had no helmet, and there was no symbol on his shield to give any clue to his identity. A sword hung from his pommel—a heavy weapon, a little shorter and thicker than Horace's cavalry sword. But strangest of all was the fact that, in place of a lance, he carried a heavy war spear some two meters long.

He had long black hair and a beard, and he looked to be in a perpetual state of ill temper, with heavy brows set in a permanent frown. Altogether, Horace thought, he was not a man to be trusted.

The riders were some ten meters away when Horace called out.

"I think that's close enough for the moment."

The leader made a brief signal, and the four men-at-arms drew rein. The leader, however, continued to ride toward Horace. When he was five meters away, Horace freed the butt of the lance from the socket beside his right stirrup and brought the point down so that it was leveled at the approaching rider.

The stranger had chosen to be provocative. He could hardly take offense if Horace reacted in kind.

The unwavering iron point of the lance, gleaming dully where it had been carefully sharpened the night before, was aimed at the rider's throat. He brought his horse to a stop.

"There's no need for that," he said. His voice was rough and angry.

Horace shrugged slightly. "And there's no need for you to come any closer," he replied calmly, "until we know each other a little better."

Two of the men-at-arms began to edge their horses out to the left and right. Horace glanced at them briefly, then returned his gaze to the other man's face.

"Tell your men to stay where they are, please."

The bearded man swiveled in his saddle and glanced at them.

"That's enough," he ordered, and they stopped moving. Horace glanced quickly at them again. There was something not quite right about them. Then he realized what it was. They were scruffy, their surcoats stained and crumpled, their arms and armor unburnished and dull. They looked as if they'd be more at home hiding in the forest and waylaying innocent travelers than wearing the arms of a castle lord. In most castles, the men-at-arms were under the orders and discipline of experienced sergeants. It was rare that they would be allowed to become so disheveled.

"You're getting off to a bad start with me, you know," the bearded man said. In another man, the remark might have had overtones of humor or amusement to soften implicit threat in the words. Here, the threat was overt. Even more so when he added, after a pause, "You might come to regret that."

"And why might that be?" Horace asked. The other man had obviously got the point. He raised the lance again and replaced it in its stirrup socket as the man replied.

"Well, if you're looking for work, you don't want to get on my wrong side, is why."

Horace considered the statement thoughtfully.

"Am I looking for work?" he asked.

The other man said nothing but gestured toward the device on Horace's shield. There was a long silence between them and finally the man was forced to speak.

"You're a free lance," he said.

Horace nodded. He didn't like the man's manner. It was arrogant and threatening, the sign of a man who had been given authority when he wasn't used to wielding it.

"True," he admitted. "But that simply means I'm unemployed. It doesn't mean I'm actually looking for a job at the moment." He smiled. "I could have private means, after all."

He said it pleasantly, without sarcasm, but the bearded man was unwilling to show any signs of good humor.

"Don't bandy words, boy. You may own a battlehorse and a lance, but that doesn't make you the cock of the walk. You're a raggletail beggar who's out of work, and I'm the man who might have given you a job—if you'd shown a little respect."

The smile on Horace's face died. He sighed inwardly. Not at the implication that he was a ragged beggar but at the insult inherent in the word *boy*. Since the age of sixteen, Horace had been used to potential opponents underestimating his abilities because of his youth. Most of them had realized their mistake too late.

"Where are you heading?" the bearded man demanded. Horace saw no reason why he shouldn't answer the question.

"I thought I'd swing by Castle Macindaw," he said. "I need a place to spend the rest of the winter."

The man gave a derisive snort as Horace spoke. "Then you've started out on the wrong foot," he said. "I'm the man who does the hiring for Lord Keren."

Horace frowned slightly. The name was new to him.

"Lord Keren?" he repeated. "I thought the Lord of Macindaw was Syron?"

His remark was greeted with a dismissive gesture.

"Syron is finished," the bearded man said. "Last I heard, he hasn't got long to live. Might be already dead, for all I care. And his son, Orman, has run off as well—skulking somewhere in the forest. Lord Keren's in charge now, and I'm his garrison commander."

"And you are?" Horace asked, his tone totally neutral.

"I'm Sir John Buttle," the man replied shortly.

Horace frowned slightly. The name had a vaguely familiar ring to it. On top of that, he would swear that this rough-mannered, roughly clothed bully was no knight. But he said nothing. There was little to be gained by antagonizing the man further, and he seemed to antagonize very easily.

"So, what's your name, boy?" Buttle demanded. Again, Horace sighed inwardly. But he kept his tone light and good-natured as he replied.

"Hawken," he said. "Hawken Watt, originally from Caraway but now a citizen of this wide realm."

Once again, his easy tone struck no response from Buttle, whose reply was short-tempered and ill-mannered.

"Not this part of it, you're not," he said. "There's nothing for you in Macindaw and nothing for you in Norgate Fief. Move on. Be out of the area by nightfall, if you know what's good for you."

"I'll certainly consider your advice," Horace said. Buttle's frown deepened, and he leaned toward the young warrior.

"Do more than that, boy. Take the advice. I'm not a man you want to cross. Now get moving."

He jerked his thumb toward the southeast, where the border with the next fief lay. But by now, Horace had decided that he'd heard enough from Sir John Buttle. He smiled and made no attempt to move. Outwardly, he seemed unperturbed. But Kicker sensed the little thrill of readiness that went through his master, and the battle-horse's ears pricked up. He could feel a fight in the offing, and his breed lived for fighting.

Buttle hesitated, not sure what to do next. He had made his threat, and he was used to people being cowed by the force of his personality—and the sight of men-at-arms ready to back his threats up. Now this well-armed young man simply sat facing him, with an air of confidence about him that said he wasn't fazed by the odds of five to one. Buttle realized he would either have to make good on his threat or back down. As he was thinking this, Horace smiled lazily at him and backing down suddenly seemed like a good option.

Angrily, he wheeled his horse away, gesturing to his men to follow.

"Remember what I said!" he flung back over his shoulder as he spurred his horse away. "You have till nightfall."

3

Malcolm the healer, more widely known as Malkallam the Black Sorcerer, looked up briefly from his work as Will rode into the little clearing in Grimsdell Wood.

Each morning at eleven o'clock, Malcolm provided his people with medical treatment. Those with injuries or illnesses would line up patiently outside the healer's comfortable house so that he could diagnose and treat their ailments, sprains, cuts, sores and fevers. Since many of the people who lived in the little forest settlement had been driven out of their previous homes because of physical disabilities or disfigurement, there was usually a long line of patients. Many had ongoing health problems that required constant care.

His last patient was a relatively straightforward case. An eleven-year-old boy had decided to use his mother's best cloak as a pair of wings while he attempted to fly from a four-meter-high tree. Malcolm finished binding the resultant sprained ankle, put some salve on the scraped elbows and wrists and ruffled the would-be adventurer's hair.

"Off you go," he told him, "and from now on, leave the magic to me."

"Yes, Malcolm," the boy said, hanging his head in embarrassment. Then, as he scuttled away, the healer turned to where Will was unsaddling his horse. The older man watched approvingly, noting the bond between the two as the Ranger spoke gently to the animal while he rubbed it down. The horse almost seemed to understand his words, responding with a good-natured snort and a toss of its short mane.

"I hear you found the Skandians, then?" Malcolm said eventually.

Will nodded. "Twenty-five prime fighting men," he said. "They were right where your messenger told us they'd be, on the banks of the River Oosel."

Malcolm's people ranged far and wide through the vast forest. There was little that happened within its boundaries that they didn't see. And when they saw something out of the ordinary, they brought word to the healer. When reports had come in of a party of Skandian shipwreck survivors, Will had set out to find them.

"And they were happy to offer their help?" Malcolm asked. Will shrugged as he sat down on the sunny veranda beside the old healer.

"They'll be happy to receive the money I've offered them. Besides, their captain felt he owed me something because he let Buttle escape."

Xander, the secretary and assistant to Orman of Macindaw, came out of the house.

"How's Orman?" Malcolm asked. The castle lord had been poisoned by Keren in his attempt to gain control of Macindaw. Will and Xander had only just reached the healer's secret clearing in time to save his life.

"He's much better. But he's still very weak. He's sleeping again," Xander said.

Malcolm nodded thoughtfully. "That's the best medicine for him now. The poison's out of his system. His body can heal itself from here on. Let him rest."

Xander looked doubtful. In spite of the fact that Malcolm had saved his master's life, he still viewed the healer with a certain amount of suspicion. He felt Malcolm should be providing more tangible treatment than the simple injunction "Let him rest." But there was something else nagging at him at the moment.

"Did I hear you say that you've offered to pay these Skandians?" he asked Will.

Will grinned at him and shook his head. "No. I've offered to let you pay them," he replied. "Seventy gold royals for their services."

Xander bristled at him indignantly. "That's outrageous!" he said. "You had no right to do such a thing! Orman is lord of Macindaw. Any such negotiations were up to him—or me, in his absence!"

The secretary had proven to be a brave little man and very loyal to his lord. But that could make him act like a bit of a prig at times. Will eyed him meaningfully. He heard Malcolm's snort of derision.

"At the moment," Will said, with a warning note in his voice, "Orman is lord of nothing very much at all, not even the borrowed bed he's lying in. So, actually, I outrank him. You seem to forget that I act with the King's authority."

Which Xander realized was true. Will was a Ranger, after all, in spite of the fact that he had come to Macindaw disguised as a jongleur. It was difficult for Xander to accept that such vast authority could be vested in someone as young as Will. He backed off now, but reluctantly.

"Even so," he said, "seventy royals? Surely you could have done better than that!"

Will shook his head at the secretary's attitude.

"You can renegotiate if you like. I'm sure the Skandians will be delighted to bargain with someone who'll sit watching while they risk their lives."

Xander saw that he was on shaky ground. But he was too stubborn to simply admit it.

"Well, perhaps. But after all, it's their trade, isn't it? They fight for money, don't they?"

"That's right," Will agreed, thinking that Xander could be a very annoying man. "And that gives them a pretty good idea of what their lives are worth. Besides, look on the bright side. Maybe we'll lose, and then you won't owe them a penny."

There was a hard edge to his voice that finally penetrated Xander's bumptious attitude. The secretary realized that it might be best not to pursue this matter any further. He sniffed and walked away, making sure that Will and Malcolm could just hear his parting remark: "Seventy royals, indeed! I've never heard such extravagance!"

Malcolm looked at Will and shrugged sympathetically. "I do hope you can get that man back in his castle before too long," he said. "One tires of him very quickly."

Will smiled. "Still, he's very loyal. And he can be a courageous little bantam, as you've noted."

Malcolm considered the fact for a few seconds. "It's strange, isn't it?" he remarked at length. "You'd expect qualities like that to make a person quite likable. Yet somehow he manages to irritate the devil out of me." He made a brief gesture dismissing Xander as a subject of conversation. "So, come inside and tell me more about these Skandians of yours."

He led the way inside the house, where he had a pot of coffee brewing. In the short time that he had known the young Ranger, he had become aware of his near-dependence on the drink. He poured him a cup now and smiled as Will tasted it, smacked his lips and let out an appreciative sigh. The two settled into comfortable chairs at Malcolm's kitchen table.

"They'll be along in a day or two," Will continued. "I left them to pack up their camp and follow on. One of your people will guide them here. I must say we were lucky to find them. I'm going to need fighting men, and they're in pretty scarce supply." In the first days after he had left Alyss imprisoned in Macindaw's tower, Will had sought furiously to find a way to release her. Gradually, his desperation eased as he realized he would need reinforcements and a plan before he could mount an attack. The news of the Skandians was like a gift from heaven.

Malcolm sighed. "True," he said. "My people aren't fighters. They're not trained or equipped for the job."

"And the people from the villages around here would hardly join us. They're all terrified of Malkallam the Black Sorcerer," Will said. He smiled to show there was no insult intended. Malcolm nodded, recognizing the truth.

"That's a fact. So what do you plan to do when the Skandians get here?"

The Ranger hesitated before answering. "Then . . . we'll see. I'll have to figure out a way to take the castle and get Alyss out of there."

"Have you ever done that sort of thing before?" Malcolm asked.

Will grinned ruefully. "Not really," he admitted. "It never came up in my Ranger training."

He didn't want to dwell on it. He hoped that the Skandians might have some ideas on the subject, but he'd cross that drawbridge when he came to it.

Malcolm stroked his chin thoughtfully. "Have you considered sending to Castle Norgate for help?"

Will shifted uncomfortably in his chair. "I have," he replied. "But Keren has the road sealed off. No riders are getting through."

Malcolm's observers had reported that riders heading west were being stopped and turned back.

"Except his own," Malcolm replied. "A rider left Macindaw while you were away."

Will nodded gloomily. "Keren's no fool. I'll wager he's reported that Orman is a traitor and has run off, leaving Keren to keep Macindaw safe. That's what I'd do in his place. The trouble is, he's well liked and respected. They'll be inclined to believe him. Whereas I'm a stranger. What's more, I'm in league with an accused traitor and a known sorcerer."

"But you're a King's Ranger," Malcolm said.

"They don't know that. My presence here was a secret." Will laughed at the thought. "Let's assume I could get a message through, and let's assume they don't dismiss it out of hand. What do you think they might do?"

Malcolm considered for a moment. "Send soldiers to help us?" he suggested, but Will shook his head.

"It's winter. Their army is dispersed to their homes. It would take a couple of weeks to assemble them. It's a big undertaking, and they're not going to do that on a stranger's say-so. The best we could hope for is they might send someone to investigate, to find out who's telling the truth. And even that will take at least two weeks— it's a week there and another week back, after all."

Malcolm pulled a wry face. "There's not much we can do, is there?"

"We're not exactly helpless," Will told him. "With twenty-five

Skandians, we can cause Keren quite a bit of trouble. Then, once I have some concrete evidence, we'll send word to Norgate."

He paused, frowning heavily. He wished he was a little more experienced in matters like this. He was the most junior Ranger in the Corps and, truth be told, he was uncertain that he was taking the right path. But Halt had always taught him to gather as much information as possible before taking action.

For the twentieth time in the past few days, he wished he could contact Halt. But Alyss's pigeon handler seemed to have disappeared from the district. Run off by Buttle and his men, most likely, he thought gloomily, then shook off the negative thoughts with an effort.

"So, what else has been going on while I've been away?" he asked.

He drained his coffee and looked hopefully at the pot. Malcolm, who was aware that his supply of coffee beans was running low, studiously ignored the hint, and the quiet sigh that followed it. He shuffled through a few sheets of notes that he had taken when his spies had reported in.

"There were a couple of things," he said. "Your friend Alyss has been showing a light at her window for the past two nights."

That news took Will's mind off the coffee. The young man sat straight up in his chair.

"A light?" he said eagerly. "What kind of light?"

Malcolm shrugged. "Looks like just a simple lantern. But it moves around the window."

"From corner to corner?" Will asked. Malcolm looked up from his notes, surprised.

"Yes," he said. "How did you know that?"

Will was smiling broadly now. "She's using the Courier's signal code," he said. "I guess she knows that sooner or later, I'll be watching. When does she do this?"

Malcolm didn't need to consult the notes this time. "Usually after the midnight watch has changed—around three in the morning. The moon's well down by then, so the light is easier to make out."

"Good!" said Will. "That gives me time to get a message prepared. I'm a little rusty on the code," he added, apologetically. "Haven't had to use it since my fourth-year assessment. You said there were a couple of items?" he prompted.

Malcolm shuffled the pages again. "Oh yes. One of my people saw Buttle and his men talking to a warrior by Tumbledown Creek the other morning. He thought they might be recruiting him, but the warrior seemed to send them packing. Then he rode off himself. I believe he's taken a room at the Cracked Flagon."

This news was less riveting, Malcolm saw.

Will, his thoughts already composing a message to Alyss, asked absently, "Could your man make out the warrior's blazon?"

"A blue fist. He was a free lance. Had a blue fist on a white shield. A round buckler."

That piece of news definitely engaged the Ranger's attention. He looked up quickly.

"Anything else? Was he young or old?"

"Quite young, apparently. Surprisingly so, in fact. A big fellow, riding a big bay. My chap was close enough to hear him talk to the horse. Called him Nicker or Whicker or something like that."

"Kicker?" said Will, a giant ray of hope dawning inside him.

Malcolm nodded. "Yes. That could be it. Makes more sense than Nicker, doesn't it? Do you know him?" he added. From Will's delighted reaction, it was obvious that he did.

"Oh, I think I might," he said. "And if it's who I think it is, things just took a big turn for the better."

4

ALONE IN HER TOWER PRISON, ALYSS WAS WAITING FOR THE moon to set. She judged that there was still an hour to go and set about making her simple preparations.

She lit the oil lamp, keeping the wick as low as possible. She had already placed a rolled-up blanket along the bottom of the door to prevent any light being seen by the guards in the room outside. When the little flame settled and burned steadily, she concealed it beneath one of the ridiculous conical hats she'd brought as part of her disguise as the wealthy but empty-headed Lady Gwendolyn.

"Knew I'd find a use for these stupid things," she muttered to herself.

Earlier in the day, Alyss's belongings had been returned to her—after they'd been searched, of course. Consequently, she had changed back into her own simple, elegant white gown, forsaking the ornate fashions that were suited to her false identity. She was glad to be wearing her own clothes again, glad to throw off the identity of the airheaded Lady Gwendolyn. She was also relieved to find that her writing satchel, with sheets of parchment, pen and ink and graphite chalks, was in her baggage as well.

She pulled the heavy curtain back and set the lamp on the floor

below the window, tossing the tall hat to one side. She set herself to
search the darkness outside, concentrating particularly on the irregular line that marked where the black mass of the forest began. For the
moment, there was no sign of any reply to the signals she had been
sending for the past two nights. But she had been schooled in patience, and she waited and watched calmly. Sooner or later, she knew,
Will would try to make contact again. As she waited, she thought
back over events of the past few days.

Since the attempt to rescue her, Keren had submitted her to one
more interrogation session, using his blue gemstone to hypnotize her
and see if she were hiding any further secrets.

It rapidly became obvious that there were none. At least, none
that he thought to ask her about. That was the one shortcoming of
hypnotism. Alyss would answer freely any questions he asked, unable to hide facts or lie to him. But she would not offer information
unless she was prompted. Consequently, in answer to his questions,
she had told him all about how Will and she had been assigned to
investigate the rumors of sorcery in Norgate Fief, and the mysterious
illness that had struck down its commander, Lord Syron. She had
also revealed the fact that Will was a Ranger, not a jongleur.

Under normal circumstances, Alyss would have been aghast that
she had revealed secrets like these. But of course she was telling
Keren little that he didn't already know. Buttle had already revealed
her identity, and had quickly guessed that Will was no jongleur, but
a King's Ranger. Nothing she said to Keren could do them any harm
now. Aside from his determination to rescue her, she had no detailed
knowledge of Will's plans.

In a show of defiance, she had told Keren that Will would certainly have sent word to Castle Norgate by now, so that authorities
there could raise a force to come and attack Macindaw. She was
puzzled by the fact that Keren dismissed this as unimportant.

Since Alyss responded to direct questions only when she was hypnotized, she had made no mention of the fact that the leather-covered glass bottle of acid that Will had used to cut through the bars on her window was concealed in the wardrobe. The bars had been replaced, of course, and she had told Keren that Will had used acid. But the renegade knight assumed Will had taken it with him. There was no way for him to know that on the night of the escape attempt, Alyss had unthinkingly placed the bottle on top of the window frame. The following day, she had remembered it was there and secreted it in the little wardrobe that completed the furnishing of her prison, along with an uncomfortable bed, two chairs and a table. It certainly wasn't luxurious, but it could have been a whole lot worse. As for the acid, there would come a time when it might be useful, she thought.

Her eyes began to water with the strain of peering into the half-light outside the tower. She stepped away for a few seconds, rubbed them, blinked away the traces of tears and then set herself to watch once more.

When the moon set, she would begin her signaling.

Will was concentrating, the tip of his tongue protruding from the corner of his mouth as he encoded his message to Alyss. The dog lay under the table, and he rested his bare feet on her warm fur. From time to time, she grumbled contentedly, as dogs do. He glanced down at her, smiling.

"Nice of you to spend some time with me," he said. "Where's your new friend?"

Her new friend was Trobar, the massively built, misshapen giant who was one of Malcolm's most faithful followers. The dog and Trobar had struck up an instant friendship. The giant had lav-ished her with all the pent-up affection of someone who had spent years with no person or creature to love. The dog seemed to sense his need and reciprocated, spending hours each day in his company. At first, Will had been slightly jealous. Then he realized how important the companionship was to Trobar and felt a little mean-spirited. The dog, he thought, was wiser and more kindly natured than he was.

He was working on Malcolm's table, and he glanced up as the healer entered the room. Malcolm looked with interest at the sheets of paper covered with letters and numbers. On one sheet, Will had written the message he wanted to send. On the second, he had translated the letters into code. He saw Malcolm's interest and, trying to seem casual, turned the original page facedown.

The Courier's code, known to the Diplomatic Service and the Ranger Corps, was a jealously guarded secret. But it was actually quite simple, and he didn't want to give Malcolm, ally though he might be, any chance to figure it out.

Malcolm smiled as he saw the gesture. As a matter of fact, he had been trying to get a glimpse. If he could see the original message, alongside the cipher version, he felt confident he could unravel the format of the code. The young man at the table was no fool, he reflected.

"Moonset in an hour or so," he said.

Will nodded. "We'll get going soon. I'm nearly finished."

"You send your message using a lamp, I take it?" Malcolm asked.

"That's right. It's only short because there's not a lot to tell her at the moment. It's just to let her know that we're watching and to set up a schedule for further messages."

The healer laid another sheet of paper on the table, along with a small, black, shiny pebble.

"Is there any way we could get this to her?" he asked. "I mean, could you tie it to an arrow and shoot it through the window? Something like that?"

Will shook his head and reached for his quiver. Malcolm had noticed that the young Ranger's weapons were always within easy reach.

"That's not a very reliable method. If you tie something to an arrow, it tends to fall off when you shoot it," he said. "We do it a little differently."

He slid an unusual-looking arrow from the quiver and placed it on the table.

Instead of the usual razor-sharp broadhead at its tip, it had an extended cylinder. Malcolm examined it curiously. The cylinder was hollow. A threaded cap, surmounted by a rounded lead weight, screwed onto the end to seal it.

"You put the written message in here?" he guessed.

Will nodded again. He leaned back to ease his cramped shoulder and neck muscles. He had been hunched at the table for some time, initially writing out a chart of the code, then the message, then the code itself. As he moved, the dog stirred. Her tail thumped the floor.

"That's right. I could use the lamp message to warn Alyss to get out of the way, then fire the arrow through her window."

"Easy as that?" Malcolm smiled.

Will raised one eyebrow. "Easy as that. If you've spent five years learning to put arrows exactly where you want them."

"And the stone?" Malcolm said. "Could you put that inside as well?"

Will picked up the little black pebble and weighed it experimentally in his hand.

"I don't see why not. I'll have to reduce the lead to compensate for the extra weight and make sure the arrow remains balanced. I assume you have some scales I could use?"

"Of course. They're basic tools of a healer's trade."

"The question is," Will continued, "why am I shooting a stone through her window in the first place?"

"Aaah, yes," said the healer, placing one finger alongside his nose. "I wondered when you'd ask that. It's to help her if Keren tries to mesmerize her again."

That gained Will's interest immediately. He looked at the stone again, examining it more carefully. There seemed to be nothing out of the ordinary about it. He frowned.

"What does it do?" he asked.

Malcolm gently took the stone from his hand and held it up, admiring its deep sheen.

"It will neutralize the blue gemstone that she said Keren is using," he said. "You see, mesmerism, or hypnotism, as some people call it, is a matter of mental focus. Keren has created a situation where the blue gemstone focuses Alyss's mind on his commands. But if she can hold this little pebble in her palm and concentrate on some kind of strong alternative image, she can resist that focus and remain in control of her own mind. If she's smart, Keren will never know she has broken his grip on her, and that could be useful. She might be able to tell him all sorts of misinformation."

He handed the stone back to Will, who turned it over, looking to see if there was something about it that he'd missed. Other than its glossy black surface, he couldn't see anything special.

"How does it do that?" he asked. It seemed a little like hocus-pocus to him, but Alyss had been very definite about the effect of Keren's blue gemstone, and when he had related the story to Malcolm, the old healer had grasped the significance of the blue stone at once.

Malcolm shrugged now, in reply to Will's question.

"Nobody really knows. It's stellatite, you see," he said, as if that explained everything. Then, seeing the question on Will's lips, he continued, "Star stone. It's all that remains of a falling star. I found it years ago. Stellatite is exceedingly valuable, probably because it has otherworldly properties. Anyway," he concluded, "I don't really know how it works. I just know it does." He smiled. "It's galling for a man of science to have to admit something like that, but what can I do?"

Will nodded, convinced. He looked at the sheet of paper Malcolm had placed on the table. It contained a description of the stone and outlined its use. But the sheet was too bulky for the message arrow. He reached into his pack and produced a flimsy sheet of thin message paper.

"Then I'd best start rewriting your message," he said. "While I'm doing that, perhaps you could weigh the pebble and the lead weight on the arrow?"

Malcolm picked up the arrow and the pebble.

"Consider it done," he said, turning toward his little workroom at the back of the house.

5

IN THE TOWER, ALYSS BEGAN HER NIGHTLY RITUAL WITH THE lamp, holding it high in one corner of the window, then moving it progressively to the other three corners.

She did this five times, then stopped, setting the lamp on the floor and scanning the dark countryside outside the walls of the castle. She had done this for the past two nights and so far had been disappointed to see no return signal. She clung to the hope that Will would reply. But the hope was getting fainter and fainter. Perhaps he was—

A light! There it was, off to her left, moving among the trees! For a moment, she felt her excitement surge, then, just as quickly, it deflated as she realized that the light was red and that it was moving along at a fixed height from the ground, alternately fading and flashing as trees obscured it. She knew that strange lights were often reported among the trees of Grimsdell Wood. Perhaps this was all it was.

Then, out to her right, she saw another. This one was yellow, and it moved up and down in a straight line. Then it disappeared for a few seconds, reappearing some distance to the left of its original position, moving up and down.

As she watched, it went out again and the red light reappeared, flitting in and out of sight among the trees. Alyss's heart sank. For a moment she had thought her attempts had been successful.

Then she saw it! At a point halfway between the other lights, a bright white light suddenly appeared. And it traced a steady square pattern, just as her own had done—from one corner of the square to another in a steady sequence. Top left. Top right. Bottom right. Bottom left.

Far below, she heard the muted murmur of voices on the battlements as the sentries also saw the lights, and she realized what Will was doing. He knew there was no way he could conceal the light from the guards. And once the news of a flashing white light was reported to Keren, it wouldn't take long for the renegade leader to guess that somebody was signaling. And there was only one person they might be signaling to.

So Will had decided to hide his signal lamp among other lights, the sort of lights people expected to see on the fringes of Grimsdell Wood. She smiled to herself—Will was hiding a tree in the forest, as the old saying went. Another light, this one blue, was flashing. Then the yellow one was back. Then the red one. And then the white one in the center. She set herself to ignore red, blue and yellow and watch only white. She picked up her own lamp, concealing it behind a stiff piece of old, dried-out leather she had found discarded in the bottom of the wardrobe.

She centered the light in the window and then flicked the leather back and forth five times, sending a series of five rapid flashes to the watchers at the edge of the forest. In the code, five rapid flashes from the center of the square meant communication had been established.

Immediately, the other light replied in kind. Five rapid flashes, then a pause, then three longer flashes—the standard response meaning, Are you ready to receive a message?

She hurried to the table and seized paper and a graphite chalk. She knew Will would wait until she was ready. Back at the window, she raised the lamp in a vertical line, up and down three times. The white light outside mirrored the action. In her peripheral vision, she could see the moving colored lights flashing and winking away. She even realized that another red light had joined the display. But her attention was focused on the white light.

It began to flash, and she noted down the letters as Will sent them.

The Courier's code was a simple but effective system. Twenty-four of the letters of the alphabet were arranged in a grid of four numbered lines, six letters to a line. To achieve an even grid, the letters *Z* and *W* were omitted. *S* and *V* would take their place if necessary.

1.	A	B	C	D	E	F
2.	G	H	I	J	K	L
3.	M	N	O	P	Q	R
4.	S	T	U	V	X	Y

This meant that the letter *A* was represented by the cipher 1-1, being the first line of the grid and the first letter in the line.

By the same token, G would be 2-1, and P would be 3-4. The person sending the message would stipulate the line number by holding the lamp in a specific corner of the square. Top left was 1, top right 2, bottom left 3 and bottom right 4.

For example, if the signal lamp were moved to the bottom left corner, then back to the center where it was flashed twice, the receiver would know it meant third row, second letter, or *N*.

Unlike Will, who had to draw up the grid to compose his message—a fact that Halt would have found highly unsatisfactory—Alyss knew the grid by heart and could note the letters down directly as they were sent.

The light flashed out steadily. To the untrained eye, it was just another random flashing light in the forest. But to Alyss, the series of flashes were as easy to read as an open book. She noted them down quickly. She smiled once. Will was not a rapid sender. Any Courier would easily beat him. Then she realized that speed was less important than accuracy and he was probably fiercely intent on his task, the tip of his tongue protruding, as it always did when he was concentrating.

The light moved vertically several times, then disappeared, signaling that the message was finished. She seized her own lamp and replied with the same signal, then turned to read what she had scribbled down. She was pretty sure she had read it accurately as it was transmitted, but it paid to make sure. She moved her finger along the letters. They were roughly scribbled and uneven, as she had written them with her eyes firmly riveted on the light.

MESSAGE ARROW TEN MINUTES CLEAR

WINDOW LOVE WILL ACK

There was no punctuation in the code, of course, but she understood that Will would be firing a message arrow through her window in ten minutes and was warning her to be clear of the window. The work ACK was a standard code shortcut for *acknowledge*. The sign-off, LOVE WILL, was highly irregular. That sort of personal touch had been frowned on during her training. She smiled once more. You could read the words before her as saying she was to acknowledge the message itself, or the two-word ending, LOVE WILL.

"Either way," she murmured to herself. Hastily, she picked up her lamp and moved it vertically in the window three times: up, down, up. It was the standard signal for *acknowledge*.

Then she drew the curtain well back from the window and scanned the forest one last time. The colored lights continued to flash, and now the white light was swinging in an arc. There was no more signaling, she realized. They were just keeping the light show going. Below, on the battlements, the sentries had grown bored with the lights. The murmur of voices she had heard before had died away as sergeants ordered the men back to their duties.

She kissed her fingertips gently and blew a kiss out into the dark night.

"Thanks, Will," she said softly. She set the lamp in the center of the windowsill to provide him with an aiming point, then moved to one side to wait for his arrow.

Once he had seen Alyss's acknowledgment, Will started to move forward from his position just inside the tree line. As he had done previously, he ghosted from one patch of shadow to the next, blending with the natural movements of the night and becoming part of the landscape.

After five years of rigorous training under Halt's watchful eye— and with occasional input from Gilan, the Ranger Corps's acknowledged master of concealed movement—he didn't need to think about his actions any longer. They had become instinctive. He had already picked the spot from where he would shoot. He had to be within a hundred meters of the castle walls, allowing for the extra distance the arrow would have to travel to reach the top of the tower. There was a slight knoll crowned by a clump of large bushes some ninety meters from the wall. The additional few meters of height would be an advantage, as would the broken, shifting shadows formed by the bushes, with their dappled patterning of white snow and dark foliage. He would blend easily into the landscape there, allowing him to stand and aim carefully.

He frowned as he thought about that. He would have to aim just above the lamp Alyss had placed in the center of the window. That would mark the gap between the heavy iron bars. It would be the height of bad luck if he got this far and fired his arrow only to have it strike one of the bars and fall to the courtyard below. He wondered if he should have written his message to Alyss in code but then shrugged away the thought. There hadn't been time to encode a full message, and besides, if the arrow missed its mark and was found, it wouldn't matter if Keren were to read about the stellatite pebble and its properties. It would have already been lost to Alyss anyway.

He had, however, encoded the last few lines of the letter, setting up a schedule for further signaling. It would definitely be a problem if that should fall into Keren's hands. If he knew Alyss had a method of signaling, Keren might be able to compel her, under the influence of his mesmerism, to send a signal that would set some kind of trap for Will.

The bushes on the small knoll were waist high, and he was able to rest for a few minutes, crouched among them, while he gathered his thoughts and prepared for the shot ahead of him.

He looked long and hard at the small lighted square that was the tower window, with the brighter point at the center bottom that marked the lamp itself. He studied it, judging distances and height and calculating how his arrow would travel in a long arc to reach the window. He would have to aim high above the point he wanted to hit, but he didn't think about that. When the time came, he would select his elevation instinctively. It would have to be a little higher than normal, he reminded himself, as he was using the take-down recurve bow that Crowley had supplied him with, and it was not quite as powerful as the longbow he had carried for the past two years. He set that thought in his mind and knew that his instincts would process it when the time came to shoot.

He closed his eyes and in his imagination saw the arcing path that would take the arrow high over the walls and into the window at the top of the tower. Halt had often reminded him of an old archery master's dictum: Before you shoot your arrow, see it fly a thousand times in your mind.

Well, he smiled wryly, he didn't have time for a thousand imaginary shots tonight. But the saying was an exaggeration in any event. It was simply a reminder to prepare for the shot by setting a successful outcome in his mind. Think of a positive outcome, and you will achieve it. Allow doubt to enter your mind, and the doubt will become self-fulfilling.

He took a few deep breaths, clearing his mind. The conscious preparation was over. Now he would allow his instincts, the result of hundreds of hours of practice and thousands of arrows fired, to take over and produce the shot that he wanted.

He rose slowly to his feet. Although at least a dozen pairs of eyes on the castle wall were turned in his direction, not a soul saw him. He drew the message arrow from his quiver and nocked it to the bowstring. The weight and balance were perfect, as a result of Malcolm's painstaking weighing and measuring back at the house in the forest. The healer was used to dealing in exact weights and measures, and Will knew this arrow would fly like any other arrow in his quiver.

He brought his left arm—the bow arm—up and, at the same time, began a smooth draw back on the string with his right, continuing to pull until the tip of his right index finger just touched the corner of his mouth. He felt for the right elevation, sensed that he was a little low and raised the bow in his sighting picture. If he had been asked at that moment why he made that final adjustment, he would not have been able to answer. It was a matter of empirical feeling, not a calculated action.

His vision was fixed on the window high above him, with the arrow now pointing well above the target. There was a slight wind from the left, and he compensated for it, knowing from experience that it would grow stronger the higher the arrow traveled.

There were two ways to destroy accuracy, he knew. One was to wait too long and concentrate too hard, so that the muscles of the arms began to tighten and tremble against the tension of the bow. The other was to shoot too quickly, so that the right-hand fingers snatched at the string during the release.

The ideal was to find a midpoint, where the action was smooth and continuous. Unhurried, but not overlong.

Then, when he felt the moment was right, when the elevation and windage and draw were all correct, he let the bowstring slip gently from his fingers, with a deep-throated twang, speeding the arrow on its way.

The moment he released, he knew the shot was perfect. He saw the arrow briefly as it streaked up into the night, then lost sight of it. Slowly, he lowered the bow, waiting. He saw a momentary flicker of movement against the lit square of the window but thought that it was more likely that his mind was playing tricks on him, causing him to see it because he wanted to see it.

He waited, standing like a statue, his cloak wrapped around him so that he merged into the background. Then he felt a vast surge of relief as the lamp began to move.

Up down, up down, up down, it went. Message received. Nodding in satisfaction, Will turned and began to make his way back to the tree line. There was nothing more to be done tonight.

6

CULLUM GELDERRIS, INNKEEPER AT THE CRACKED FLAGON, wasn't altogether happy about his most recent, and, in fact, his only guest.

The young warrior had arrived late the previous afternoon, seeking a room for a few days. His bay battlehorse was bedded down in the inn's small stable. The young man had lugged his weapons and armor up the stairs, along with a saddle roll containing a change of clothes and washing items, and settled into the inn's largest room.

As he had entered, the landlord noted the blue fist symbol painted on his white shield. A free lance, he thought. There was only one place in the fief where a man like him might find employment, and that was at Castle Macindaw.

The new castle lord, Sir Keren, was recruiting fighting men, Cullum knew. His inn had already been visited several times by Keren's second in command, the ill-tempered John Buttle, who was scouring the surrounding countryside in search of men with some skill at arms. He seemed disbelieving when Cullum had told him that all his customers were simple farm folk. There were a few yeomen in the area who could put up a decent showing with a pike, but they, like the innkeeper, tended to view recent events at Macindaw with the deepest suspicion and stayed well clear of Buttle when he was on his recruiting trips. Cullum was glad to maintain their anonymity.

There were a lot of questions being asked by the folk who lived in and around Tumbledown Creek, the small village several kilometers from the Cracked Flagon.

First, there had been the mysterious business of Lord Syron's illness, then the rumors that the black sorcerer Malkallam had returned from the past to wreak vengeance on Syron's family. Next, word had spread that Orman, son of the castle lord and temporary commander of Macindaw, had escaped into Grimsdell Wood, where he was in league with Malkallam.

Escaped? Cullum asked himself. Why would a man escape from his own castle? And if he did, why would he join with the sorcerer who was sworn to destroy his family?

Then again, why was Keren looking for fighting men? The castle under Orman and Syron had maintained a perfectly adequate garrison of professional soldiers. But many of these had been weeded out and sent packing when Keren took control. And the villagers had seen the quality of men that Keren had replaced them with. Soldiering was no gentle trade, to be sure, but the men now serving Castle Macindaw seemed to be particularly rough, unruly types. Most of them, Cullum guessed, were former criminals or brigands.

Buttle himself was a good example. Surly and ill-tempered, he was also authoritarian and arrogant, demanding the best seat in the house and the finest food, wine and ale when he visited, then waving the bill away with an airy gesture, telling Cullum to present it at the castle, a good day's ride away.

Buttle also had assumed the title of Sir John—an obvious

pretense. "If he's a knight," Cullum told his wife, "I'm the Dowager Duchess of Dungully." His wife agreed, but urged him to be cautious.

"We want nothing to do with those people," she said firmly. "We keep ourselves to ourselves, and we don't interfere."

Good advice, Cullum thought gloomily, as he set the table for the midday meal. But now this young free lance was here, asking about events at the castle.

It seemed strange, because he was unlike the type that Buttle had been recruiting. He had paid for his room in advance. And he seemed quite well mannered, always referring to Cullum's wife as "Mistress Gelderris" and speaking politely to the few customers who came in contact with him. Not that there had been many of them last night. Word spread quickly in a small community like this, and people assumed that the free lance's presence would draw Buttle to the inn to recruit him. Most people sought to avoid "Sir John" whenever possible.

"Good afternoon, innkeeper. What's on the menu today?" The voice, coming from so close behind him, made him jump nervously. He turned to see the young warrior had entered the room and was standing a meter away, smiling.

"No menu, I'm afraid, sir," he said, trying to recover his poise after the nervous start the young man had caused. "Just lamb shanks braised with winter vegetables and gravy."

The young man nodded appreciatively.

"Sounds excellent," he said. "And d'you think there might be some of your good wife's delicious berry pie remaining from last night?"

"I'll set you up a table, sir," he said, hurrying to clear a smaller table closer to the fire. But the young man cheerfully declined.

"Don't go to any fuss," he said, dropping onto the bench along the main table. "I'm happy to eat here. Come and join me for a moment."

Cullum hesitated. "Ah, well, sir, it's the busy time of day, you see...."

The warrior nodded, looking around the empty taproom and grinning at the innkeeper.

"So I see. The place is packed to the rafters. Come on, Cullum, I'm a stranger in these parts and I'd like a little local information."

Cullum could think of no way to refuse without offending him. And offending trained warriors was not a good idea. Reluctantly, he agreed.

"Well, just a few minutes, then. The customers will be arriving soon."

His regular customers may have stayed away the previous night—people could always do without a drink for a night or two. But the lunch trade was different. They had to eat somewhere, and the Cracked Flagon was their only choice.

Cullum sat down, a little reluctantly. He preferred to keep his distance from strange warriors, no matter how friendly they might appear.

"I'm told there was a jongleur passed through here some time back. Perhaps two weeks ago?" the warrior said.

Cullum, suspicions instantly on the alert, replied cautiously.

"Aye, sir. There was, I recall."

Last he'd heard, the jongleur in question had been heading for Macindaw as well—although there were rumors that he had been part of Lord Orman's mysterious escape.

"No need to call me sir. Hawken's my name. Now, about this jongleur, young fellow, was he? About my age—but not quite as big?"

The innkeeper nodded. "I'd say so. Yes."

"Hmmm," Hawken said. "Any idea where he might be now?"

Cullum hesitated. In truth, he couldn't say for sure. He decided he'd simply stick to what he knew.

"He was headed for the castle, sir—" He noticed the warrior tilt his head at the word and hurried to change it. "I mean, Hawken. But I've since heard that he might be somewhere in Grimsdell Wood."

The young man pursed his lips at the news.

"Grimsdell?" he said. "I thought that was the lair of that fellow Malkallam?"

Cullum looked anxiously around at the name. Malkallam was not someone that he wanted to discuss. He wished fervently that his normal lunchtime customers would arrive and give him a reason to get up and go to the kitchen.

"Please, Hawken, we don't usually . . . discuss Mal . . . that person," he said awkwardly. Hawken nodded his understanding, rubbing his hand over his chin as he considered the innkeeper's words.

"Still," he said, "what would a jongleur be doing in those woods?"

"Possibly minding his own business. A practice I can recommend to you, Hawken."

Cullum felt the icy swirl of wind from outside as the main door opened. Both men at the table whirled around to see a cloaked, cowled figure silhouetted against the light from the doorway. The tip of a recurve bow was visible, slung over one shoulder. At the other, the fletched ends of a quiver full of arrows could be seen. Hawken slowly rose from the bench, stepping clear and turning to face the new arrival, left hand dropping casually to the scabbard of his long sword, angling it slightly forward to facilitate drawing the weapon.

Cullum stood up rapidly, tangling his feet and stumbling as he looked fearfully at the two men facing each other.

"Please, gentlemen," he said, "there's no need for unpleasantness here."

The silence in the room grew unbearable. He was about to add another plea for reason, thinking of the damage that would be done to his taproom, when he heard a surprising sound.

Laughter.

It started with the tall swordsman, Hawken. His shoulders began to shake, and in spite of a massive effort to suppress it, a snort of laughter burst from him. It was echoed by the silhouetted figure, whom Cullum now recognized as the jongleur, Will Barton—the jongleur they had just been discussing. The two now abandoned their threatening positions and moved forward, throwing their arms around each other exuberantly, hands pounding on backs in greeting. Finally the jongleur, the smaller of the two, pulled away, a wry grimace on his face.

"Careful, for pity's sake! Stop pounding me with that giant leg of mutton you call a hand! You'll break my spine, you oaf!"

Hawken recoiled from the other man in mock horror.

"Oh, did the big brute of a warrior damage the delicate little jongleur?" he asked. The two of them burst into more snorfles of laughter.

Cullum, totally puzzled, looked at them. The door to the kitchen opened, and his wife, hearing the noise in the taproom, peered through. Her eyes widened as she took in the two armed men, now standing back a little from each other and giggling in a most unwarlike way. She looked a question at Cullum, but all the innkeeper could do was shrug in bewilderment.

Hawken, however, noticed the movement from the corner of his eye and turned toward her. He placed a muscular arm around the shoulders of the jongleur and led him toward the bar as he spoke. He seemed to tower over the smaller man.

"We'll have another guest for lunch, mistress," he said cheerfully. "He may look like a midget, but he has an appetite like a giant."

"Of course, sir," she said, as puzzled as ever. She withdrew into the kitchen, shaking her head.

Hawken led his friend to the separate table that the innkeeper had been about to set a few minutes ago.

"My god, Horace! It's wonderful to see you!" Will exclaimed as they sat down. Then he couldn't contain his excitement any longer. "You're just the person I need! What brings you here? And what's all this Hawken nonsense? And since when did you become a free lance? What happened to your oak leaf?"

"Careful, Will! Mind what you're saying!" Hawken held up his hands to stem the flow of questions. He directed a warning look at Will as his old friend queried his name. He glanced meaningfully in the direction of the innkeeper, who was listening keenly, eager to know more about these strange young men and what they were doing in Norgate Fief.

Already, Cullum felt a stirring of interest. The name Horace and the mention of an oakleaf symbol struck a chord in his memory. Sir Horace, the Oakleaf Knight, was a legendary figure in Araluen, even in a place as remote as Norgate. Of course, the more remote the location, the more garbled and fantastic the legends became. As Cullum had heard tell, Sir Horace had been a youth of sixteen when he defeated the tyrant Morgarath in single combat, slicing the head off the evil lord's shoulders with one mighty stroke of a massive broadsword.

Then, in the company of the equally legendary Ranger Halt, Sir Horace had traveled across the Stormwhite Sea to defeat the Riders from the East and rescue Princess Cassandra and her companion, the apprentice Ranger known as Will.

Will! The significance of the name suddenly registered with the innkeeper. The jongleur's name was Will. Now here he was, in a cowled cloak, festooned with recurve bow and a quiver of arrows. He looked more closely and saw the hilt of a heavy saxe knife just visible at his waist. No doubt about it, Cullum thought, these cheerful young men were two of Araluen's greatest heroes! Trying to look casual, he turned toward the kitchen, eager to share the news with his wife. Horace saw him go and shook his head at Will.

"Now see what you've done?" he said. "Hawken is my cover name. I'm supposed to be incognito. That's why I'm wearing a free lance's blazon. After all, there'd be no point taking a false identity and then covering myself with oakleaf symbols, would there?"

Will shook his head, perplexed.

"A cover name? Who gave you a cover name? Who sent you?"

"Didn't you get the message?" Horace asked. "Halt and Crowley thought you might need some help—"

Before he could finish, Will interrupted, grinning. "So they sent you to tell me it was on the way?" he asked innocently. Horace gave him a pained look, and he was instantly contrite. "Sorry. Go on."

"As I say," Horace continued deliberately, "they thought you might need a grown-up to look after you, so they sent me along. They thought I'd better travel incognito until I saw what was happening. But . . . there should have been a message pigeon telling you all this at least a week ago."

Will raised his hands in a frustrated gesture. "We've lost contact with Halt," he said. "Things have been a little hectic around here lately, and Alyss's pigeon handler had to run for it."

"Where is Alyss, by the way?" Horace asked. Before he could stop himself, he looked around, as if she might suddenly materialize in the room. The moment he did it, he realized how senseless the action was. Will's expression darkened.

"She's being held prisoner," he said quietly. Horace started to his feet.

"Held prisoner?" he said. "By whom? By Malkallam? Well, let's go and get her! What are we doing wasting time here?"

Will put a hand on his arm and drew him back down to his seat again. He couldn't help grinning. That was so like Horace, he thought. If he thought a friend was in danger, his first instinct was to charge to the rescue. And Alyss, of course, was a friend. The three of them had grown up together in the Ward at Castle Redmont.

"Settle down," he said. "She's being held in the tower at Macindaw by Keren. Malcolm and I are working on a plan to get her out. Now that you're here, we might stand a better chance."

Horace frowned. "Malcolm?" he said. "Who's Malcolm? And who's this Keren fellow? I keep hearing about him. I ran into some character yesterday called Buttle who said Keren was running things at the castle now."

Will nodded. "As I said, things have been a little hectic. Malcolm is Malkallam's real name. But," he hastened to add as he saw Horace about to interrupt, "he's no sorcerer. Just a healer. He's on our side. Keren has taken over the castle. We're pretty sure he's got something planned with the Scotti, but we're not sure what."

There was a bustle of movement and conversation outside the inn. The taproom door opened and four local farmworkers entered, looking for their meal. They noticed the two young men already seated and mumbled greetings to them. Then they took their places at the long table Cullum had set up.

"However," Will said, "I don't think this is the place to discuss it." He was conscious that country folk were notoriously curious about strangers. As a result, every ear in the taproom would be listening to their conversation. "Let's eat and I'll fill in the details on the ride back."

7

AFTER A SUBSTANTIAL LUNCH AT THE INN, WILL AND HORACE prepared to mount for the ride back to Grimsdell. Before they did, however, Horace untied the bow case hanging behind his saddle and passed it to Will.

"This is yours," he said. "Halt thought you might need it."

A delighted grin broke over Will's face as he slid the massive longbow from the case and felt its weight and balance for a few seconds. Then, he deftly slipped one end into a leather loop on the back of his right boot and leaned forward, bending the heavy bow across his shoulders as he slid the string up into the grooved recess at the tip. He drew back on the string once or twice, testing the familiar weight of the draw. Then he quickly unstrung the recurve bow and placed that in the bow case.

"That feels a lot better," he said. Horace nodded. He understood the satisfaction and comfort that a familiar weapon brought with it. They mounted and rode away from the inn together. Horace, on his massive battlehorse, towered over Will, who, of course, was riding Tug. The dog loped along in front of them, questing back and forth across their path as she found new scents to chase down and identify. She had deigned to accompany Will on the trip to the Cracked Flagon, as the giant Trobar was busy on some chore for Malcolm.

"I heard you had a dog these days," Horace said. "What's his name?"

"He's a she," Will replied. "And I haven't got around to choosing a name yet."

Horace studied the dog thoughtfully. She was almost all black, apart from a white chest and a white flash on her face.

"Blackie would be good," he offered after a while. Will raised an eyebrow.

"That's an original thought," he said. "How in the world did you ever think of that?"

Horace ignored the sarcasm. "It's better than calling him 'the dog.'"

"Her," said Will. "He's a she, remember?"

"Whatever," Horace continued. "A dog should have a name. And you can hardly criticize me for being unoriginal if you haven't even thought of a name yet. Blackie is better than nothing."

"That's debatable," Will answered. But secretly, he was enjoying this friendly bickering with Horace. It was just like old times.

"Well, I'm going to call him . . . sorry, her . . . Blackie," Horace decided.

Will shrugged. "If you choose to. But she's an intelligent animal. I doubt that she'll answer to such a mundane name."

Horace looked sidelong at him. His friend seemed very sure of himself. Suddenly, the tall warrior let out a piercing whistle, then called, "Blackie! Stay, girl!"

Instantly, the dog stopped her questing and turned to face him, one forepaw raised, her head tilted inquisitively. Horace made a triumphant gesture in Will's direction. Will snorted in derision.

"That doesn't prove anything," he protested. "She heard the

whistle, that's all! You could have called out . . . Bread and Butter
Pudding, and she would have stopped!"

"Bread and Butter Pudding?" Horace repeated with mock incre-
dulity. "That's your suggestion for a name, is it? Oh yes, that's *much*
better than Blackie."

"I simply meant she stopped because you whistled," Will
persisted. In the past, he had usually won these verbal encounters
with Horace. His friend now smiled at him in an annoyingly superior way.

As they rode up to the dog, who was still waiting for them, Will
muttered out of the corner of his mouth, "Traitor."

But unfortunately, Horace overheard him.

"Traitor? Well, that's a slight improvement on Bread and Butter
Pudding, wouldn't you say, Blackie?" he said.

And to Will's chagrin, the dog barked once, as if in agreement,
then darted ahead again to resume her questing. Horace let out
a contented chuckle. Then he decided he should let Will off
the hook.

"So the whole story about the sorcerer was nothing but rumors?"
he said. They had managed to discuss some of the events at
Macindaw over lunch, but there were still details that Horace wanted
to know.

"Not quite," he said. "The lights and strange sounds and apparitions in the forest were all real enough. But they were illusions created by Malcolm. Alyss figured that out," he added.

Horace nodded. "She was always quick on the uptake,
wasn't she?"

"Absolutely. Anyway, Malcolm used his illusions to frighten people away and keep his little community safe. Pretty soon, people
started believing that Malkallam was back.

"Then Keren took advantage of the situation to seize control of the castle. He slowly poisoned Lord Syron until the poor man was helpless, virtually dead. Keren knew that Orman would be an unpopular lord in his father's place. And he knew that people would be prepared to believe it when Keren spread rumors that Orman was dabbling in the black arts. That gave Keren a chance to take control."

"But you got Orman out?" Horace asked.

Will nodded. "Just in time. Keren had poisoned him as well. But he didn't get the chance to finish the job."

"What's happened to Syron?" Horace asked. "That Buttle character said he may already be dead."

Will could only shrug. "We don't know. He could well be. Now that Keren has shown his hand, there's no reason for him to keep Syron alive."

Horace frowned. "This Keren sounds like a thoroughly nasty piece of work," he said.

"He didn't seem that way when I met him," Will admitted, a little crestfallen. "He had me fooled at the start. I was convinced that - Orman was behind all the hocus-pocus and that Keren was on the side of the angels. I was wrong. Now the first priority is to get Alyss out."

Horace nodded agreement. "How do you plan to go about it?"

Will glanced sidelong at him. "I thought we'd assault the castle," he replied, adding casually, "You know about that sort of thing, don't you?"

Horace thought for a moment before answering. He pursed his lips. "I know the theory," he said. "I can't say I've ever actually done it."

"Well, of course not," Will agreed. "But the theory is pretty simple, isn't it." He managed to make it sound like a statement, not a question. He didn't want Horace to know that he was working entirely in the dark. But Horace was too busy gathering his thoughts to notice.

People often assumed that Horace was not a great thinker—even that he was a little slow. They were wrong. He was methodical. Where Will tended toward flashes of brilliance and intuition, jumping from one fact to another and then back again like a grasshopper, Horace would carefully think a problem through in strict sequence, one concept leading logically to another.

His eyes narrowed as he recalled the lessons he'd learned in Battleschool under the tutelage of Sir Rodney. Even after he had been knighted and appointed to Castle Araluen, Horace had spent several months each year with his original mentor at Castle Redmont, learning the finer points of the warrior's craft.

"Well," he said at length, "to assault a castle, you need siege engines, of course."

"Siege engines?" Will repeated. He knew vaguely what Horace was talking about. He knew definitely that he didn't have any.

"Catapults. Mangonels. Trebuchets. The sort of things that throw rocks and giant spears and dead cows at the defenders and batter down the walls."

"Dead cows?" Will interrupted. "Why would you throw dead cows at the walls?"

"You throw them *over* the walls. It's supposed to spread disease and lower the defenders' morale," Horace told him.

Will shook his head. "I don't suppose it does much for the cows' morale either."

Horace frowned at him, feeling they were getting off the point. "Forget the dead cows. You throw boulders and such to breach the walls." Another detail occurred to him, and he added, "And siege towers are always handy too."

"But not absolutely necessary?" Will interjected. Horace chewed his bottom lip for a moment.

"No. Not absolutely. As long as you have plenty of ladders."

"Yeah. We'll have them," Will said, making a mental note: Build plenty of ladders.

"And as far as numbers go, Sir Rodney always felt you needed at least a three-to-one majority."

"Three to one? Isn't that a little excessive?" Will asked. He didn't like the way this conversation was progressing, but Horace didn't register his growing doubt.

"Well, at least. You see, the defenders have all the advantages. They've got the high ground. They're concealed behind the walls. So you need to draw as many of them as possible away from the place where you make your real assault. For that, you need at least three times as many men as they do. Four times is even better."

"Oh." That was all Will could come up with.

Horace frowned, remembering what he had been told about Castle Macindaw when Crowley and Halt had briefed him some weeks back.

"I figure a place like Macindaw has a permanent garrison of, what, thirty, thirty-five men?"

Will nodded slowly. "Ye-es. That sounds about right."

"So we'll need about a hundred and five, maybe a hundred and ten men to be on the safe side."

"That would be three to one, I suppose," Will agreed.

"That way, we can mount fake assaults on two sides and draw most of the defenders away from the point we really want to attack."

"But don't they know that's the way it's done?" Will asked, trying to salvage something from this conversation.

"Of course they do."

"So couldn't we, for example, just assault in one place so they'll think it's a mock attack to draw off their numbers, but then keep on and make it the real assault?"

Horace considered that. "We could, I suppose. But they can't take the risk that we won't do exactly that. They'd have to counter each threat as it arises, and assume it's the real assault. Then, when we've got them strung out all over the walls, running from place to place and totally confused and disorganized, we hit them with the real attack."

"Yes. That makes sense," Will said. Despondently, he realized that it did, in fact, make sense.

"Of course," Horace said, warming to his theme now as he remembered more details, "the quality of your attacking troops is a big factor. And the quality of the defenders. What sort of men does Keren have?"

"On the whole, we think they're pretty low quality," Will said. "Not the friendliest of types, but not the brightest either."

"That matches what I saw of them. The ones I saw would look right at home trying to stick a dagger in your back on a dark night. They didn't look like prime fighting men." They had already discussed his meeting with John Buttle the previous day.

"Most of the original garrison have gone," Will said. "They weren't too fond of the new men Keren's been recruiting."

"Would they fight for us?" Horace asked.

Will shook his head. "No, unfortunately. They all think Malkallam is a sorcerer. Most of them have left the immediate district, looking for other work."

"So who do we have? Are they trained? Do they know one end of a sword from another, or are they all local farmers and plowboys?"

"They're Skandians," Will said.

Horace gave a small whoop of triumph. "Skandians! That's

terrific! Well, if we've got troops like that, we'll get away with a three-to-one majority, I should think. Maybe even a little less." He paused, then asked the question Will had been dreading. "How many do we have?"

"A little less than three to one, as a matter of fact," Will hedged.

Horace shrugged. "No matter. I'm sure we can manage. So, how many, exactly?"

"You mean, counting you and me?" Will asked. For the first time he saw a flicker of suspicion in Horace's eyes.

"Yes. I think we'd better count you and me. How many?" Horace's tone of voice told Will that he would tolerate no further prevarication.

The Ranger took a deep breath.

"Counting you and me, twenty-seven."

"Twenty-seven," Horace repeated, his tone devoid of any expression.

"But they're Skandians, after all," Will said hopefully.

His friend looked at him, one eyebrow raised in disbelief. "They'd better be," he said heavily.

8

ALYSS WAS STUDYING THE SMALL, BLACK STELLATITE PEBBLE once again.

When Will's arrow had soared through her window the night before, she had been surprised to find it contained what appeared to be a pebble. Then she read Malcolm's brief explanation of its purpose, and she felt a surge of hope.

She was more ready to believe that the stone could help her refocus her mind than Will had been. After all, she had experienced the effects of the blue gem that Keren used on her. She had seen how quickly her mind could be enslaved by it. Now she was grateful that she might have a way to resist his efforts. Alyss was a strong-willed and intelligent girl, and the thought that her mind had been captured so easily by Keren made her feel vulnerable and exposed.

She examined the little pebble, turning it over in her fingers. It was definitely pleasant to the touch—smooth, glossy and comforting.

And was that a hint of warmth she felt radiating from it? Or was she just imagining it? She wasn't sure. She read through the last few lines of Malcolm's instructions, carefully transcribed by Will onto the thin message sheet.

Touch the stellatite pebble when Keren attempts to use the gemstone. Focus on a positive, pleasant image. When he questions you, speak normally. Do not pretend to be in a daze or he will know you are trying to trick him.

There were a few final lines written in code. She had decoded them to find they outlined a signaling schedule. Will wanted to avoid regular signaling, knowing that Keren would eventually become aware of it. The colored lights in the trees would appear at irregular intervals, not at the same time and place each night. And sometimes, there would be no message and the white light's movements would alter from the strict pattern needed for the code.

"Clever, Will," she said softly. She knew Keren was no fool. Will also told her that he would keep someone watching the tower each night in case she had anything urgent to communicate.

She burned the thin paper in the flame of the lamp. When it was reduced to ashes, she crumpled them to dust and scattered them out the window.

She already knew what positive image she would use when Keren next tried to mesmerize her.

Less than an hour later, she heard Keren's voice in the anteroom outside and the startled clatter as the sentries came to attention.

Alyss was willing to bet that he'd heard about the lights in the forest—maybe he'd even watched them himself. Now, she figured, he was here to make sure there was no significance to them. As the key turned in the door lock, she slipped the pebble under the tight cuff of her left sleeve, where it was concealed yet accessible.

Keren nodded briskly to her as he entered the room. He jerked his head toward the table.

"Sit down, Alyss," he said. "I have a few questions for you."

Today, he was all business. Obviously, he didn't have time to waste and there would be none of the previous mock-friendly formalities. She was grateful for that. His good humor and self-satisfied air had begun to grate on her. They were enemies, after all, and she would prefer it if he treated her accordingly, without the pretense at airs and graces and knightly charm.

He reached into the leather wallet at his belt and produced the blue stone, letting it roll onto the table between his fingers. There was no need for preamble now. The stone had become the trigger for his posthypnotic suggestion. All he had to do was order her to look at it and, within a few seconds, she would be mesmerized again.

He leaned forward. "Look at the stone, Alyss," he said softly.

Her eyes fell to the beautiful orb as he rolled it gently back and forth on the tabletop. As ever, she could feel it drawing her in, filling her consciousness.

Beneath the table, she slid the forefinger of her right hand under the cuff of her left sleeve, to touch the smoothness of the little pebble. Instantly, she saw a glossy black sheen overlay the blue depths of the gem and her mind stepped back from the abyss of Keren's control.

Think of a pleasant, positive image, Malcolm had instructed. Will's face, deep brown eyes smiling, came to life before her.

And her mind was free.

"Keep looking at the blue," Keren said softly. "Are you ready to answer my questions?" She continued to stare at the gem. But now the depth had gone from it, and it was a dim background to her image of Will's face. She'd always loved that cheeky grin of his, she realized.

"Yes," she replied simply. She was glad that Malcolm had instructed her not to try to appear as if she were in a trance. She had no way of knowing how she had behaved on the previous occasions when Keren had controlled her mind, but she had assumed she must have been in some kind of trancelike state. Apparently not.

"Good. There were lights in the forest last night," he said. She had been right. He knew about them.

"There were," she repeated, neither questioning the fact nor confirming it. So far, there had been no direct question, so there was no specific answer required.

"Did you see them?" he asked.

Suddenly, she felt the urge to answer truthfully. To say, "Yes. I saw them. They were signals." She stroked the stellatite, felt the compulsion recede as her resolve strengthened.

"No," she said, and her heart leapt. She had broken his hold over her. She could tell him anything, answer anything, as long as she kept her wits about her. Inside, she was exultant and she felt her heart pounding. But her diplomatic training helped her keep a totally neutral expression on her face.

Keren frowned. He was sure the lights had been some form of signal being sent to her. But he knew she couldn't lie to a direct question. He tried again.

"You're sure?" he said. "There were red, blue, yellow and white lights moving in the trees. Did you see them?"

Alyss, on the point of saying, "It was late. I was asleep," stopped herself just in time. If she hadn't seen the lights, she would have no way of knowing when they had appeared. She realized that her hold on control was a tenuous one. The effort of countering Keren's insistent assault on her mind was very distracting, and she must not let her guard slip.

"I didn't see them," she replied. Then she added, in a conversational tone, "I've seen them before."

Her eyes on the gem, she felt rather than saw Keren's head snap up at that revelation.

"When?" he asked her instantly. "When did you see them?"

"Ten days ago. Will and I went into the forest. There were lights."

She knew he had a pretty good idea that she had been into Grimsdell Wood with Will. His men had shadowed her on that occasion. At the time, of course, she and Will had assumed it was Orman having them followed. And while they hadn't actually seen her enter or leave the forest, Keren must suspect that was where they had gone. It would do no harm now to admit it. It might even divert him from the line of questions he was following.

He drummed the fingers of one hand on the table. As he became more distracted, Alyss noticed that it became easier for her to control her words and her thoughts.

He tried one more time. But she could feel his conviction was waning. "What do the lights mean?"

She shrugged. "I think Malkallam uses them," she said. "They frighten people away from the forest."

The fingers drummed again. "Yes. They do that all right. My men won't go near the place."

That was definitely worth knowing. Since Will had escaped into the forest with Orman, she had thought that Keren might have seen through Malkallam's ploy and convinced his men to follow them in and hunt for them.

Keren let go a long, pent-up breath. He was on edge. She sensed he was expecting something, some event to take place. His next words confirmed her suspicions.

"Well, I can't waste any more time with this. General MacHaddish is due in the next day or two." He was speaking to himself, secure in the knowledge that his words wouldn't register with her in her mesmerized state. He rolled the blue stone back toward him and removed it from the table.

"All right, Alyss. Until next time. You can wake up now."

She assumed that she should not make any pretense of coming out of a trance but simply continue with normal conversation. But her mind was racing. MacHaddish was a Scotti name. There was a Scotti general due here in the next few days. Will would have to be told.

"So," she said evenly, "what did you wish to talk about?"

Keren smiled at her. "We've already talked," he said. "But of course, you don't remember it."

That's what you think, Alyss thought.

9

WILL AND HORACE RODE ALONG THE WINDING PATH THROUGH Grimsdell Wood, following the dog's unwavering lead. Horace shook his head at the impenetrable tangle of trees and foliage around them.

"No wonder Malcolm's been safe in here all these years," he said.

Will smiled. "It's been his best defense," he agreed. "Of course, he has a few other ways to discourage visitors."

"He'd hardly need them. You could lose an army in here, and they'd never find their way out . . . good grief!"

The last two words were drawn from him as they rounded a bend in the track and he saw the gruesome skull warning sign among the trees. He suspected that Will had intentionally neglected to tell him about it.

"Oh, that's Trevor. Pay him no mind. He's harmless," Will said.

Horace could hear him chuckling quietly to himself as they rode on.

"Hilarious," he muttered to himself.

They came to the clearing in the woods quite abruptly. One moment they were in the semidark tunnel formed by the track among the gloomy old trees. Next, they were in the sunlight, and Malcolm's pleasant little thatched cottage was before them, smoke curling from its chimney.

A table had been set up in the late-afternoon sunshine, and Will could see Malcolm, Xander and, to his surprise, Orman sitting around it. The sallow-faced castle lord appeared to have lost weight. His face, beneath the receding hairline, was even paler than normal and there were dark shadows under his eyes. The eyes themselves, however, were bright and alert.

There were two vacant chairs. Will guessed that Malcolm had delayed lunch until they arrived. In all probability, Will thought, he had been receiving constant updates on their progress.

After introductions all around, Will and Horace sat at the table with the others. The dog took off like an arrow, catching sight of Trobar on the far side of the clearing.

"Go ahead, then," Will said belatedly.

"We waited lunch for you," Malcolm told them.

Will made a disclaiming gesture. "We ate lunch at the inn," he began, but Horace interrupted before he got any further.

"Still, there's no harm in an early supper," he said. He was forever hungry, although his lean, muscular frame showed no evidence of the amount he could eat.

"It's good to see you up and around, my lord," Will told Orman. The castle lord allowed himself a wry grimace.

"Up, perhaps, Will Barton. But I'm definitely a long way from being around."

"We're very pleased with his progress," Malcolm put in.

Will indicated Horace, who had already begun demolishing a bread roll.

"And the good news continues, my lord. With Horace to help us, we'll soon have you back in your castle." Horace reddened slightly at Will's fulsome praise, and Will realized he might be laying it on a little thick, but he was inordinately pleased and relieved to have his old comrade by his side again. He sensed that the others hadn't realized the significance of Horace's identity, so he added, "You might know him better as the Oakleaf Knight."

The name meant nothing to Xander, who scowled and muttered, just loud enough to be heard, "And how much are we paying this one, I wonder?"

Horace reddened further, but said nothing.

Orman shot Xander a warning look. The little man subsided, mumbling. Then a thought struck Orman.

"The Oakleaf Knight?" he said thoughtfully. "Then surely you're the one who was involved in that business with Morgarath some years back? And with the Skandians, as I recall."

Horace shrugged. "A lot of that was exaggerated, my lord."

But now Orman's gaze had turned to Will as realization dawned.

"And I recall that he had a friend who was a Ranger," he said. "That was you, wasn't it? Will Barton, my foot! You're the one they now call Will Treaty?"

It was Will's turn to shrug.

"All of that was exaggerated," he said. He noticed that Malcolm was oblivious to the events that Orman was discussing. Of course, Will thought, he'd been secluded in the forest for years. Xander, however, was looking disconcerted as he realized he had just insulted one of the Kingdom's most capable warriors. Will grinned. Served him right.

Horace coughed gently. He had more important matters on his mind than a surly insult from Orman's attendant.

"There was some mention of food?" he reminded them. Horace always did have a good grasp of priorities.

10

THE MEAL WAS EXCELLENT, CONSISTING OF COLD ROAST venison, some plump wood ducks and a salad of slightly bitter winter greens. There was warm, fresh, crusty bread as well. All in all, it more than lived up to Horace's expectations. He tipped his chair back contentedly and grinned at Will.

"Good food," he said. "What's for dessert?"

Will rolled his eyes to heaven.

Malcolm smiled indulgently. "He's a growing boy," he said. He had been impressed by Horace's self-effacing, cheerful demeanor. He gathered that the young man was something of a celebrity in the Kingdom and it was his experience that famous people usually behaved as if the rest of the world should step aside and be impressed by them. Nothing could be farther from the truth with Horace.

The young warrior reached across the table and poured himself another mug of black coffee. Like Will, he drank it generously laced with honey, a habit he had learned from the Ranger when they had traveled to Celtica years previously.

Malcolm winced slightly as he watched. Pleasant young man or not, if Horace and Will kept drinking coffee at this rate, he was going

to run out. He made a mental note to send one of his people to the
Cracked Flagon to trade for more beans.

There was a small commotion at the far side of the clearing, and
they all looked up.

A file of roughly dressed, heavily armed men emerged from the
forest, led by a smaller man with a withered right arm held close to
his body. As Horace looked at him, he realized that the man also had
a hunched right shoulder.

The new arrivals peered around the clearing uncertainly, shading
their eyes from the sudden light after hours in the dimness of the
woods. Some of Malcolm's people, alarmed at the sight of a group of
armed men, had let out startled cries, then faded away into the forest.
The Skandians, in turn, muttered among themselves at the sight of
them. Each of Malcolm's followers suffered some significant form of
disfigurement, and the superstitious sea wolves, who believed all forests were inhabited by spirits and ogres, closed ranks a little and
made sure their weapons were free and ready for use.

Unlike the others, Trobar didn't attempt to hide. Instead, he
moved to interpose himself between the new arrivals and his master.
At the sight of the giant, the muttering and uncertainty among the
Skandians increased. They were all big, burly men, but Trobar towered over the biggest of them.

By now, Will knew that, in spite of his terrifying appearance,
Trobar was at heart a gentle person. Yet he had no doubt the giant
would give his life if anyone attempted to harm the man who had
taken him in and given him a home. The dog, Will noted, had gone
with him. Sensing Trobar's concern, her hackles had risen, and the
ruff of fur around her throat seemed to be twice its normal size.

The young Ranger rose hurriedly and stepped forward to prevent any unfortunate misunderstanding.

"It's all right, Trobar," he said quietly. "They're friends." Then, in a louder voice, he called across the clearing, "Gundar Hardstriker, welcome to Healer's Clearing."

He came up with the name on the spot, thinking that such an unthreatening name might serve to relax the situation. As he spoke and the Skandians recognized him, he could see the tension in them drop away a little. Trobar, for his part, stopped his advance across the clearing and stepped to one side. Will went forward to greet the Skandian crew. Horace followed, a pace or two behind him.

"I take it these are our men?" he said mildly.

Will glanced back over his shoulder. "Your men," he amended. "You'll command them, not me."

Horace grinned at him, not taken in for a second by that ploy. "I'll command them," he said, "as long as we do exactly what you tell us to do, right?"

He had experience with Rangers and how they operated. They claimed to be nothing more than advisers who stayed in the background. Yet he knew they were experts at manipulating any situation. He had seen Halt do it with the Skandians five years ago. Will's mentor was a master of the art of commanding while not seeming to. Horace had no doubt that his apprentice had learned the skill as well.

Will had the grace to smile at the comment. "Yes. Something like that," he admitted.

Gundar had stepped forward a few paces as the two Araluens approached. He made the peace sign.

"Good pastnoon, Will Treaty," he said. "This is a strange place you've brought us to."

Will nodded. "Strange, Gundar, but not unfriendly. Nobody here wishes you ill."

"Unless it's that idiot secretary," Horace put in, in an undertone.

"Shut up," Will told him in the same tone, then, speaking more loudly, he said, "Gundar, meet my friend, Sir Horace."

Horace and Gundar shook hands, each studying the other, each liking what he saw.

Horace was young, Gundar saw. But his face bore the signs of experience in combat—the scar and the slightly broken nose. Yet there weren't so many as to suggest that he was continually on the receiving end. Gundar subscribed to the view that a face covered in battle scars usually belonged to a man who didn't know how to duck.

Horace, for his part, saw a typical Skandian: powerful, fearless, experienced, a man who handled his massive battleax with practiced ease and who met your gaze frankly while giving you a handshake that could crack walnuts. With twenty-five men like this, he thought, he could probably just knock the castle down.

"Sir Horace is the commander for the assault?" Gundar asked, and Will nodded.

"That's right. Even a small army like ours needs a general, and Horace is trained for the job."

Gundar shrugged, content with the arrangement. "That's agreeable," he said.

In Gundar's view, a commander was really nothing more than an entrepreneur. He could worry about all the minor points like tactics and strategy. Skandians weren't interested in niceties like that. A commander's chief task, so far as Gundar was concerned, was to supply opportunities for Skandians to hit people.

Yet acceptance was not total. Inevitably, there was one Skandian who looked at Horace and saw only his youth. In typical Skandian fashion, he wasted no time making his views known.

"It may be agreeable to you, Gundar," he said in a loud voice, "but I'm not taking orders from a boy who's still wet behind the ears."

Will heard Horace give vent to a small sigh—there were equal amounts of exasperation and boredom in the sound. Quietly, Will hid a smile. Horace had plenty of experience in dealing with this particular situation.

A less confident man than Horace might have blustered and shouted and attempted to enforce his authority on the Skandian. Which, of course, would have been the wrong approach entirely. Skandians placed little value on words.

Instead, Horace smiled and stepped forward, gesturing for the Skandian to do likewise.

He was a big man, perhaps a few centimeters shorter than Horace, but broader in the shoulders and in the body. Horace noted with interest that he was the bearer of many scars. Horace shared Gundar's opinion about such men. His hair was long and gathered in two tarry pigtails, one on either side of his head. His long beard was a tangle of greasy whiskers and bore visible evidence of his last few meals. He carried a massive battleax and a large round oaken shield that looked more like a wagon wheel than a shield. Perhaps it had begun life that way, Horace thought.

The Skandian ignored Horace's smile, keeping his face set in a tight scowl of disapproval as he responded to Horace's gesture and stepped to meet him.

"And your name is?" Horace asked mildly.

"I'm Nils Ropehander," the man replied in a loud, aggressive voice. "And my life's too important to place it in the hands of a *boy*."

There was no doubt that the last word was intended as an insult. Horace, however, continued to smile.

"Of course it is," he said reasonably. "And may I say, that's a lovely hat you have."

Like most of the Skandians, Nils Ropehander wore a heavy iron helmet, adorned with two massive horns. As Horace mentioned it and gestured toward it, it was only natural for the Skandian's eyes to glance upward.

As he did so, he momentarily broke eye contact with Horace, which was what the knight intended. Horace stepped forward, grabbed a horn in each hand and lifted the helmet clear of his head. Before the man could properly protest, Horace had slammed the unpadded heavy iron headpiece back down, causing Nils's knees to buckle and his eyes to cross slightly under the impact. The Skandian staggered for a second, but that was long enough. He felt an iron grip seize hold of his beard, and he was jerked violently forward.

Horace stepped forward too, into the off-balance Skandian's path. The heel of his right hand, fingers spread upward, slammed forward into the Skandian's broad nose, making solid contact. At the exact moment that he struck, Horace released his left-handed grip on the beard so the Skandian was hurled backward, sprawling, on his back onto the hard ground.

One inevitable side effect of a solid blow to the nose, as Horace knew, was to fill the eyes with unavoidable tears. As Nils scrabbled on the ground, blinded by tears, he heard a slithering sound of metal on leather. Then he felt a strange prickling sensation in his throat. There had been something familiar about that sound, and instinct told him not to move. He froze and, as his vision cleared, he found himself staring up the glittering length of Horace's sword, its point held lightly just beneath his chin.

"Do we need to take this any further?" Horace said. The smile had gone. The young man was deadly serious, and Nils knew his situation was a very unhealthy one. Horace moved the sword slightly away from his throat to give him room to answer.

The Skandian shook his head and spoke thickly through the blood that was running down the back of his throat from his nose.

"Nuh . . . no fur'der."

"Good," said Horace. He rapidly sheathed the sword, then held his hand out to Nils, helping the burly sea wolf to his feet. The two stood, chest to chest, for a few seconds, and a look of understanding passed between them. Then Horace slapped the Skandian on the shoulder and turned to his shipmates.

"I think that settles things?" he said. There was a chorus of approval and agreement from the others. They all knew Ropehander's propensity to complain and object to any change in routine, and they felt the young knight had handled the situation perfectly. They were impressed by his startling speed, his strength and his expert grasp of Skandian debating tactics. Skandians invariably preferred a good thumping to any amount of well-reasoned argument.

Horace looked around the bearded, approving faces and grinned at them. "Let's see what a bunch of bad bargains I've been given as an army. Step closer," he said.

Grinning in turn, the Skandians moved around him in a half circle. Horace gestured for them to make room for Will.

"He's not too big," he said, "but he can turn very nasty if he's excluded."

The grins widened as they made room for the Ranger. Horace, hands on hips, paced around the circle, frowning as he studied them. They were a scruffy bunch, he thought, and none too clean. Their hair and beards were overlong and often gathered in rough and greasy plaits, like Nils's.

There were scars and broken noses and cauliflower ears in abundance, as well as the widest assortment of rough tattoos, most of which looked as if they had been carved into the skin with the point of a dagger, after which dye was rubbed into the cut. There were grinning skulls, snakes, wolf heads and strange northern runes. All of the men were burly and thickset. Most had bellies on them that suggested they might be overfond of ale.

All in all they were as untidy, rank-smelling and rough-tongued a bunch of pirates as one could be unlucky enough to run into. Horace turned to Will and his frown faded.

"They're beautiful," he said.

11

THE LITTLE SPACE WILL HAD CHRISTENED HEALER'S CLEARING was growing considerably more crowded. Malcolm's small cottage was already stretched by having to accommodate Lord Orman and Xander. As a consequence, Will and Horace chose to pitch their own one-man tents on one side of the clearing, close together, where they could talk in private.

The Skandians had brought canvas and ropes from their ship and they set about building a large, communal shelter for themselves on the far side. At least, Will thought, there was no lack of timber available in Grimsdell Wood.

A large fire pit was constructed in the middle of the clearing for heating and cooking purposes, and to provide an area for relaxation as well. On the first evening, Horace looked a little askance at the roaring blaze that the Skandians built. The northmen seemed to have a love for setting big fires, whether they were burning down villages or just sitting around having a drink.

"It's a big fire," he said doubtfully to Will. "It could be visible for miles."

The Ranger shrugged. "No harm in it," he replied. "It'll just add to the legend of Grimsdell—strange sounds, strange lights."

At that moment, the Skandians, who had brought a few kegs of aquavit, the rough grain spirit that they flavored with caraway seeds, broke out into a sea chantey.

"Strange sounds, indeed," Malcolm put in. "If I could have come up with something like that, I would have kept people away from my home for another ten years."

One of the Skandians broke away from the circle around the fire and lurched toward the small group of onlookers. He thrust a beaker full of the spirit into Horace's hands.

"Here you go, General," he said, "take a drink."

Horace sniffed carefully. "My god. Do you drink this stuff, or strip paint with it?"

The Skandian bellowed with laughter.

"Both!" he replied. Horace handed him back the beaker.

"I think I'd rather live through the night," he said. The Skandian beamed at him.

"All the more for me, then!" he said, and weaved his way back to join his friends.

Xander had come out onto the veranda of the cottage as the singing had started. He glared disdainfully at the Skandians and walked over to join the little group.

"Is this going to continue for very long?" he asked. Malcolm, Horace and Will regarded him with distaste, then, deciding that he had asked no one in particular, they each decided to let someone else answer.

Xander's scowl deepened.

"Malcolm," he said, "how is my lord supposed to sleep through this infernal racket?"

Malcolm regarded him thoughtfully. "In my experience," he said, "if one is tired enough, one can sleep through a little noise."

"A little noise!" the secretary spluttered. "Do you call what those barbarians are doing—"

He got no further. Will's hand suddenly clamped over his mouth, and the rest of his question was reduced to unintelligible mumbling. Eventually, he stopped, peering fearfully above the hand into the Ranger's eyes. Will's eyes, usually so warm and cheerful, were suddenly cold and threatening. It was as if a curtain had been pulled aside to reveal a previously unseen side of the Ranger's character.

"Xander," Will said, when he was sure he had the man's full attention, "since we have been here, you have done nothing but moan and complain. Malcolm has saved your lord's life. He has given you shelter and food and a safe place to stay. These Skandians—the barbarians to whom you refer—are friends of mine. They are going to help you regain your castle. Some of them will probably die doing it. Sure, we're paying them, but the fact remains, we need them. Now we are all sick and tired of you, Xander. You'd better realize that, unlike the Skandians, we do not need you. So if I hear one more word of complaint, one more snide remark, I swear I will drag you back to Macindaw and hand you over to Keren. Is that clear?"

Xander's eyes still bulged above Will's hand. The Ranger shook him roughly. "Is that clear?" he said very slowly and distinctly. Then he took the hand away.

Xander breathed in, deeply and raggedly, his chest heaving. After a pause, he replied in a small voice.

"Yes."

Will took a deep breath in his turn and exhaled slowly.

"Good," he said, and Horace and Malcolm both nodded agreement. Will started to turn away from Xander, but the little man could not resist trying to have the last word.

"All the same—" he began in that pompous tone they knew so well.

Will threw his hands to heaven in a gesture of despair, then swung back on the little man.

"Right!" he said angrily. His hand shot out and grabbed a handful of Xander's collar, twisting it so that the secretary was thrown off balance and turned slightly side on. Then Will started toward the forest trail that led to the black mere and, eventually, out of Grimsdell Wood to the plain beside Macindaw.

"I'll be back in an hour or so," he called over his shoulder to Horace and Malcolm. "I've got some garbage to take out." Neither of them moved to stop him.

Xander squirmed and wailed, but Will's grip was like iron. He held the secretary off balance and continued to walk quickly away, keeping him that way. Xander could do nothing but totter precariously along in his wake. He sensed that if he stumbled and fell, Will would not stop but would simply drag him until he regained his feet.

Horace wondered later if Will would have made good on his threat. He thought that perhaps he might have, except that Xander would have been able to provide Keren with a lot of useful information, including the whereabouts of Malcolm's clearing and the fact that Will now had a force of armed and eager Skandians at his disposal and was planning to attack the castle with them. Most likely, Horace thought, his friend would have thrown Xander into the mere. Whether he would have fished him out again was a moot point.

But it was one they would have to wonder about. Because just as Will reached the beginning of the track through the woods, one of Malcolm's people dashed into the clearing, coming from the other direction.

It was Poldaric, a young man whose spine had been badly twisted in a childhood accident. He was permanently stooped to one side and could not look straight ahead, as his head was set crookedly on his shoulders. Yet Horace had noted how quickly the young man could move among the trees. Amazing how the body could adapt, he'd thought. Poldaric saw Will now and sidled up to him so he could look up at the young Ranger.

"Your friend," he said, "she's signaling!"

Two hours later, Malcolm's small living room was crowded with people. Horace, Malcolm, Orman, Gundar and Xander were grouped around the fireplace.

Will finished deciphering the last few words of Alyss's message and sat back, frowning.

"Bad news?" Horace prompted. His friend shrugged.

"Could be. Apparently Keren is expecting a visit from a General MacHaddish in the next few days." He glanced at the faces around the table. "Does that name mean anything to anyone?"

Gundar shrugged, as did Malcolm. Orman frowned thought-fully, then shook his head.

"Other than he's obviously a Scotti and the son of someone called Haddish, no. Have you heard the name, Xander?"

The little man thought carefully and shook his head. After his recent confrontation with Will, he was grateful to be included in the discussion and wished he could provide more information.

"I'm afraid not, my lord."

"Well," said Horace, practical as ever, "at least it confirms your theory that Keren's in league with the Scotti."

"True," Will said. "But I wish I knew a little more. For example, it'd be nice to know if this MacHaddish is bringing an army with him."

Orman rubbed his jaw thoughtfully. "I shouldn't think he'd be bringing a large party at this stage," he said, and they all turned to him. "The main route through the border will be almost impassable at this time of year. The snows won't melt for at least another three weeks."

He reached for Will's pen and a spare sheet of paper and drew a quick sketch of the surrounding countryside.

"The mountains here form the natural border," he said. "As you can see, Castle Macindaw lies right across the road from the main pass into Araluen. But the pass is closed during the winter by snow. That's why we've never needed a large winter garrison at Macindaw. We've never had to contend with more than small raids."

He quickly drew a series of thin slashes through the mountains on his chart. "There are a lot of small side roads, but they're steep and tricky. You might get a small party through one of them, but not an army with its baggage train."

Horace had leaned over his shoulder to study the chart. He nodded thoughtfully.

"In addition," he said, "no general would move a large force into hostile territory without initial reconnaissance."

Will nodded agreement. "So we can assume MacHaddish will have a small party with him. Which means they'll probably travel by night." He glanced around and saw the others nodding. Except Gundar, who was looking totally disinterested by now. Skandians hated planning, Will remembered.

"So what do you have in mind?" Horace asked.

"We keep watch on the castle so we know when he arrives," Will said. "Then, when he's heading back to Picta, we take him prisoner and ask him a few questions."

Horace nodded agreement. "Not bad," he said. "But don't expect to get too much out of a Scotti. From what I've heard about them, you'll never get one to talk."

It was Malcolm's turn to smile. "Oh, I think I might know a way," he said.

12

IT WAS SNOWING AGAIN. THE HEAVY CLOUD COVER MASKED THE arrival of dawn, particularly in the forest where Will and Horace were camped. Consequently, there was no moment when Will knew the sun had risen, just a gradual brightening in the dull gray light that covered the countryside. Without noticing the transition from dark to light, Will realized he could see his hand clearly when he held it up, where, a few minutes previously, he had been conscious only of a dark blur.

Their little camp, consisting of a low two-man tent and a canvas shelter strung between two trees, was in a clearing they had hacked out, twenty meters to the side of the track that led toward the border with Picta. They were far enough from the track to remain unseen by anyone passing by, close enough to hear if anyone did.

Two days had passed since Will had read Alyss's message. The two companions had decided to keep watch over the track, in order to intercept and observe the mysterious Scotti general whenever he arrived. Once they knew the size of his party, they could organize an ambush for his return trip.

In addition to their observation post, Malcolm had placed a screen of observers in the woods, keeping watch over the trails and paths that led down from the mountains that barred the way into Picta. His people were used to seeing without being seen, he told them. Their safety had depended for years on their ability to remain hidden.

In the tent, Will heard Horace stir. Then the warrior's face, tangle haired and bleary eyed, appeared at the small triangular entrance. Will was sitting on his heels under the canvas shelter.

"Morning," Horace said grumpily. Will nodded, saying nothing. Horace crawled out through the tent entrance. He reflected that it was impossible to exit from a small tent like this without ending up with two wet patches on the knees. He stood stiffly, stretching himself and groaning slightly.

"Any sign of them yet?" he asked.

Will looked at him. "Yes," he said. "A party of fifty Scotti came through just twenty minutes ago."

"Really?" Horace looked startled. He wasn't fully awake yet.

Will rolled his eyes to heaven. "Oh, my word, yes," he said. "They were riding on oxen and playing bagpipes and drums. Of course not," he went on. "If they had come past, I would have woken you—if only to stop your snoring."

"I don't snore," Horace said, with dignity.

Will raised his eyebrows. "Is that so?" he said. "Then in that case, you'd better chase out that colony of walruses who are in the tent with you."

Horace reached for the canteen hanging from a tree nearby and took a long draft of the icy water. Then he rummaged in a pack for a piece of hard bread and some dried fruit. He frowned at it. "Breakfast," he said distastefully.

Will shrugged unsympathetically. "I've had worse."

Horace bit off a piece of bread and hunkered down beside the Ranger under the canvas awning. Already, there were snowflakes in his hair and dusting his shoulders from the few minutes he had spent in the open air.

"So have I," he said. "But I don't have to like it."

They sat in silence for a few minutes. Horace shifted restlessly every so often. Will, trained to remain silent and unmoving for hours at a time, regarded his old friend sympathetically. Warriors were, by definition, men of action. It went against all their training to simply sit and wait for events to take place.

More to take Horace's mind off the boredom of waiting than for any other reason, he asked, "Do you see much of Evanlyn these days?"

Horace glanced at him quickly. Evanlyn was the Crown Princess Cassandra of Araluen. When Will and Horace had first met her, she had been traveling under the name Evanlyn. Horace knew there had been a special bond between Will and the Princess when they had both been captives of the Skandians. He wondered how strong that bond was these days. It was the first time Will had mentioned her since Horace had arrived. Not surprising, really, he thought. They'd had little opportunity to discuss personal matters since he'd arrived in the fief. The recruiting of the Skandians, Alyss's signals and now the imminent arrival of the mysterious Scotti general had taken up most of their attention.

"I see her from time to time," he said briefly.

Will nodded, giving nothing away. "Unavoidable, I suppose," he said. "After all, you are based at the castle. I suppose you'd bump into her occasionally, wouldn't you?"

"Well . . . a little more than occasionally," Horace said carefully. In fact, he and the Princess saw a good deal of each other socially, but he wasn't sure that he wanted to go into that with Will. In the past, he had sensed a slight tension between himself and his friend when it came to Evanlyn, and he didn't want to re-create it now. He realized that Will was watching him and felt the need to add more.

"I mean, there are balls and dances and such," he said. He didn't add that he was usually invited by Cassandra as her partner for these occasions. "And picnics, of course," he added, immediately wishing that he hadn't. Will arched an eyebrow.

"Picnics?" he said. "How lovely. Sounds like life is one big picnic at the castle these days."

Horace took a deep breath, then decided it might be better if he didn't respond. He stood up and rubbed the small of his back, where the muscles were still stiff.

"I'm getting too old for this camping-out lark," he said. Will noticed the deliberate change of subject and had the grace to feel embarrassed at the way he had been acting. After all, it wasn't Horace's fault that he was based at Castle Araluen. And as an old friend of Evanlyn—Cassandra, rather—it was only logical that he should spend time with her.

"Sorry, Horace," he said, "I spoke out of turn there. I suppose I'm a little edgy. I hate all this waiting around doing nothing."

As a matter of fact, he was completely accustomed to it, and it didn't bother him. Horace looked at him, recognizing the gambit as a peace gesture. His face lit up with that easy grin of his, and Will knew that the awkward moment had passed.

And of course, it was at that instant that Malcolm's man Ambrose slipped into the clearing, calling to them in a hoarse whisper, "Ranger! Sir Horace! The Scotti are coming!"

There were nine of them all told: General MacHaddish and eight warriors forming his escort.

MacHaddish marched at the head of the small column. He was a muscular man but quite stocky—few Scotti were tall. His head was shaven, apart from one long, tightly plaited pigtail that hung down on the left side of his crown. He was wrapped in a coarse woolen tartan upper garment that was nothing more than an elongated blanket. It wound around his shoulders and torso, leaving his arms bare, even in this freezing cold weather. He wore a long kilt of the same material and sheepskin boots. A two-handed broadsword was slung at his back, its massive hilt protruding above his head. The left side of his face was painted in thick stripes of blue, marking him as a general of the second, or lower, rank. On his right cheek and his bare arms, darker-toned tattoos were etched permanently into his skin.

In his left hand, he carried a small, iron-studded shield, a little bigger than a dinner plate.

His men were similarly dressed, in the same dull red-and-blue-checked tartan. But the paint on their faces extended around the eyes only, forming a blue mask on each of them and marking them as common soldiers. One or two wore swords, although none as large as the general's broadsword. Most of them carried clubs—heavy affairs studded with spikes—and the same small, round shields. In each boot top, Will could make out the hilt of a long dirk, for fighting at close quarters.

The Ranger stood, unmoving and wrapped in his cloak, less than two meters from the edge of the track, as the nine men moved past him at a steady jog. Horace, some five meters farther back in the trees, marveled at the way his friend could merge so successfully into the background as to become virtually invisible. Even Horace, who knew exactly where Will was standing, found it hard to pick him out. The ability to get so close to a potential enemy was a real benefit, Horace thought. One could observe so much more detail at that distance.

The shuffling crunch of the Scottis' boots in the thickening snow died away as the small column rounded a bend in the track. Horace watched the last trace of dull red tartan fade among the trees, then stepped forward to where Will was waiting.

"What now?" he asked.

The Ranger glanced up at him. "We'll follow at a distance, make sure they've gone to Macindaw. Then we'll arrange a reception for them when they head home."

Horace voiced a doubt that had been nagging at him for some time. "What if they go home by a different route?"

Will was silent for a few seconds.

"Then we'll have to improvise something," he said, then added, with a flash of annoyance, "For god's sake! Stop trying to make me worry!"

13

ALYSS WAS STANDING BY THE WINDOW, STARING OUT OVER THE bleak snowscape that surrounded Macindaw. Through the low-lying cloud cover, she could make out a diffused, watery glow low in the eastern sky that told her the sun had risen. At any other time, she thought wryly, she might well have been entranced by the wild beauty of the scene, the white fields flanked by the dark mass of trees, their own tops crowned with snow.

But in her current situation, she found the view bleak and depressing. She longed for some spot of color in the world outside. The gray walls of the castle were grim and forbidding, and even the standard that Keren had chosen for himself added to the lack of color—a black sword imposed on a shield background of alternating white and black diagonal strips.

The window was a tall one, with the lower sill coming up barely past knee height. This afforded her an excellent view of the courtyard below, although there was usually little of interest to see there, just the regular changing of sentries and the occasional figure passing from the keep tower to the gatehouse or stables. There were few visitors to Macindaw at this time of year, which was probably why Keren had chosen winter as the time to stage his coup.

The key rattled in the door to the outer room and she turned, incuriously. It was probably one of the servants come to clear away the remains of her breakfast. But any break in the monotony was welcome. She was surprised, then a little alarmed, as the door opened to admit Keren.

Her first assumption was that something had happened to arouse his suspicions once more, and she slipped her hands behind her back, feeling for the small, shiny black stone concealed in the cuff of her sleeve. Her surprise grew as she realized that the renegade was carrying a tray, bearing a coffeepot and two mugs. He smiled at her as he closed the door with his foot, then moved to set the tray down on the table.

"Good morning," he said cheerfully.

She said nothing, nodding warily at him, wondering what this was all about. Unbidden, her eyes dropped to the wallet on his belt, where she knew he kept the blue gemstone. He saw the movement and spread his hands out in a reassuring gesture.

"No tricks. No mesmerism. I just thought we could have a mug of coffee together," he said.

Alyss eyed the coffeepot suspiciously. Perhaps Keren had placed some kind of drug in it, a drug that couldn't be countered by the stellatite pebble.

"I've just had breakfast," she said coldly. Keren smiled at her, understanding her doubts.

"You think the coffee might be drugged?" he said. He poured a cup and took a deep sip, sighing with pleasure as he tasted it. "Well, if it is, it's an excellent-tasting drug."

He paused thoughtfully, as if waiting for something to happen. After several seconds, he shook his head, smiling.

"No. I don't feel any ill effects at all—other than the desire for another sip."

He took another and gestured to the chair opposite him.

Alyss was still unconvinced. "Of course," she said, "before you came in, you could have taken an antidote to any drug that might be in the coffee."

He nodded, conceding the point. Then he said, quite pleasantly, "Alyss, if I wanted to drug you, do you think I'd come in here with a jug of coffee to do it?"

"I don't see why not," she replied.

"Well, think of this: If I did plan to drug you, why would I put you on your guard? Wouldn't it be a lot simpler to slip the drug into the breakfast you've just eaten?"

He indicated the empty platter, cup and teapot on the table, awaiting collection, and Alyss realized that he was right. His appearance with the coffee had set her on guard. But she'd eaten the meal quite happily, with no thought of drugs entering her head.

"I suppose so," she said reluctantly. Once again, he gestured to the chair, and this time she sat, puzzled as to his motives.

He poured a cup for her and gestured for her to drink. She did so, warily, sitting on the edge of her chair, alert for anything. The coffee was excellent, as he had promised. And, apparently, it was nothing but coffee. She felt no sudden dizziness, no compulsion to speak only the truth.

But still, she waited for him to have another sip before she drank again. The effect could be cumulative, she reasoned. Once again, he seemed to read her thoughts, and he smiled.

"We'll drink sip for sip, if that makes you feel more secure," he said. "You really don't trust me, do you?"

He smiled at her, but she remained stone-faced.

"You're an oath breaker," she said. "No one will ever trust you again. Not even the Scotti."

For a brief moment, she saw the light of pain in his eyes, and she realized that Keren was only too aware of what his actions had cost him. He was an outcast now, enemy to everyone he had known. He would have all of Araluen against him. People whose trust and respect he had won over years of service would now be his sworn enemies. People he had never known would revile his name.

And his new comrades would never replace the old, because they would never thoroughly trust him. A man who breaks his oath, who turns traitor once, can always do the same thing again. He knew it because he knew the caliber of men he had recruited to his banner. Men like John Buttle. Keren could never really trust his second in command. John Buttle, Sir John as he liked to style himself now, would stand by Keren only so long as it benefited John Buttle. Then, when he saw a better, more profitable alternative, he would betray him.

Alyss wondered if that was why he was here now. Keren was a leader who had nothing in common with his own followers. They were rough, uneducated men, men without principles or morals. Aside from providing a constant reminder to Keren of what he had become, they would provide him with no company, no stimulation, no amusement.

Surrounded by followers, he was alone.

She looked at him now with a new interest. Perhaps there was a chance here for her to turn this whole debacle around, without further loss of life.

"It's not too late," she said, leaning forward on her elbows, looking into his eyes. "You can put an end to this."

His eyes slid away from hers. He wouldn't meet her gaze. *I knew it,* she thought.

"I can't go back now," he said. "I can only keep going along the path I've chosen."

"That's ridiculous!" she said, with considerable spirit. "It's never too late to admit you've made a mistake! Are you concerned about Buttle? He wouldn't dare dispute with you! The man's a coward."

He laughed harshly. "I'm not worried about Buttle," he told her. "Nor any of the brigands and gutter sweepings he's recruited. But you said it yourself, I'm an oath breaker. Who'll trust me now?"

"All right," she admitted, "your life will never be the same. You've made a mistake, and it's one that could take years to live down. But if you abandon this course now, if you declare your loyalty to Araluen once more, at least you won't be an outcast for the rest of your life."

He said nothing, but she could see he was deep in thought. She pressed harder.

"Keren," she began. She used his name intentionally. She needed to reach him, to convince him. "You're expecting some Scotti general—" She paused as he looked up at her, suddenly suspicious. She made a dismissive gesture. "Oh, for god's sake, I'm not stupid!" she said impatiently. "One of your men said the name the other day." He relaxed as he remembered the occasion and she continued. "Look, send him packing. Tell him the deal's off. Or lie to him. Say you'll go ahead with the plan, whatever it is. Just stall him for the time being and get some loyal troops back in the castle. The men you got rid of can't be too far away. Will can help you."

But Keren was already shaking his head.

"It's too late," he said. "There's no turning back now. If I betray the Scotti, they'll kill me. Buttle's men won't fight to save me. He'll take my place. The Scotti won't mind, so long as they know there's no Castle Macindaw threatening their supply lines when they invade."

She recoiled. "Invade?" she repeated, incredulously. "I thought they were planning to simply raid across the border."

He smiled sadly.

"Oh, no, my dear girl. This is much more serious than a few skirmishes and raids. They plan to occupy Norgate Fief and make it part of Picta."

She felt the blood drain from her face. Her training as a Courier meant that she understood the strategic importance of the situation. If the Scotti were to occupy Norgate, the way would be open for them to raid any of the adjoining fiefdoms, and Araluen could never tolerate that. It would trigger a war that would drag on for years, bleeding both countries dry.

"Keren," she said, leaning forward again and taking his hands in hers to impress her sincerity on him, "you have to stop this!" As he began to shake his head, she raised her voice angrily. "And stop saying it's too late! It's *not* too late! For god's sake, I'll speak for you. Stop this now and I'll speak to the King himself."

"A slip of a girl like you?" he said sardonically.

Alyss bit back the angry retort that sprang to her lips.

"You forget, I'm a Courier," she said instead. "And a Courier's word carries a lot of weight, even with the King. If you give up this madness now, I will do all I can to help you. I swear it."

There was a rattle at the door lock, and one of Keren's men threw the door open and entered. Keren looked up at him, his face dark with anger.

"Get out, damn you!" he flared. The man made an apologetic gesture but remained in the doorway.

"Sorry, Lord Keren, but Sir John thought you should know. The Scotti general is approaching the castle."

Keren stood quickly, the tray rattling as he jostled the table in his haste. He gestured briskly to the man, who left the room, leaving the door open behind him.

"Well," said Keren, "it seems the die is cast."

Alyss tried one more time. "Keren, I can help you. Trust me."

He smiled at her again, but she realized the smile was a mask for the pain he was feeling.

"You know, up until two days ago, that might have been true. But Lord Syron died the night before last."

Alyss stood up as well.

"He's dead?" she asked. Keren nodded.

"I didn't mean it to happen that way, but it is my fault. So unless you can bring a dead man back to life, you really can't help me at all."

14

WILL AND HORACE STAYED SEVERAL HUNDRED METERS BEHIND the Scotti party as they followed them through the woods. Had he been alone, Will could have maintained much closer contact, but with Horace along, he felt it wiser to remain at a distance. The tall warrior wasn't clumsy by any means. In fact, as far as knights went, he was quite graceful.

But that meant nothing in comparison with a Ranger's ability to move silently through the forest. As he followed Will along the narrow track, Horace felt as coordinated as a one-legged bear.

"I don't know how you do it," he said at length. Will looked back at him, his eyebrows raised in inquiry, so that Horace felt compelled to elaborate. "How you Rangers move so quietly," he explained. Will frowned slightly, then moved back to his side.

"Well, for a start," he said in a low voice, "we Rangers don't blunder along, yelling out 'I don't know how you do it.'"

Horace was a little crestfallen. He lowered his voice to a whisper. "Oh . . . right. Sorry."

Will shook his head and moved off again. Horace followed some five meters behind, watching where he placed his feet and stepping with exaggerated care. The thick carpet of snow on the track helped matters, he thought. And the falling snow would conceal them from sight. In fact, Will, in his black-and-white-mottled cloak, kept disappearing from Horace's view even at five meters' range.

Leading the way, Will gritted his teeth with every twig that snapped under Horace's feet. The warrior seemed to have exceptionally big feet, he thought. They certainly seemed to find a lot of twigs to snap. Still, he knew they were far enough behind the Scotti to make Horace's noise indiscernible as Will followed their tracks in the new snow. Fortunately, it wasn't falling fast enough to blanket them completely. They were obviously heading for Macindaw, as this track led to the castle and nowhere else. The woods they were in were relatively new growth, nothing like the thick, impenetrable tangles that marked Grimsdell Wood, which lay to the east. In Grimsdell, if you found a path to follow, it would be half the width of this relatively clear track. And it would twist and turn and wind upon itself like a demented serpent so that after a few minutes, you had no sense of where you were heading.

They were approaching the end of the trees now, and Will moved more slowly, motioning for Horace to remain where he was for a few minutes while Will scouted ahead.

As the trees thinned out, he could see the small party of Scotti warriors more clearly. They were still moving at that slow jog, crossing the open ground, where the gorse and bracken grew only knee high. They were almost up to the castle, whose main entrance was on the southern side. As he watched, the Scotti detoured toward the main entrance.

Even from this distance, Will could see the flurry of movement on the ramparts of the castle as the small party approached. But there were no sounds of alarm. No gongs, no shouts. The Scotti were obviously not regarded as a threat.

Turning, he trotted back through the forest to the spot where he had left Horace.

"They're going to Macindaw, all right," he said. "And they're expected. Let's go."

He led the way to the southeast, angling through the forest to the spot where it gradually merged into the thicker growth that was Grimsdell. There was no way he and Horace could move across open ground to follow the Scotti. They would have to stay under cover of the tree line. That meant covering two long sides of a triangle while the Scotti took the shorter, more direct route.

By the time they reached a point where they could keep the south wall in sight, the castle gates had opened, admitted the Scotti general and his men, and closed again.

The two friends lay belly down in the shadow of the trees, staring at the castle.

"What do you think they're up to?" Horace asked.

Will shrugged. "MacHaddish is a general, and generals usually command more than a handful of men. My guess is he has a larger force waiting across the border and he's making final arrangements with Keren to bring them south—discussing numbers of men, how much they're going to pay Keren. That sort of thing."

"So it's a raiding party?" Horace asked, and Will nodded thoughtfully.

"At least. Maybe something bigger. Whatever it is, I don't like the look of it."

Horace wriggled uncomfortably. Unlike Will, he could never lie unmoving in one place for long.

"We need to know what they're up to," he said.

Will smiled at him. "I'm sure Malcolm will be able to find out for us when we capture our friend MacHaddish."

Horace nodded thoughtfully. "We've got to manage that first," he pointed out.

"True. How many men did you count?" Will asked. He thought he knew himself but it never hurt to make sure.

"Counting the general? Nine."

"That's what I thought. So I figure you, me and ten of the Skandians should be able to do the job."

Horace looked skeptical. "Twelve of us? Do we really need that many? After all, we'll be taking them by surprise."

"I know," Will told him. "But we want to take him alive, remember?"

"That's true. When d'you think we'll do it?"

Will shrugged. "I can't see them spending more than a day here. The castle guards were expecting them. I'd say they've been planning this for some time and now they're settling last-minute details. We'd better be in position before dark. Back at the spot where we camped."

"That's as good a place as any," Horace agreed. "So do you want me to go and collect Gundar and some of his men while you keep an eye on things here?"

Will rolled on his side to study him. "You're sure you can find your way back to Malcolm's clearing?" he asked, and Horace grinned at him.

"I think even clumsy old noisy me can manage it," he said. "Will we meet you here or back at our campsite?"

Will thought about it for a few seconds. On his own, he'd be able to ghost across the open ground once it was dark. That way, he could wait till he was sure the Scotti were on their way and still beat them to the ambush site.

"Take them to the campsite," he said. "Leave a lookout at the tree line to warn you when they're coming, just in case I miss them." For a moment, he was tempted to go into detail about how to set up the ambush itself, but he realized that Horace could organize that side of things as well as he could.

Horace clapped a hand on Will's shoulder and rose from the ground, taking care to keep in the shadows under the trees.

"We'll see you there," he said.

By midafternoon, even Will's patience was being tested. He was wishing he'd asked Horace to send someone back from the clearing to watch with him. At least then he'd be able to take a break and even sleep for an hour or so.

Strangely, after a while, simply lying in the tree line staring at the castle became immensely tiring. At one point, Will found himself on the verge of nodding off. He shook himself, took a few deep breaths and resumed his vigil. Within a few minutes, he felt his focus drifting and his chin dropping onto his chest again.

"This is no good," he said angrily. Rising to his feet, he began pacing back and forth. Staying active seemed to be a better way of staying awake. The snow had continued to fall intermittently throughout the day, and the countryside was draped under a thick cover by now. The light began to fade, and Will realized that it might be best if he headed back to the trees north of the castle. If the Scotti emerged now, there was a chance that Will might miss seeing them until it was too late.

Of course, he thought, he was only surmising that they would leave this evening. Perhaps Keren would entertain them at the castle with a banquet. They might well stay another day or two to rest before the journey home. But somehow he doubted it. He'd seen the Scotti general's face close-up, and he didn't look like the sort of man who would waste his time at banquets or relaxing.

He spent the usual few minutes preparing, observing the natural rhythms of the land around him—the movement of the falling snow, the way the gentle wind stirred the bushes and the treetops. Then, when he felt attuned to it all, he rose to a crouch and glided across the open ground in the uncertain light.

Seen from ten meters' distance, he seemed to fade into the background. From the castle walls, several hundred meters away, there was no chance that an observer would have noticed him.

Back at Healer's Clearing, as it was now generally known, Orman and Malcolm watched Horace lead the party of Skandians away into the trees. It was remarkable, Orman thought, how one so young could exert such effortless authority over the battle-hardened Skandians. Malcolm seemed to have reached the same conclusion.

"You're lucky to have those two on your side," he said, and Orman knew that he was referring to Will and Horace. "They're very accomplished young men."

Orman nodded. "They make an excellent team, all right." Then he eyed the small healer with a sidelong glance. "It occurs to me that I've been lucky with all my new allies."

Malcolm shrugged diffidently. But Orman felt it was time he pursued the matter.

"After all," he said, "you owe me nothing. You chose years ago to seclude yourself in the forest here and cut yourself off from contact with the outside world." He sighed heavily. "I can't say I altogether blame you for that."

"I've been reasonably content, I suppose," Malcolm replied.

"And now you're risking all that," Orman said.

Malcolm pulled a wry face. "Am I?" The thought seemed to be occurring to him for the first time. "I suppose I am, really," he agreed.

"All your protective devices and illusions have been exposed as tricks."

"Were you planning on telling the world?" Malcolm asked with a little smile.

Orman shook his head. "Of course not. But once a secret is broken, it has a way of getting out. All your people here will be at risk again."

Malcolm's smile faded at that. "I know," he said at last. "I considered that, but really, what could I do? Will and your man Xander arrived here with you at death's door. What choice did I have?"

"You could have turned us away," Orman said, but Malcolm was shaking his head before he had finished the sentence.

"I'm a healer," he said simply. "I swore to dedicate my life to the art. If I turned you away, I'd be an oath breaker. You see?" he added, with a trace of the sad smile creeping back onto his face. "You put me in an impossible position."

Orman nodded. He did realize the fact, which was why he had raised the matter with Malcolm.

"I understand that. But I want you to know, things will be different in the future. You'll be under the protection of Castle Macindaw."

Malcolm thought about that for a few seconds. "I appreciate the offer," he said. "But you won't mind if I remain in the forest? I've grown rather accustomed to things here. And I couldn't leave my people."

"I wouldn't expect you to," Orman told him. "I just want you to know that you won't need to hide here anymore. I'll give you all the protection you need. And any other practical help you could ask for."

The two men shook hands solemnly. Malcolm opened his mouth to say something, then hesitated.

"What is it?" Orman prompted.

"Well," the healer said reluctantly, "I hate to ask, but these Skandians are eating me out of house and home—and our two young men are going through my supplies of coffee beans like a plague of locusts."

Orman grinned. "I'll take care of it," he said. "I'll have Xander buy some supplies from Tumbledown Creek village. He can dip into my purse to pay for it. Mind you," he added, and the grin widened considerably, "it'll probably break his heart to do it."

15

THE WORST PART ABOUT BEING A PRISONER, ALYSS THOUGHT, was not knowing what was going on. She had watched MacHaddish and his party arrive after Keren had been summoned by Buttle's messenger. Her window commanded a view of the courtyard and the main gate by which they entered. But once they were ushered into the keep, she was left in a fever of curiosity. What were they discussing? What were their plans? How would Will counter them? Did he even know the Scotti were here?

As a Courier, she was accustomed to being privy to confidential information. Her enforced inactivity, and her ignorance of what was happening, gnawed away at her, sending her pacing helplessly about the small circular room.

Looking for something to distract her, she knelt to inspect the two center bars in the window. In recent days, she had begun to work on the bars with the remaining acid. Each time Keren came to see her, she waited half an hour after he had left, then poured the acid into the shallow well around the base of the two bars. She only used a little at a time, as the action of the acid on the iron created pungent fumes that took at least an hour to disperse. This was the reason why she could only work on the bars after Keren had visited her. She reasoned that there was little prospect of his returning on those occasions.

As the acid ate away at the iron and the mortar, she concealed the missing material with a mixture of soap, dirt and rust. She gouged the soft material away now with her spoon, piling it carefully to one side for reuse. The bars were three quarters eaten away. Another two or three applications should see the job complete and there was plenty of acid left to do the job.

She wasn't sure what she would do once the bars were eaten away. She was terrified of heights and the thought of descending the outer wall made her weak at the knees. But it didn't hurt to be prepared.

Perhaps she could risk another application now. Keren was tied up with the Scotti general, and the odds were he wouldn't come to see her again in the immediate future. But she resisted the temptation. For all she knew, Keren might want to parade her in front of MacHaddish. Reluctantly, she replaced the soap, dirt and rust paste, concealing the gap in the iron. Then, to put temptation behind her, she moved away from the window, stretching out on the bed, fingers laced behind her head.

She didn't sleep. Her thoughts whirled through her head, spurred by her own sense of inactivity and frustration.

The hours dragged by. She paced the room again. Lay on the bed again. Rearranged the furniture. One table. Two chairs. One bed. That didn't take long. She considered moving the wardrobe but decided it was too heavy. Besides, the noise might bring the sentries in to see what she was doing, and she had no wish to see them. She inspected the iron bars once more. At one stage, she examined the little bottle of acid, which she had returned to its hiding place on the top of the window lintel. She shook it to see how much remained. Then, taking control of herself, she put it away.

She was lying on the rearranged bed when she heard orders being shouted from the courtyard. She rose hurriedly and moved to the window. The Scotti party was leaving.

"That was quick," she muttered. MacHaddish had been here less than six hours. Either the talks with Keren had been successful or the reverse. From the way the two men shook hands, with Keren clapping his free left hand on the Scotti's shoulder, she assumed it was the former. She glanced at the sky. The light was fading fast, and she hoped Will could see what was going on. She'd have to send him a signal later tonight. She knew that even when he wasn't watching the castle, he left someone in the trees who would note down the light patterns she sent so Will could decipher them later.

The drawbridge rumbled and the portcullis creaked again as the way opened for the Scotti to leave. She watched them for a few minutes as they jogged through the knee-high gorse, angling back to the north and to the path that led to the Pictan border. Then the bulk of the northeast tower hid them from view.

Half an hour later, she heard the key in the lock and Keren entered. She expected him to be triumphant and boastful but instead he was strangely subdued. When she tried to pump him for information about MacHaddish, he waved her questions aside, preferring to reminisce about his childhood, talking about the years he spent growing up in the countryside around Castle Macindaw. She was puzzled by this unexpected attitude, and the renegade's strange air of sadness. Then, slowly, realization dawned on her.

Instead of feeling triumph that his plan was working, Keren was feeling regret—regret at the fact that he was now committed irrevocably to a path that would take him away from all that he knew and had held dear for years. A path from which there was no return.

Abruptly, as if suddenly fearing that he might have said too much, he stood up, excused himself and departed. Alyss continued to sit at the table after he'd gone. Things were coming to a head faster than she had expected. Later tonight, she'd start work on the bars again.

16

THE PLAN FOR THE AMBUSH WAS SIMPLE. WILL HAD SELECTED A
spot close to their temporary campsite, where the track ran in a
relatively long, straight stretch. Gundar and nine of his Skandians
would be concealed in the trees to either side. They would be at
the beginning of the straight section so that, once the Scotti had
passed by them, the sea wolves would be able to surprise them from
behind.

Will and Horace would take a position at the far end, where
they could draw the enemy's attention. The idea was that Will and
Horace would step into sight and call upon the Scotti to halt. Then,
while their attention was diverted, the Skandians would quickly
emerge from the trees behind the invaders—who would realize they
were outnumbered and surrounded and that resistance was futile.
The two young men had yet to figure what they would do with
the nine captives when they were secured. Somehow, they would
have to keep them prisoner, but Will decided to face that problem
later.

He knew, from his own experience and from watching and listening to Halt, that the mere appearance of a Ranger was often
enough to stop enemies in their tracks. In extreme cases, parties

larger than this one had surrendered without a fight. Will didn't expect that to happen but he thought that the sight of a Ranger would at the very least cause the Scotti party to hesitate, and that moment of uncertainty would give the Skandians the opportunity to move in and disarm them.

Will made it to the tree line well in advance of the Scotti. One of the Skandians was posted there, as he had instructed. The man leapt to his feet in alarm as the Ranger suddenly seemed to materialize out of the twilight, right in front of him. He grabbed for the ax leaning against a tree beside him, but fortunately, Will stopped him in time.

"Relax!" he said, throwing back the cowl on his cloak so that the sentry could see his face. "It's only me."

"Gorlog's beard, Ranger," the Skandian said, shaking his head. "You startled the hell out of me."

Gorlog was a lesser Skandian deity who had a long beard, curved horns and fanglike teeth. On different occasions, Will had heard all of those features invoked by startled Skandians, but he didn't waste time discussing the issue now.

"They're on their way," he said briefly. "Let's go."

The Skandian looked back across the open ground to the castle. Dimly, he could make out a small group of men moving toward them. He turned back to the Ranger, but Will was already running down the track to the ambush site.

Hastily, the Skandian followed in his tracks. Like Horace, he was intrigued by the way the cloaked figure seemed to shimmer in and out of sight as he moved. He blundered along the narrow track in pursuit of the elusive shape ahead of him.

Horace was waiting at the turn in the track that marked the beginning of the straight stretch. He also started in alarm as Will suddenly seemed to rise out of the ground beside him.

"Don't do that!" he said angrily. Then, as he saw Will's puzzled expression, he explained, "You know we don't hear you coming and we can hardly see you. Make some sort of noise so we know you're there!"

"Sorry," Will said. "The Scotti are on their way."

Horace nodded, his momentary annoyance forgotten. He turned toward the trees.

"Gundar! Did you hear that? They're coming!"

There was a rustle of movement in the trees, and Will saw the shadowy figures of the Skandians moving into position. They had been relaxing in the cleared campsite. Now they moved closer to the track itself. Will nodded approvingly as he saw that, on Horace's instructions, they had taken off their distinctive horned helmets. Nothing would give the ambush away faster than the sight of massive ox horns nodding among the bushes. Gundar stepped out of the trees with four of his men. The other five found positions a few meters back from the track and settled down to wait.

"All right, Horace," Gundar said, "we hear you. How long before they're here?"

Horace glanced enquiringly at Will, who answered for him.

"Maybe ten minutes. Get into position. And once you're there, don't keep moving around." He searched for a way to emphasize the order, then said, "By Gorlog's fangs and beard, all right?"

Gundar grinned at him. "Nice to see you're learning the language," he said. "Don't worry. We've ambushed people before." He gestured for the four men with him to move to the opposite side of the track, thus putting five men on either side. Before he plunged into the bushes, he called softly to the others, "Anyone makes a noise, I'll crack his skull. All right?"

There was a muttered chorus of understanding, then the burly Skandians sank slowly out of sight behind bushes and trees.

"Remember," Will said, "we want this man alive. He'll be the one in the lead. He has half his face painted in blue stripes."

"How attractive," Horace murmured. Will glared at him.

"And a large broadsword slung over his shoulder," he added. Horace made a small moue of mock concern.

"Not so attractive," he said.

Will ignored him. Gundar rose out of the bushes beside the track, rather like a whale surfacing.

"So we take this blue-face alive," he said. "But you won't be brokenhearted if some of his men don't survive?"

"I'd prefer to avoid bloodshed," Will said. But he knew in a situation like this, things rarely went exactly to plan. "Do what you can," he said. "Wait till you hear me call on them to stop. Give it a moment or so until I've got their attention, then move in behind them. If we time it right, they should surrender without a fight."

He said the last to reassure himself more than anything else. Gundar's expression left no doubt that he wasn't convinced.

"That's as may be," he said skeptically, "but if they even look like fighting, my boys will start hitting."

Will nodded. He couldn't ask for more than that. In a situation like this, he wouldn't expect the Skandians to take unnecessary risks just because he'd prefer to avoid bloodshed.

"Fair enough," he told the skirl. "Now get back into cover before they're here."

Gundar sank back into the undergrowth and, once more, Will was reminded of a whale surfacing then submerging. But he didn't have time to ponder the matter. Horace plucked at his sleeve.

"Let's go," he said briefly, and led the way to the far end of the track.

Horace stepped off into the trees a few paces to get out of sight. Will simply remained by the side of the track, his cowl pulled up over his head and the cloak pulled around him. He held his bow in his left hand, with a pair of arrows ready, between the fingers of his right hand. He glanced into the undergrowth and noticed that Horace had covered his white enameled shield with dull green cloth. He nodded approvingly. In the rapidly failing light, there'd be no gleam of white to warn the Scotti.

He tensed suddenly as he heard them coming. There was the dull shuffle of jogging feet on the thick, dry snow cover. Horace saw his involuntary movement.

"Are they here?" he said softly.

"Any moment. Keep quiet," Will warned him. He slipped the cowl back slightly so he could hear more clearly. Now he could just make out the soft squeaking sound of boots against the dry snow. He stood stock still beside a large tree trunk, eyes intent on the dark aperture among the trees that marked the bend in the track, twenty meters away.

A figure appeared. Indistinct and blurred at first in the falling snow and dull light, it soon could be recognized as the Scotti general, MacHaddish. His men followed close behind him, in four pairs. Will waited until they were all clear of the corner, then stepped out into the center of the track, nocking an arrow and bringing the bow up at half draw.

"King's Ranger!" he shouted, in case there were any doubt in their minds. "Stand where you are."

There was a moment of shocked surprise among the Scotti as the strange figure suddenly became visible in front of them. MacHaddish heard the shouted command but made no sense of it. The words "King's Ranger" meant nothing to him. Will might as well have shouted "King's Rabbits."

The truth was, Will's excellent plan would have worked perfectly, if only the Scotti had understood their part in it all. In Araluen, the mere presence of a Ranger would often be enough to settle a matter like this without fighting. Unfortunately, the Scotti, in their remote northern country, had been involved in very few dealings with Rangers and so were in no awe of them. They were taken off guard by Will's sudden appearance and, for a moment, they froze.

Will saw that initial hesitation among the Scotti and relaxed a little, smiling to himself as he thanked the generations of past Rangers who had built such a remarkable reputation.

Then, everything went very wrong.

MacHaddish recovered from his moment of surprise. His right hand reached back over his shoulder and closed on the massive hilt of his broadsword, sliding it free of its scabbard in a movement so smooth and rapid that it had to have been rehearsed hundreds of times in the past.

"*Na cha'rith Nambar!*" he screamed, brandishing the huge blade aloft, circling it in the air. His men, galvanized into action, echoed the words, the war cry of the MacHaddish clan. The scream rose from eight throats, and MacHaddish hurled himself forward at the indistinct figure on the track ahead of him. Two of his men followed close behind as he charged. The others turned to face Gundar and his Skandians as they crashed from the undergrowth, axes whirling.

Will, faced with an armed and seemingly enraged Scotti general, brought the bow to full draw instinctively. At the last moment, he remembered his own instructions to the Skandians and, just before he released, moved the aim point from the center of the general's chest to his right wrist.

The arrow seared through the tendons and nerves in the wrist, the immediate shock of the wound depriving the hand of all feeling, numbing the entire arm and robbing MacHaddish of the strength to brandish the huge sword. With a startled cry of pain, he doubled over, letting the broadsword fall to the track as he clutched his right wrist with his left hand.

But Will had no further time for MacHaddish. The other two Scotti were almost upon him. He nocked and fired his second arrow in one movement, dropping one of them to the snow, dead in his tracks. Then the other was all over him, screaming hate and revenge, sword going back for a killing stroke. Will hurled himself to the side, hitting the deep snow on his shoulder and rolling, discarding the bow as he went, his right hand drawing the saxe knife as he rolled to his feet again.

But the Scotti's blow had been intercepted by Horace's shield. The blade snagged and tore a huge gash in the cloth cover. The Scotti took Horace's sword on his own small shield as Horace struck at him in reply. But he was in no way prepared for the Araluen knight's blinding follow-up speed. Even as the Scotti prepared to strike back, he realized that he was already behind the rhythm of the fight and the taller man's sword was slashing around at him again. He blocked desperately with the shield, grunting as the force of the blow jarred his arm. Then, unbelievably, another stroke was on its way from yet another angle and he had to parry quickly with his sword. He felt as if he were fighting two men, felt the gut-freezing terror of impending death as the sword was jarred from his grip and went spinning into the trees.

Blindly, he stooped to reach for the dirk in the top of his boot, but as he did so, Horace planted his own sword point first in the ground and stepped forward to throw a solid right uppercut to his jaw.

The Scotti's eyes rolled up in his head and his knees collapsed under him. He went facedown in the soft snow, unconscious.

At the far end of the track, Will and Horace became aware of shouts and the clash of weapons.

The Scotti were severely outflanked and outnumbered, with six men facing ten. But they continued to fight, wounding two of the Skandians. That was probably a mistake, as it goaded Gundar into a fighting rage. His ax whirled around his head, and he carved a path through the clansmen, smashing aside the inadequate hand shields that they carried.

There were only two left standing by the time they opted to lower their weapons and call for mercy. Gundar, blind and deaf with fighting rage, didn't hear them. But one of the Skandians threw his arms around his skirl and dragged him away to calm down. The other Skandians surged around the surviving clansmen, knocking the weapons out of their hands and forcing them to their knees.

Horace and Will exchanged a look, shaking their heads.

"Well," said Horace, "that wasn't quite the way we planned it."

Will was grateful that he had said "we" and not "you." He resheathed his saxe knife.

"Not quite," he said. "But at least we've got MacHaddish."

He looked around to the spot where the general had sunk to his knees, cradling his wounded right arm. There was a large red stain on the snow.

But no sign of MacHaddish.

17

"WHERE THE BLAZES DID HE GO?" HORACE SAID. "I HARDLY TOOK my eyes off him."

But Will was already crouching over the spot where the general had fallen, his eyes following the clear trail that the escaping Scotti had left in the new snow. In addition to the footprints, now becoming difficult to see in the failing light, there was a bright red trail of blood drops. He started forward in pursuit, then hesitated, looking down the track to where the Skandians surrounded the surviving Scotti warriors.

Gundar was off to one side, being calmed down by the man who had dragged him away from the Scotti. Will wanted to make sure someone was left in charge of the prisoners.

"Hold them there, all right?" he called. He gestured to the warrior Horace had knocked out. "This one too."

One of the Skandians stepped forward. To his surprise, Will recognized Nils Ropehander. The scar-faced man had been one of the first Horace had chosen for the ambush. In Horace's experience, men like Nils, at first cynical and reluctant, often became the most dependable followers once they were converted to a cause.

"You go after Blue Face, Ranger," he said now. "We'll keep an eye on these beauties until you get back."

Will nodded once, then plunged into the trees, closely followed by Horace. He had a moment's hesitation when he realized that he had left his bow by the side of the track, then shrugged it aside. In the close quarters of the forest, the bow would be next to useless. His saxe and throwing knife would be more suitable weapons in these conditions.

He ran in a half crouch, frowning with concentration as he searched for MacHaddish's tracks in the snow. At first, the bright blood trail made progress easy, even in the near dark. But then the general must have realized he was leaving a trail that a blind man could follow and bound the wounded hand up to stop the flow. Probably in the massive tartan he wore around his shoulders, Will reflected.

He had no sooner had the thought than he saw the broken arrow shaft caught up in a bush to one side, where the Scotti had thrown it. Will winced. The task of removing the arrow must have been agonizing.

Now, without the blood trail to follow, tracking MacHaddish grew more difficult. In daylight, a tracker of Will's ability would be able to read the footprints in the snow without hesitation. But now it was almost full dark.

In addition, he realized, MacHaddish was actively trying to throw them off the trail, at times standing still, then leaping as far as he could to one side or the other before continuing. At other times, he had laid false trails, heading off to the side for a dozen or so paces, then rapidly backtracking, stepping backward in the same footprints, or jumping or using overhanging branches or occasional rock outcrops to change direction without leaving footprints. The Scotti had the luxury of being able to head in any direction he chose at any time.

In normal light Will would have instantly detected the signs of backtracking and ignored the false trail. But at night, in winter, in the woods, he had no choice but to follow the trail as he saw it.

He stopped as he came to a point where the trail twisted hard left. Instinct told him that MacHaddish had laid another false trail here. He'd noticed that the man seemed to instinctively return to the same general direction each time he threw out a false lead. He was heading north, for the border. And north was straight ahead, not to the left. Will was tempted to continue that way, ignoring the footprints angling off to the side. He could see a bare patch of rocks straight ahead, where MacHaddish could have headed to obliterate his tracks. In the intervening space, there was plenty of ground litter—fallen branches and leaves lying on the snow—that he could have stepped on to conceal his trail. Probably, on the far side of the rocks, the footprints would resume.

But if they didn't, if this were the real trail, he would waste precious minutes locating it again in the dark. He hesitated, unsure of himself, sensing that the Scotti was drawing farther and farther away from them with each minute.

"Which way?" Horace asked, but Will instantly signaled him to remain silent. He had heard something in the forest, ahead and to the right. He turned his head slightly from side to side, trying to pick up the noise again. He cupped his hands behind both ears to capture any slight sound that . . .

There! He could just hear a body forcing its way through the trees and the tangled undergrowth. He had been right. The trail to the left was a false one. And now he saw how he could gain ground on MacHaddish. Not by looking for his trail. But by listening.

In the same instant, he realized how he could conceal his approach from MacHaddish.

He beckoned Horace closer, pointing in the direction the sound had come from. "He's gone that way," he said. "I can hear him. Follow behind me but stay back ten to twenty meters. And make a bit of noise, all right?"

Horace frowned. Will could see the question forming in his mind and answered it before his friend could ask.

"He'll hear you coming," he said. "He won't hear me."

Will saw understanding in Horace's eyes and he plunged off into the woods again, hearing his friend resume the pursuit behind him. Horace stayed far enough back that he didn't drown out the sound of MacHaddish shoving through the trees and bushes, and now Will sensed that he was gaining on the fugitive. He redoubled his pace, the noises made by MacHaddish becoming clearer, while those made by Horace faded slightly as Will widened the gap between him and his friend.

This time, the Scotti's ignorance of Ranger skills was working to Will's advantage. MacHaddish continued to plunge headlong through the undergrowth, unaware that his pursuer was gaining on him, not knowing that Rangers could move through country like this making virtually no sound. MacHaddish could hear someone crashing noisily through the forest, far behind him. He didn't realize it was Horace.

Then Horace, knowing what Will had in mind, had a flash of inspiration. He began calling encouragement to himself, shouting out vague directions and instructions.

"There he goes! I see him! This way, lads!"

He said whatever came into his head. The words didn't matter, but the direction was all important and Horace was intentionally straying from the direct line of pursuit.

Will heard his friend's voice and smiled, realizing what he was up to.

Not far ahead of Will, MacHaddish smiled too. The shouting

was far away now, moving to the west and growing fainter. His pursuers were gradually losing contact, confused by the false trails he had left.

The general paused for a moment in a small clearing, leaning against the bole of a tree. His arm throbbed painfully, and his breath was ragged with the exertion of his escape and with the shock of the wound. Carefully, he unwound the blood-soaked tartan from his wrist and examined the injury. He tried to flex the fingers. There was no movement. Shock had numbed the wound.

He tried again and this time thought he felt a slight movement, which encouraged him. He tried once more, and a blinding flash of agony shot along the inside of his forearm as the numbness faded.

He gasped in pain and surprise. But he was encouraged nonetheless. Anything, even the pain, was better than that frightening lack of feeling. If his right hand was permanently crippled, that would be the end of him. Among the Scotti, even generals had to take part in hand-to-hand fighting. Trying to ignore the pain, he took a deep breath and looked up from the wounded hand.

There was a shadowy figure moving toward him, barely three meters away.

MacHaddish's hand may have been crippled, but his reflexes were still razor-sharp. He reacted almost without thinking, hurling himself forward at the dim figure. He saw the man's hand drop to his waist and realized he was reaching for a weapon. Left with one hand useless, he lowered his shoulder and drove it into the cloaked figure.

The sheer speed of the attack took Will by surprise. As he had approached the Scotti, he had heard the man's low-pitched grunt of pain, and seen his obvious distress as he tried to move the injured right hand. The impression was of a man who was virtually helpless. Will's lack of experience with these fierce fighting men from the north now led him to make a second mistake. An injured hand would not put a Scotti warrior out of action. The Scotti would fight with hands, feet, head, knees, elbows and teeth as the need arose.

MacHaddish's shoulder hit him just below the breastbone and drove the air from his lungs with an explosive *whoof*. Will staggered, felt his legs go from under him and crashed backward into the thick snow. Unsighted for a moment, he rolled desperately to the side, sure that the Scotti would be following up his advantage. Then, as his vision cleared, he saw that the other man was doubled over awkwardly, his right knee raised as he scrabbled at the top of the boot with his left hand.

It was the fact that MacHaddish had to reach across with his left hand to draw the dirk in his right boot that probably saved Will's life. It was a clumsy action, and it gave Will time to regain his feet.

Almost as soon as he did, he had to leap aside to avoid MacHaddish's slashing attack with the dirk. He felt the blade slice easily through his cloak and kicked out flatfooted at the Scotti's left knee. MacHaddish danced sideways to avoid the crippling blow, giving Will the moment he needed to draw his saxe knife.

MacHaddish heard the sinister whisper of steel on leather, and his eyes narrowed as he saw the heavy blade gleaming in the dull light under the trees.

They circled awkwardly. The dirk was almost as long as the saxe, although the blade was narrower. Normally, the two might have closed, grappling with each other, each seizing the other man's knife wrist with his free hand and turning it into a contest of strength. But the fact that MacHaddish was using his left hand against Will's right made this impractical. For either to grab the other's knife wrist would mean turning his unarmed side toward the enemy, exposing it to instant attack.

Instead, they dueled like fencers, alternately darting their blades forward, lunging at each other, clashing blades as one lunged and the other parried. Their feet shuffled in the snow as they made sure they retained their footing, not daring to raise their feet in case they landed on uneven ground. As they circled, the two antagonists' eyes narrowed in concentration. Will had never seen an enemy move as quickly as this Scotti general. For his part, MacHaddish had never before faced an adversary who could match his own lightning speed.

Left hand or not, Will thought, this man is very, very skilled. He knew that if his concentration lapsed for an instant, the Scotti could well be upon him, the dirk sliding through his guard and between his ribs. He could die here tonight, he realized.

He tried to reach for the throwing knife in its concealed scabbard beneath his collar. The movement nearly cost him his life. The cowl of his cloak impeded the movement and as he fumbled, trying to clear it, MacHaddish lunged forward with the dirk.

Desperately, Will skipped backward, feeling the blade slash through his jerkin, a trickle of blood running down his ribs. His mouth had gone dry with fear. He slashed sideways at the Scotti, driving him back in his turn. Then they began circling each other again.

The problem Will faced was that he needed to take MacHaddish alive. Not that killing him would be any easy matter, he reflected grimly. MacHaddish, on the other hand, was under no such restriction. He had one aim only: to kill his opponent as quickly as possible and fade away into the forest before reinforcements arrived.

Where the devil is Horace? Will thought. He realized that the young warrior may well have lost touch with them. He'd given Will the chance he needed to catch up to MacHaddish, by making as much noise as he could and moving off to the west so that

MacHaddish would think he had given them the slip. Now, the chances were that Horace had no idea where he was or what was happening. Will realized that he was going to have to do this alone—and that there was a distinct chance that he would lose this fight, and be left here among these gloomy trees, his lifeblood leaking away into the snow.

If you worry that you'll lose, you probably will. Halt's words came back to him now, and he realized with a shock that he was actually preparing to lose. He was letting MacHaddish dictate the fight; all he was doing was reacting to the other man's attacks. It was time to go on the offensive. Time to take a chance.

18

His opportunity came when MacHaddish stepped onto an icy patch of snow. Their sliding, shuffling feet had churned and compacted the snow in the small clearing and, for a fraction of a second, the Scotti was distracted as his boot slid on the frozen patch that had been exposed.

It was only a small moment, but Will realized it might be the only one he would get. In one fluid movement, he stepped forward and threw the saxe knife underhand at the general.

He had seen the man's speed already and he had no real hope that the throw would penetrate his defense. Quite the opposite in fact, as he still planned to capture the Scotti alive. As the gleaming blade shot toward him, MacHaddish swept the dirk across his body in a desperate parry, blocking the heavy saxe at the last second. But the throw had served its purpose, distracting MacHaddish's attention and deflecting the dirk. The instant the Scotti sent the saxe knife spinning away, Will was upon him, his right hand grabbing the general's left wrist like a vise.

But MacHaddish was fast as a snake. The moment Will gripped him, he twisted and jerked violently away, pulling Will forward and off balance. At the same time, knowing his own right hand was useless, he jammed his right forearm up under Will's chin, across his throat, choking Will and forcing his head back.

With his right arm extended and his head being forced farther and farther back, Will could feel his grip on the knife hand weakening.

The Scotti's skin was lightly covered in grease—no doubt as protection against the penetrating cold—and this made it even harder to maintain his grip. MacHaddish twisted his left hand back and forth. Will could feel it turning inside his own grip, and he knew it would be only a matter of seconds before he jerked free of Will's hold completely.

Quickly, Will threw two hard, hooking punches into the Scotti's exposed right side, hitting the ribs and feeling one give slightly. MacHaddish grunted in pain, and the pressure of his forearm across Will's throat lessened slightly. It was enough. Will reached up and grabbed MacHaddish's right wrist, dragging the forearm down from under his chin and twisting MacHaddish off balance.

As Will's iron grip fastened onto his injured arm, MacHaddish screamed in agony and doubled over in an instinctive movement to protect himself. The galvanic twisting action caught Will off guard and he lost balance, releasing his grip on MacHaddish's injured wrist, his feet slipping in the compacted snow. They staggered around the clearing, each trying to gain the advantage. MacHaddish's knife hand was still locked in Will's grip, and now the Scotti went on the attack again. He threw his right forearm at Will's face. The young Ranger ducked the blow, then just managed to twist his body to one side in time as MacHaddish's right knee jerked up at him. Now all of Will's focus was directed at maintaining his grip on the hand that held the razor-sharp dirk. He knew if he lost that grip, he would be finished. All thought of taking MacHaddish alive was now gone. Will was thinking only of survival.

He grabbed the long pigtail that hung down the left side of MacHaddish's head and jerked it up and over, dragging the Scotti's head to the right. The general howled in pain and turned his head, teeth snapping, trying to lock onto Will's hand. As he did so, Will swept his left leg across in a scything action that took the general's feet from under him, sending him crashing to the snow, Will on top of him, his weight driving the air from the general's lungs.

Again, he felt MacHaddish twisting and turning the knife hand in his grip, trying to break free. Then the general heaved convulsively and rolled to the right at the same time, reversing their positions so that he was on top, the dirk hand poised above Will's throat, slowly starting to move downward as he put all his weight and strength behind it.

Will gripped the knife hand with both his hands, trying to force the dirk away to the side. But he felt a hollow sense of despair as he realized how much stronger the Scotti was. Fighting on their feet, Will would have had a slight edge in speed and mobility. But here, all the advantages were with the Scotti.

Will heaved and bucked desperately, trying to throw the other man off. But MacHaddish was expecting the movements and countered them easily. Each time, Will gained a little respite as the knife moved away from him. Then, inexorably, MacHaddish's brute strength would bring it back, forcing it down toward Will's throat. And Will was tiring.

The sweat of fear, panic and exertion ran into Will's eyes as he watched the gleaming tip of the dirk inch closer and closer. Behind it, vaguely, he could see MacHaddish's face, his features obscured by the paint. There was a light of triumph in his eyes, and MacHaddish's lips drew back in a fierce smile as he realized that any second now, it would be all over.

And then, sooner than he had expected, it was.

Bang! Bang! The heavy brass pommel of Horace's sword slammed into the Scotti's temple twice in rapid succession.

Will felt MacHaddish's strength suddenly fade to nothing, and all that was left was his dead weight bearing down on the knife as his eyes glazed and he slumped unconscious. With one final convulsive heave, Will threw him off to the side and staggered to his feet, reeling a little as he moved away from the inert body in the snow.

Horace stepped toward his friend and put an arm around his shoulders to steady him.

For the past five minutes Horace had been blundering blindly through the trees and bushes, heading in what he hoped was the right direction. Thank god, he thought, he had made it just in time.

He saw, with some concern, that the front of Will's jerkin was covered in blood.

"Are you all right?" he said, taking his arm from Will's shoulders and turning him so he could see more clearly, looking for some sign of a wound.

Will coughed and retched in reaction to his close shave. He knew how near to dying he had been, and his legs were weak from the thought of it.

"Will!" Horace said, concern making his voice harden. "Are you okay?"

The young warrior was frantically running his hands over Will's chest and stomach, trying to see where he might be wounded. There was a lot of blood soaked into his jerkin front, and it had to be coming from somewhere. Still in slight shock, Will reacted angrily to the question.

"Of course I'm not all right, you idiot!" he snapped. "He damn near killed me! Or didn't you notice?"

He tried to slap Horace's searching hands away but didn't succeed.

"Where did he get you?" Horace asked frantically. He knew he had to find the source of that blood and stanch the flow. Wounds to the stomach and torso were all too often fatal, he knew, and he felt panic rising in him as he continued to search.

"Stop pawing at me!" Will shouted angrily, stepping back from him. "It's MacHaddish's blood, not mine!"

Horace looked at him, uncomprehending for a moment. "Not yours?" he said.

"No. Look at his hand where the arrow hit him. He was pouring blood all over me as we fought. I'm fine."

And illogically, right on the heels of a sudden rush of relief, Horace felt his anger welling up.

"His blood? Why didn't you say so? I was frantic here, thinking you were bleeding like a stuck pig!"

"When did you give me a chance?" Will said. "You were all over me, grabbing at me, turning me this way and that!"

The anger, of course, was nothing more than reaction to the shock and fear they had both felt. But it was no less real for all that.

"I'm sorry," Horace snapped back. "Forgive me for being concerned about you. It won't happen again!"

"Well, if you'd got here a little sooner, there wouldn't have been a problem," Will retorted quickly. "Where the blazes were you, anyway?"

"Where was I? I nearly went crazy trying to find you! Is this the thanks I get for saving your life? Because let me tell you, it didn't look as if you were having the best of it with our friend here."

He nudged the unconscious MacHaddish with the toe of his boot. The Scotti general made no sound. But Will had the grace to look suddenly chastened as he realized his friend was right.

"I'm sorry, Horace. You're right. You saved my life, and I'm grateful."

"Well. . . ." Now it was Horace's turn to shuffle his feet uneasily. He knew the reason for Will's apparent anger. He had seen it in many soldiers who had come close to death and he knew Will hadn't meant to be ungracious. "That's okay. Think nothing of it." He looked for a way to change the subject and realized the perfect opportunity was lying unconscious in the snow.

"I suppose we'd better get him back to Grimsdell," he said. He stooped and grabbed the Scotti's arms to heave him up and over his shoulder, then realized the man's right arm was still pulsing blood. "Better bind this up or he'll bleed all over me," he said.

Quickly, he cut a strip off the man's tartan and wrapped the injured wrist in it. Then, with Will's help, he managed to get the dead weight of the general over his shoulder. He wrinkled his nose with distaste.

"He's a bit ripe close to, isn't he?" he said.

Will shrugged. "I was a little too busy to notice."

19

IN ADDITION TO THE UNCONSCIOUS GENERAL, THREE OF THE Scotti patrol had survived the vicious fight among the trees. Two were unwounded, although one had a large bruise on his jaw where Horace had hit him. The third was semiconscious from loss of blood, with a massive ax wound to his arm.

Gundar, having recovered from his brief flare of berserker rage, ordered the two unwounded Scotti to make a stretcher for their companion and to carry him back to Malcolm's cottage. As they were doing so, he beckoned Will to one side.

"One of them got away," he said. "I can send a few of my men after him if you want."

Will hesitated. The Skandians were excellent fighters, but he doubted their ability to track one running man in the dark. He would have preferred it if none of MacHaddish's party had escaped, but he knew that was asking too much. In the confusion of the battle, it would have been easy for one man to slip into the trees. It was a pity the man had gotten away, but it was no huge problem. He gestured toward MacHaddish, whom Horace had now lowered to the ground with a small sigh of relief.

"We've got the one we came for," he said. "Let it go. He can't do us any harm." He frowned thoughtfully, hoping he was right.

When the stretcher was ready, Horace heaved the Scotti general onto his shoulder again. Nils Ropehander offered to relieve him, but Horace shook his head.

"Maybe later," Horace replied. "He's all right for the moment."

But it was a long way back to the clearing in Grimsdell, and Horace and the Skandians ended up passing the general from one to another, each taking turns carrying him. Eventually, MacHaddish regained consciousness and was able to walk. But his hands were tied and a rope around his neck was secured to Horace's belt. Horace shrugged several times, turning his neck from side to side to relieve the cramped shoulder muscles.

"What are we going to do with this lot?" he asked Will softly, indicating the prisoners. Will didn't answer immediately.

"I suppose we'll have to build some kind of stockade," he said uncertainly. "We'll certainly have to keep guard over them."

Horace grunted. "The boys will love that," he said, indicating the Skandians marching ahead of them, joking and laughing quietly among themselves. "They won't want to spend their time guarding prisoners. They like their food and drink too much."

Will shrugged. "That's too bad," he said. "Maybe we can rig some kind of shackles for them—leg irons or something like that. Then we'd only need one man at a time to keep an eye on them."

"That shouldn't be too much of a hardship," Horace agreed.

It was late night before they reached the clearing. The moon had risen and set, unseen by them as they moved beneath the thick blanket of trees. The glowing remains of the Skandians' cooking fire cast a flickering light over the clearing as they emerged from the trees. There were lights in the windows of Malcolm's cottage as well. The front door opened as they walked into the clearing, spilling an elongated rectangle of light across the dark ground.

Malcolm stepped out to greet them.

"I heard you were on your way," he said. Will and Horace exchanged tired grins.

"We should have known nothing would get past your network of watchers," Will said.

Malcolm pulled a wry face. "Force of habit," he said. As he spoke, he had moved beside the litter and was examining the wounded Scotti. "You'd better get him into my house where I can take a look at him," he said.

Gundar regarded the wounded man with disinterest.

"Why bother? He's an enemy," he said. Malcolm's eyes rose to meet his. There was a hard light in them.

"That makes no difference to me. He's injured," he said.

Gundar met his gaze for a few seconds, then shrugged. "Suit yourself," he said. "But if you ask me, it's a waste of time."

As they moved farther into the light spilling from the house, Malcolm noticed the rough bandages that several of the Skandians wore and understood the reason for Gundar's seeming callousness. The Skandian captain felt a strong sense of responsibility for his men.

"I'll look at your men too," he said, with a note of apology in his voice.

Gundar nodded his acceptance. "I'd appreciate that."

During this exchange, MacHaddish had been peering around, taking in the scene. His eyes were bright and intelligent and his face was fixed in a heavy frown under the blue paint. Malcolm studied him with interest.

"I take it this is MacHaddish?" he said. The general looked sharply at him as he recognized his name.

Will nodded. "That's him," he said. "And a right dance he led us, I can tell you."

For a second, he remembered the moment in the clearing when MacHaddish's knife was bearing down on him, closer and closer to his throat. He shuddered at the memory.

"Hmmm," said Malcolm, taking in the keen, calculating light in the general's eyes. "I'd trust him about as far as I can throw him." He inspected the rough bandage Horace had bound around the Scotti's wounded hand. "That'll do for now," he said. "I'll take a closer look later." He turned away and called across the clearing. "Trobar! Bring the chains!"

The massive figure appeared at the opposite side of the clearing and lumbered toward them. One of the Scotti prisoners took a step backward, muttering something in surprise at the sight of the huge figure. Trobar was carrying several lengths of iron chain. As he came closer, Will saw that the chains had thick, hard leather collars attached.

"I thought we might need something to keep our hostages out of mischief," Malcolm explained, "so I set Trobar to making these up earlier this afternoon."

Will and Horace exchanged a quick glance. "I'm glad someone thought about it," Will said.

Malcolm smiled. "You catch them. I'll keep them," he said. "Shackle them, please, Trobar," he added.

The Scotti warriors recoiled from the giant figure at first, then as one of the Skandians growled a warning, they submitted to having the heavy leather collars attached around their necks. Assisted by two of the Skandians, Trobar then led the prisoners across to a huge fallen log under the edge of the trees. He hammered large iron staples through the end links of each chain to fasten them to the log.

"The snow's stopped, so they can sleep in the open," Malcolm said. "They're used to it." He glanced at MacHaddish. "I think it might be better if we keep the general separate from the others."

Horace nodded. "Good thinking. He can have his own log. It's a privilege of rank," he added, with a small grin.

When MacHaddish had been secured in a similar fashion, several other members of Malcolm's secret community emerged from the trees, as was their custom, bringing food and drink for the tired ambush party. Malcolm, sensing Gundar's priorities, tended to the two injured Skandians, cleaning their wounds thoroughly, dressing them with a healing salve and bandaging them neatly and efficiently. Then he addressed the wounded and still unconscious Scotti, cleaning the ax wound in his arm and gently sewing the edges together with clean thread. Horace winced at the sight of the needle passing in and out of the man's flesh.

When Malcolm had finished, Trobar carried the Scotti to a bunk bed under the shelter of the veranda. He laid him in it and covered him with blankets. Then, unconscious or not, he fastened another collar around the man's throat and attached it by a short length of chain to the bed.

"If he goes anywhere, he'll have to take his bed with him," Malcolm observed, a glint in his eye. "I doubt he's up to the effort."

The other Scotti soldiers, having been fed by Malcolm's people, had already wrapped themselves in their massive tartans and leaned back against the log they were fastened to. By now, they were philosophical about their fate as captives and reasonably reassured that they weren't going to be killed or tortured. As a result, they reacted like soldiers everywhere: They took the chance to catch up on some sleep. Their snores were audible across the clearing.

By contrast, MacHaddish sat straight-backed by a second log, his eyes darting around the clearing.

"He'll need watching," Horace said, chewing on a chunk of tender grilled lamb wrapped in a soft piece of flat bread. Close by, Trobar grunted something unintelligible and moved out to sit on the ground a few meters from MacHaddish, his eyes fixed on him. Silently, a black and white shape detached itself from the shadows and slipped across the clearing to his side. Will smiled at the sight of her.

"The dog can take care of that," he said. "But perhaps we'd better set a watch through the night. At least, out in the open the way they are, they're easy to keep an eye on."

Malcolm joined them, working his shoulders up and down, easing the arm and back muscles that were cramped and stiff from bending over, tending to the wounded men.

"Trobar can watch him for a couple of hours," he said. "You two should rest. I'll organize a guard roster."

Will smiled gratefully. "I won't argue," he said. "It has been a long day." He turned away, heading toward his and Horace's tents. Then a thought struck him, and he stopped and looked back at the healer.

"When do you want to question him?" he said, jerking a thumb at the stiff-backed figure chained to the log.

Malcolm answered without hesitation.

"Tomorrow night," he said. "The little surprise I've planned to play on his nerves will be much more effective in the dark."

20

WILL SAT CROSS-LEGGED IN THE LATE-MORNING SUN OUTSIDE
his tent, poring over the message Alyss had sent the night before.

Mortinn, a former inn-boy who had come to Malcolm after
being hideously disfigured by a spilled cauldron of boiling water, had
kept watch at the forest's edge during the night, dutifully noting
down the light patterns as Alyss sent them from her window. He'd
made a few mistakes, but the gist of the message was clear enough.

The temptation for Horace, sitting outside his own tent with
nothing to occupy him, was to watch the process. But, knowing
Will's concern over the secrecy of the code, he wandered off to check
on the chains holding MacHaddish and his two warriors. Satisfied
that they were still secure, he stopped to scratch the dog's head as he
passed. The heavy tail thumped several times on the ground. The
dog had remained on vigil all night while the human guards had
changed every few hours. Now, Horace saw, Trobar had resumed the
guard position.

"Good dog, Blackie," Horace said. The words were greeted by
another tail thump from the dog and an angry glare from Trobar.
The giant rarely spoke, Horace knew. His palate was deformed, and

this made speaking an effort for him. In addition, his words were so slurred they were difficult to understand, and the inevitable questions that resulted tended to embarrass the big man. This time, however, he was sufficiently annoyed to make the effort.

"No' Bla'ie," he said.

Horace hesitated, then thought he knew what had been said. He had noticed that Trobar had trouble with hard consonant sounds like *t* and *k*.

"Not Blackie?" he ventured, and the angry face nodded vehemently. Horace shrugged apologetically, a little put out. Everybody seemed to deride his choice of name for the dog, he thought. "Then what is his name?" he asked.

Trobar paused, then, trying his hardest to enunciate clearly, he said, "Sha'th'ow." There was just the faintest hint of a *d* sound in the *th*.

Horace considered for a moment, then asked, "Shadow?"

The big moon face lit up in a smile and Trobar nodded enthusiastically. "Sha'th'ow," he repeated, pleased that he had communicated something. The dog's tail thumped again as he said the word. Horace studied the dog, thinking how she slipped along, belly close to the ground, moving silently as a wraith.

"That's a good name," he said, genuinely impressed by the giant's creativity. Trobar nodded assent once more.

"Be'er tha' Bla'ie," he said disdainfully.

Horace raised his eyebrows at the taunt.

"Suddenly everyone's a critic," he said, and turned away to see if Will had finished decoding the message. Behind him, as he walked away, he heard the deep rumble of Trobar's laughter.

Will was stashing his crib into an inner pocket when Horace returned.

"What's the news from Alyss?" he asked.

"Mainly she wanted to tell us about MacHaddish's visit. But there's news for Orman as well. I'm afraid his father is dead."

Horace's face hardened. "Keren had him killed?"

Will shrugged. "Not directly. It was more an accident than anything else, but in the long run he is responsible. Alyss says that he'll never give in now. His only hope is to go ahead with his plan with the Scotti."

"And I don't suppose she has any idea of their timetable?" Horace asked.

Will shook his head. "With any luck, Malcolm will get that from MacHaddish tonight," he said.

But Horace looked doubtful. "I wouldn't depend on that. He looks like a tough nut to crack. D'you have any idea what Malcolm has in mind?"

"No idea at all. I expect we'll find out tonight. For now, I'm going to have to tell Orman about his father."

He stood slowly, glancing down at the message sheet again as if it would tell him some easy way to impart the painful news to Orman. Horace dropped a large hand on his friend's shoulder.

"I'll come with you," he said. There was nothing concrete he could do to make the situation any better. But he knew that his presence would provide some comfort and support for Will.

"Thanks," Will said, and they started across the clearing together.

MacHaddish, alert to every movement in the clearing, watched them go.

Orman was in the little cabin with Malcolm and Xander when Will broke the news of Syron's death. Orman accepted it fatalistically.

"Alyss says he would have felt no pain, at least," Will told him, hoping to make the news easier to bear. "He was unconscious at the end and just slipped away."

"Thanks for telling me," Orman said. "I think I knew it anyway. I'd sensed something—a lack or a loss. I knew in my heart that my father must be dead."

Xander's eyes had filled with tears at the news. He had served Syron's family since he had been a teenager. His sadness didn't stem so much from a sense of affection for the family—Xander was too much a servant to presume affection for his masters. His sadness came from a sense of duty. Syron's death brought with it a loss of direction in the little man, as if an arm or a leg had been cut off.

In spite of the fact that he had been serving as Orman's secretary for the past few months, his initial loyalty had been to Syron, and as Will and Horace had noted on several prior occasions, that loyalty was deep-seated and integral to his character.

He coped now as he usually did, by trying to find some way to serve Orman, now officially established as his permanent master.

"My lord, is there anything I can get you? Anything I can do?"

Orman patted his shoulder gently.

"Thanks, Xander, but you need to grieve as well. He was your master before I was, and I know you always served him faithfully. Don't bother yourself about me for a while."

The little steward's face seemed to crumple before them, and Orman realized that the most effective way for Xander to cope with the loss would be to busy himself doing things for his master.

"On second thought," he said, "I think I could use a large cup of tea right now. If it's not troubling you too much."

Xander's face cleared instantly.

"At once, my lord!" he said. He looked at the others. "Anyone else?" he asked.

Will and Horace hid their surprise. The little steward had been decidedly prickly over the past few days. Malcolm, however, understood his need for something to do.

"I'd like a cup too, Xander, if you don't mind," he said softly.

Xander nodded several times and bustled toward the small cottage's kitchen, rubbing his hands energetically together.

"What's the plan of action for tonight?" Will asked Malcolm when the steward had left the room.

"There's a clearing a little way east of here," Malcolm told them. "My people are setting up a few things now. We'll take MacHaddish there once the moon has set."

Horace frowned thoughtfully. He'd been wondering for some time how Malcolm intended to get MacHaddish to answer questions.

"What exactly do you have in mind?" he asked.

The healer regarded him. His normally kindly face was devoid of expression. "I'm planning to prey on MacHaddish's superstitions and fears. The Scotti have a host of demons and supernatural beings that I can use."

"You know what they are?" Orman asked, eyeing the healer with some interest.

Malcolm shrugged diffidently. "Well, yes. One of my people spent his early years living north of the border. He's familiar with the Scotti demons and superstitions." A thought struck him, and he looked at Will. "I suppose we'll need a few Skandians tonight as guards," he said. "Ask Gundar if we can have two or three of his most simple-minded and superstitious men."

"I'll tell him," Will said doubtfully. "But wouldn't we be better with more intelligent guards?"

Malcolm shook his head. "Terror feeds upon itself. If Mac-Haddish sees the Skandians are terrified, it'll make it easier to frighten him. And it'll be better if they're not acting."

Xander returned at that moment, with a tray bearing two mugs of steaming tea. He offered the tray to Orman, who took a cup carefully.

"Thank you, Xander," he said. "I don't know what I'd do without you."

Xander smiled. It was an unusual expression on his face, and Will and Horace exchanged a surprised glance. They had just witnessed an object lesson in leadership and authority.

"And thank you," Malcolm said in his turn. He sipped appreciatively at his tea, then asked Will and Horace, "I assume you two will be along to watch tonight?"

"Of course," Will answered. "We wouldn't miss it for the world."

Malcolm nodded. "Thought you might say that. Well, I'll have Trobar bring you all along when the time's right. I'll be leaving shortly to get a few things ready at the clearing." He glanced down at his teacup and smiled. "Just as soon as I've finished this excellent tea."

21

TROBAR LED THE LITTLE PARTY ALONG A TYPICAL GRIMSDELL track. Narrow, constricted and overgrown, it wound its way beneath the massive trees that loomed above it. At ground level, the track was barely two meters wide. Above the ground, the canopy of the forest overhung the track, the branches and vines intertwining to block out the view of the stars.

At odd intervals, they passed arcane symbols and warning signs—skulls and bones figuring prominently among them. MacHaddish seemed unperturbed by these, although they caused a certain amount of nervous comment from the three Skandians.

More ominous to Will was the fact that the forest was completely silent. There was no rustling of nocturnal animals among the undergrowth, no soft, swishing flight of bats or owls through the trees. Nothing.

And yet the silence did not suggest the absence of life. Far from it. In fact, there was a sense of some large presence around them—of eyes that watched them from the impenetrable darkness that began outside the narrow circle of light from the torches they carried. The forest itself seemed to personify a massive, ancient evil.

Will shivered at the thought of it and pulled his cloak more tightly around him. The darkness and the silence were causing him to have fanciful thoughts, he told himself. There was nothing here to be afraid of. He knew that the manifestations he had seen and heard when he first entered the forest had been the result of Malcolm's trickery. And yet, the forest had been ancient long before Malcolm had come to live in it. Who could tell what prehistoric evil might have taken root here, deep under the trees, where the warming, cleansing light of the sun never penetrated?

He glanced surreptitiously at Horace, marching beside him. In the light of the torch he carried, Horace's face was pale and set. He could feel the atmosphere too, Will thought.

They wound through the trees. Trobar walked at the front of the party, with MacHaddish behind him. The giant had levered MacHaddish's chain free of the log that had secured him through the night and stapled it to a slightly smaller log. Trobar now carried it by one hand as if it were weightless, but Horace and Will both realized that its weight would take all the strength of a normal man to lift. It was a simple way to ensure that MacHaddish didn't try to escape. All Trobar had to do was drop the massive piece of hardwood, and MacHaddish's progress would be reduced to a staggering crawl.

The three Skandians followed directly behind the Scotti general, their weapons ready for any sign of treachery on his part—and for any supernatural interference that might manifest itself in the meantime.

Will and Horace brought up the rear.

"How far's the clearing?" Horace asked quietly. The darkness of the forest was becoming oppressive. It seemed to press in on them, and he would have welcomed the sight of a patch of clear sky and a little room around him to let him breathe.

Will shrugged. "He said it was close by. But the way this trail twists and winds, we could be walking for miles."

At the sound of their voices, muted as they were, Trobar turned to look back at them. He placed his finger to his lips in an unmistakable sign for silence. Will and Horace exchanged a glance and shrugged. But they said nothing.

A few meters farther, Trobar held up his hand and they all stopped. He peered from side to side into the blackness, holding his torch higher to try to penetrate farther into the gloomy depths that surrounded them. Instinctively, the other members of the little party copied his actions. For the first time, Will noticed that MacHaddish had lost his customary lack of concern. His glance flicked quickly from Trobar to the surrounding darkness and back again.

The man had some nerves after all, Will thought to himself. The Skandians muttered in an undertone until Trobar rounded on them fiercely and made the gesture for silence again. He started forward, then stopped, uncertainly. His nervousness communicated itself to the rest of the group. Will felt an overwhelming sense that something was coming up on him in the darkness behind them, but when he turned quickly to look, he could see nothing but blackness beyond the flare of his torch.

Then the sound began.

It was a deep, rhythmic noise, the sound of some massive creature's breathing. It came from the sides and from behind. Then it was ahead of them. Then to the right. The hair on Will's neck prickled upright. It's the forest itself, he thought. It's alive. He shook himself angrily to get rid of the ridiculous fancy. He knew how Malcolm arranged for sounds to move around the forest. The healer had shown him the network of hollow tubes he used to broadcast and amplify sounds to different positions. Somewhere out in the dark, Will told himself, Luka, Malcolm's barrel-chested assistant, would be breathing into the tubes, sending the sound through a network of tubes to different points in the trees around them.

Then the breathing stopped as suddenly as it had begun. Trobar stepped off again, MacHaddish and the three Skandians following reluctantly. Will realized, in a flash of inspiration, that the giant's reluctance and uncertainty were a pretense. It was brilliant playacting on his part—pretending to be nervous, pretending to be uncertain as to whether to carry on or not. As Malcolm had told them, fear communicates itself to others. The fact that the massive, gargoyle-like Trobar was afraid was enough to make the others fearful as well.

Trobar stopped again. Then he turned his head from side to side, listening.

The sound came from nowhere and everywhere. The breathing was gone, replaced now by a deep sighing sound, an extended, visceral growl that was right at the lower register of human hearing.

Trobar looked back at the small party, his eyes wide with fear.

"Hur'y!" he croaked at them, and then, in case they hadn't understood him, set off along the track at a shambling run. MacHaddish was caught by surprise and remained rooted to the spot for a second or two. Then the chain leading to the collar around his neck tightened and nearly jerked him from his feet. He recovered with difficulty, staggering and blundering into trees as he tried to regain his balance, knowing that if he lost his footing, Trobar would not wait for him. He would be dragged along by the chain until the collar choked him.

The Skandians needed no extra urging. They careered behind the reeling general, shoving him with their weapons, exhorting him to go faster or to make way for them. Will and Horace, after a moment's indecision, took off in pursuit, stumbling on roots and depressions in the uneven track, the flames from their torches flaring behind them, trailing showers of sparks as they tried to keep up.

Will told himself that it was all a trick, an illusion. He knew that Malcolm and a party of his followers had been at work all day preparing for this. Yet even so, while logic told him there was nothing to be frightened of, his sense of terror in these cold dark woods could not be denied.

The groaning had changed. It had become a guttural laugh as the forest seemed to express its contempt for their efforts to escape.

Ahead of them, Trobar's hoarse, slurring voice could be heard as he continued to exhort them to hurry. Will glanced back over his shoulder, but with the glare of the torch beside his head, he couldn't see more than a meter or two behind him. Again, he had the sense of unavoidable dread—the feeling that something large and hostile was looming in the night behind him.

His feet caught in a tree root and he pitched forward. But before he reached the ground, he felt Horace's hand grab his upper arm and drag him upright again.

"Watch where you're going!"

The fear was infectious. Will sensed it in Horace's high-pitched voice. Horace saw it in Will's fearful backward glances. Each of them had the highest regard for the other's courage, so the thought that Horace was terrified added spurs to Will's fear, and vice versa for Horace. The night, the darkness, the narrow, winding track all magnified their fear. And it fed upon the oldest fear of all, fear of the dark unknown.

Now the voice in the night had changed again. The laughter had changed to a pulsing, wordless snarl. It was a sound that mingled frustration with hatred that told them beyond doubt that whatever was out there in the forest was weary of toying with them and was about to close in for the kill.

And then, blessedly, there was light and open space as they blundered into the clearing they had been searching for, and the sounds of the forest gradually died away.

The little party stood, heads hanging, chests heaving, as they recovered their breath. The clearing was barely twenty meters across, but they could see the night sky above them and feel relief from the threatening wall of trees that had enclosed them. There was a small fire burning in the center of the clearing. After the oppressive blackness of the forest, it seemed twice as bright as normal, and instinctively, seeing it as sanctuary, they moved toward it. Then a figure stepped into the light between them and the fire, one hand up in an unmistakable gesture, his shadow long and wavering in the flickering light of the fire.

The figure was tall and narrow shouldered, dressed in a long black gown that was festooned with gold thread tracing out the shape of the moon and stars and comets. A high, flat-topped tubular hat crowned his head, with a narrow brim circling it about ten centimeters above its base. The hat was bright-burnished silver, and it caught the red glare of the fire, throwing weird dancing reflections of light into the trees around them with every slight movement of his head.

His face was painted in alien patterns of black and silver, completely covered so that only the eyes were left glaring out from the terrifying mask.

The figure held out his hands to the side, and Will could see that the arms of the long garment he wore were flared at the cuffs so the sleeves hung like a bat's wings from his arms. And his voice when he spoke was harsh and querulous, a voice that would brook no argument.

Gone was Malcolm, the gentle healer Will had come to know. In his place was the character he had created to keep intruders away from Grimsdell Wood.

Malkallam, Will realized. The sorcerer.

22

"TROBAR, YOU FOOL!" GRATED MALKALLAM AT HIS COWERING assistant. "I told you to be here before moonset—before it awoke!"

He gestured to the dark circle of trees around them as he spoke, and, faintly, the small group heard that deep, evil chuckle again. Trobar hung his head in shame and fear.

"Sor'y, Ma'ther," he said miserably. But there was no forgiveness in the sorcerer's glaring eyes.

"Sorry? No good to be sorry, fool. You have woken him, and now I must protect us all."

The Skandians had listened wide-eyed to this exchange. Perhaps more terrifying than the events in the forest, and Malkallam's arcane appearance, was his callous, unforgiving treatment of Trobar. The Skandians had been around long enough to know that Malcolm usually treated the deformed giant with kindness and soft words. This was a different person altogether.

Will, having regained a little equanimity now that they were out of the trees, watched with narrowed eyes. He realized that Malcolm and Trobar were playing a part for the benefit of MacHaddish. He leaned close to Horace and whispered, "Go along with it."

Horace nodded, but at the slight sound, Malkallam rounded

upon them, one arm outstretched, the forefinger adorned with a long nail pointing at them like an arrow.

"Silence, you idiots! This is no time for chatter! Serthrek'nish is awake!"

And at the name, there was a reaction from MacHaddish. The Scotti let out an involuntary cry of terror and sank to his knees, huddled over the heavy log that Trobar had dropped. Malkallam stepped toward him, standing over the crouching figure as he spoke.

"Yes, MacHaddish. The dark demon Serthrek'nish is abroad in this forest, watching us as we stand here. You know of him, I think? The shredder of bodies and renderer of limbs? The red-fanged destroyer of men?"

He paused. There was a strangled sob of fear from the Scotti. He remained bowed over the heavy log that secured his chain, refusing to look up, as if fearful of what he might see.

Malkallam continued inexorably.

"Only the light of my fire is keeping him back from this clearing. But Serthrek'nish won't be denied for long. He's gathering his courage now, and he knows the flames will soon die down."

As if in answer, a deep-throated chuckle sounded from the darkness outside the clearing.

MacHaddish's head snapped up. Even from several meters away, Will could see the whites of the man's wide-open, terrified eyes against the blue paint that covered his face.

"We've no time to waste. I have to build our defensive perimeter," Malkallam said. He ignored the staring general, gesturing to his assistant. "Trobar! Take those men over there!"

Trobar led the Skandians to a point near the edge of the clearing indicated by his master. The sea wolves looked fearfully at the dark wall of the trees as they approached it. They would have preferred to remain right in the middle of the clearing, near the fire.

"Sit," Malkallam commanded them, and, following Trobar's lead, they sat cross-legged on the damp ground. The sorcerer then moved around them, muttering incomprehensible incantations as he poured black powder from a sack in a large circle around them.

"Don't touch the circle," he warned them. "The soul stealer can't touch you if your circle is unbroken."

He ushered Will and Horace to another point in the clearing. Motioning them to sit on the ground, he poured more black powder in a circle around them. He began the mumbling incantations again as he moved around Will and Horace, then in the middle of it all, without changing intonation or volume, he said quietly, in his normal voice, "Don't try to guess what I'm doing. Don't discuss it. Just look scared to death."

Will nodded and saw an almost imperceptible nod in return. It made sense, he realized. If he and Horace were to sit here calmly and analytically trying to second-guess his actions, they would destroy the atmosphere he was working to create.

Malkallam—it was almost impossible to think of him as Malcolm in this context—moved away from them now and formed another black circle around MacHaddish. The Scotti had recovered a little by now and watched him as the black powder fell around him. Malkallam met his gaze as he completed the circle.

"You're safe if the black circle is complete," he said. "Do you understand?"

MacHaddish nodded, swallowing heavily. Malkallam's face darkened.

"Say it!" he ordered. "Say you understand!"

"I . . . understand," the Scotti said. There was a thick accent to his speech that made the words almost unrecognizable.

Will's eyebrows shot up. It was the first time the Scotti had spoken since they had captured him, the first sign that he understood the Araluen language. Although, he thought immediately, it would have made little sense to send someone who didn't speak Araluen to negotiate with Keren.

Now, not only had MacHaddish spoken, he had done so in response to an order from Malkallam. It seemed that the sorcerer was beginning to assert dominance over the stiff-necked Scotti. Will glanced quickly at Horace, saw that the young warrior's eyes were lowered, his head bowed, and realized that he was looking altogether too interested in the proceedings himself. He copied his friend's example and lowered his head, pulling the cowl of his cloak farther forward. From inside the shadow of the cowl, he could watch Malkallam at work without risking his features being seen.

The tall figure strode across the clearing now, reflections from the silver hat flickering across the trees, and picked up a long black-thorn staff. The wood was gnarled and highly polished from constant handling over the years. He held it above his head.

"The three black circles are complete," he called to the forest. "I hold the sacred blackwood scepter. We are protected from you, Serthrek'nish!"

An angry snarl resonated through the trees in answer. On the southern side of the clearing, the side they had approached from, there was a sudden glare of red light as something flashed between the trees. Then it came again, closer this time, circling the clearing as it moved to the west.

Malkallam backed away from the trees toward the fire in the center of the clearing. Will looked around at the others. In their circle, Trobar and the Skandians were wide eyed and staring, their eyes searching the trees for the next sign of light or movement. MacHaddish was the same. Will glanced at Malkallam and saw that he was watching MacHaddish carefully. Once he was assured that the Scotti's attention was distracted, he reached into his cloak and took a small package from an inner pocket. Moving closer to the fire, he dropped the packet into the embers at its edge.

There was another flash of red in the trees, moving to the north-west side of the clearing now. Then, at the spot where it disappeared, a thin curtain of fog began to rise from the ground, just inside the tree line.

Malkallam began to back away again, moving toward the huddled figure of MacHaddish.

"Stay back, Serthrek'nish!" he called. "The flames of fire and the circles of power forbid you to enter this clearing!"

Even as he said it, there was a sudden flare of red from the fire itself. A red flash leapt from the flames, followed by a thick red mist that bloomed up from the side of the fire—right at the point, Will realized, where Malkallam had tossed the small packet only a few seconds before.

The Skandians, Trobar and MacHaddish all cried out in shock. A little belatedly, Will and Horace added their voices to the reaction. Then, as the strange red mist spread over the fire, the flames began to dwindle, as if being smothered. The clearing grew darker as the flames died down. Malkallam's tall figure threw a distorted, elongated shadow across the ground and the trees seemed to press in closer to them.

"Gorlog's claws!" shouted one of the Skandians. "What the devil is that?"

Everyone followed the direction of his pointing arm. In the bank of fog that was rising among the trees to the north, they saw a sudden red flare of light.

But this was more than just light. This was the shape of a terrible face, looming through the mist. It was there for an instant and then gone, but it was indelibly printed on their memories. A triangular face, with hollow, slanted eyeholes and a leering black mouth set with long, canine fangs. Wild tendrils of beard covered the chin, and the hair was a red mass of tangles, with two curved horns visible through them.

Then it was gone and a shattering laugh split the night. The laugh ran around the circle of trees that surrounded them, and their eyes followed its movement involuntarily.

Then, high in the sky above the clearing, the face reappeared, this time glowing as if lit by an inner light. It swooped low, then soared across the clearing, climbing back into the trees and seeming to explode and disappear in a shower of sparks that left the darkness even blacker as they died away.

Malkallam had recoiled as the apparition swooped low overhead, then tried unsuccessfully to strike at it with his blackthorn staff. He staggered and dropped to his knees. Then, maintaining his hold on the staff, he pointed to the fog bank again, where the horrible grinning face had appeared once more.

"Go, Serthrek'nish! I forbid you entry! Go!"

The face disappeared again, and the watchers cried out in terror as a new apparition formed. Black and shimmering in the fog—or rather, Will realized, *on* the fog—a huge figure took shape: Massively built, wearing a huge horned helmet and holding a jagged-edged ax, it towered above them for a second, then faded to nothing.

The Night Warrior, Will realized. He had seen the dreadful figure the first time he had ventured into Grimsdell Wood, and it had terrified him. A few days later, Alyss had discovered it was nothing more than an illusion, using fake lights and a magic lantern projector, created by Malcolm to scare away intruders.

The fire was nothing but a small pile of coals now. Malkallam rose unsteadily to his feet. He pointed the black staff, threatening the trees that encircled them.

"Stay back, I warn you!" he called. But now a series of red flashes and flares ran through the trees, circling the clearing, throwing huge, twisted shadows across the small open space, shadows that were there and then gone in an instant. And as this happened, they heard Serthrek'nish speak for the first time, his voice deep, resonant and blood-chilling.

"The flames have died. The power of the circles is weak. I will have the blood of one of you."

One of the Skandians went to rise, battleax ready in his hand, but Malkallam's outstretched hand stopped him before he had gone above a crouch.

"Stay where you are, you fool!" his voice cracked like a whip. "He says he wants one and one only. He can have the Scotti."

"No-o-o-o-o-o!" MacHaddish's cry was high-pitched and agonized. To the Skandians, the demonic red face was a terrifying apparition. But to MacHaddish, it lay at the very heart of terror. It was the basis of all fear for Scottis, instilled in them when they were children. The flesh eater, the renderer, the tearer of limbs—Serthrek'nish was all these things and more. It was the demon, the ultimate evil in Scotti superstition. Serthrek'nish didn't just kill his victims. He stole their souls and their very being, feeding on them to make himself stronger. If Serthrek'nish had your soul, there was no hereafter, no peace at the end of the long mountain road.

And there was no memory of the victim either, for if a person were taken by Serthrek'nish, his family were compelled to expunge all memory of him from their minds.

With Malkallam's words, MacHaddish knew he was not facing just a terrible death. He was facing a forever of nothing. He looked up now into the implacable face as the wizard stepped toward him.

"No," he pleaded. "Please. Spare me this."

But the blackthorn rod had moved out and begun to scrub an opening in the circle of black powder that surrounded MacHaddish.

Frantically, MacHaddish tried to restore it, pushing the powder back into place with his hand, but his efforts only succeeded in widening the gap. His breath sobbed in his throat, and tears of abject terror scored a path through the blue paint on his face.

Then the face reappeared in the mist, seeming to be more clearly defined now. It flickered, faded and disappeared again.

MacHaddish looked up at the wizard's painted face. All traces of the proud, unbending Scotti general were gone now.

"Please?" he said. And the staff stopped its work.

Malkallam paused. "No," he said impassively.

MacHaddish, already on his knees, now bent forward until his forehead touched the ground—making sure that he remained within the circle, Will noted.

"I'll give you anything," he said. "Anything you ask. Just keep the demon away."

Malkallam's staff moved toward the thin black line once more, touching it, stirring the grains of black powder that marked it out, slowly separating them, deliberately working to form a breach in the circle. The general watched the tip of the staff at work, watched his safe haven slowly being scraped away.

"Please?" he said, in a voice that was cracking with fear.

The staff stopped moving.

"Tell me," Malkallam said in a deliberate voice, "what are you planning with Keren?"

23

MACHADDISH LOOKED UP QUICKLY, SUSPICION MIXED WITH FEAR on his face as he heard the terms. He had expected something else from the wizard—a demand for riches or power or both. Information was the one thing he hadn't expected Malkallam to ask for.

"It's a simple question," Malkallam continued. "Tell me what you have planned."

In spite of the terror that gripped his insides, the discipline MacHaddish had learned over long years as a warrior and leader reasserted itself. To disclose plans like this was treachery, nothing less. His jaw set in a hard line, and he began to shake his head.

Malkallam's staff begin its inexorable work again, wiping out the circle that protected the Scotti. MacHaddish knew his own folklore. He knew the black circle was his only protection against Serthrek'nish. He knew that once there was a gap in the circle wide enough for the demon's hand to enter, it would be the end of him.

Serthrek'nish would drag him, screaming, from the circle and into the black night under the trees—and into a greater blackness beyond.

He watched the gap widen. A lifetime of loyalty and discipline struggled with a lifetime of superstition, and superstition won. He reached out and grabbed hold of the tip of the staff, stopping its deliberate movement.

"Tell me what you want to know," he said in a low voice, his shoulders slumped in defeat.

"Your plans for attack," Malcolm said. "How many men are coming? When are they going to be here?"

There was no further hesitation from the Scotti. He had committed to betray his trust, and he could see no point in hedging.

"Two hundred men, initially, from the clans MacFrewin, MacKentick and MacHaddish. The commander will be Caleb MacFrewin, warlord of the senior clan."

"And the plan is to occupy Castle Macindaw, then spread out farther into Norgate Fief, correct?"

MacHaddish nodded. "Macindaw will be our anchor point, our stronghold. Once we have neutralized that and occupied it, we can bring more and more men through the passes."

A few meters away, Will and Horace exchanged worried glances. Both knew the potential danger of having an armed force of two hundred men loose in the province. And those two hundred would be just an advance party. Once a foothold was gained, more would follow in their tracks.

It would take a major army to dislodge them, and that army would have to come from the south. It would be months before King Duncan could put a large enough force together and then march them north. By then, the Scottis would be firmly entrenched and it might well prove impossible to drive them back through the passes to the high plains of Picta—particularly if they held Castle Macindaw in strength. If this went unchecked, it could mark the beginning of a long, drawn-out war, with no guarantee of victory for the Araluen forces. You could almost redraw the maps of Araluen and Picta and move the permanent border fifty kilometers to the south.

But most of this they had already guessed. There was one question still remaining that needed answering. And that answer might well hold the key to Norgate's future.

"When?" Malcolm posed the question. This time MacHaddish did hesitate. He knew as well as they did that this was the vital question, and for a moment his loyalty reasserted itself.

But not for long. Malcolm twisted the point of the staff from his grip and moved it toward the thin black line of powder once more.

"Three weeks," MacHaddish said, a note of surrender in his voice. "Three weeks from yesterday. Caleb MacFrewin is already gathering the clans. They're marching to the border now. It will take time for them to get through the few passes that are open and then reassemble into marching order. They'll be at Macindaw in three weeks."

Malcolm stepped back a pace, studying the crouching figure before him. He saw the slumped shoulders, the downcast eyes and the look of defeat. MacHaddish was a broken man, a man who had betrayed his own honor, and Malcolm had no intention of crowing over the fact. Nor did he plan to reveal to MacHaddish that he had been tricked. But that was less because of any sympathy for the man and more because he realized that there might come a time when he needed more information.

"Thank you," he said simply. He took a sack from an inner pocket and bent forward, pouring black powder onto the ground to restore the gaps he had forced in the circle.

Then he walked quickly to the smoldering remains of the fire and threw another handful of powder onto the coals. There was a deep *whoof!* and a vivid yellow flash, and the flames reignited instantly, climbing high into the dark sky above Grimsdell Wood. He looked at the three Skandians, who had watched the proceedings in terrified silence.

"We're safe," he said. "Serthrek'nish can't harm us now."

The tension went out of the Skandians' bodies as he spoke. They gripped their weapons a little less fiercely, although Will noticed that they didn't actually let go of them. Then, from behind Malcolm, they heard an unexpected sound.

MacHaddish was sobbing. But whether from shame or relief, no one could tell.

They spent the rest of the night in the clearing. Throughout the hours of darkness, Malcolm replenished the flames whenever it seemed necessary with the strange chemicals he carried. He was determined to maintain the illusion that he had created for MacHaddish's benefit.

As the first gray light of day crept over the treetops, they climbed stiffly to their feet and headed back to Healer's Clearing. They traveled silently. Even by daylight, Grimsdell was a foreboding place that discouraged idle conversation, and the events of the night before were fresh in all their minds.

There was a general lightening in their collective mood when they finally stepped into the open space that marked Healer's Clearing. The other Skandians called greetings to the three who had accompanied the small party, while the Scotti soldiers looked curiously at their general, who kept his eyes averted from them as he sank to his knees, allowing Trobar to transfer his chain once more to the larger log. The stiffness and pride were gone from MacHaddish's body language. He was a shattered man.

Malcolm, who had wiped off his wizard's makeup and resumed his normal gray robe before they left the clearing, beckoned to Will and Horace as he turned toward his little cottage.

"We'd better talk," he said. "Orman will be anxious to hear the news."

The two young men agreed and followed him to the cottage. As they entered the warm parlor, the healer slumped gratefully into one of his carved wooden armchairs.

"Oh, that's better," he said, the relief obvious in his voice. "I'm getting too old for all this playing around in the forest. You've no idea how exhausting it can be prancing around in high boots pretending to be an evil wizard."

He twisted awkwardly in his seat, grimacing as he favored one side of his back.

"Then Nigel let that flying face get too low and nearly took my head off with it, so I had to duck out of the way. Think I might have ricked my back," he said sourly.

At the sound of their voices, Orman and Xander had appeared from an inner room. Orman looked from one to the other.

"I take it the expedition was a success?" he asked.

Malcolm shrugged, then obviously wished he hadn't, as his back twinged in pain.

"You could say that," Horace answered for him. "Malcolm got the names, the numbers and the timetable. Took him less than twenty minutes too," he added admiringly. "On top of that, he scared the daylights out of MacHaddish and our Skandian friends."

Malcolm smiled at him. "That's all?"

Horace grinned sheepishly. "As a matter of fact, you made me a little nervous too," he admitted.

"And me," Will added. "And I know how most of the illusions are done."

"Well, you're one up on me," Horace told him. "Everything came as a wonderful surprise as far as I was concerned."

"The demon face in the fog—and the giant warrior—they were your normal projection illusions, weren't they?" Will asked Malcolm.

Horace snorted. "Normal!" he muttered under his breath.

Malcolm ignored him and replied to Will's question. He was justifiably proud of the technology he had created to form the illusions, and he couldn't help preening just a little.

"That's right. The fog serves a double purpose. It gives me a kind of screen to project on, but it also dissipates and distorts the projections so they're never seen too clearly. If MacHaddish had got a clear look at them, he might have seen how crude they are. The suggestion is all important. The viewer tends to fill in the empty spaces for himself, and usually he does a far more terrifying job than I could."

"The lights in the trees I've seen before too," Will continued. "After all, we use them when we're signaling Alyss. But the flying face—the one that nearly hit you—how did you manage that?"

"Ah, yes, I was quite pleased with that one. Although it nearly brought us undone. Nigel and I spent most of the afternoon rigging that. He's only seventeen, but he's quite an artist. It was nothing more than a paper lantern with the face inscribed on it in heavy black lines. We mounted it on a fine wire that ran across the clearing. It was invisible in the dark. The idea was it was supposed to swoop down, then disappear into the trees opposite."

"But it . . . just seemed to fly apart into sparks," Will said.

Malcolm nodded enthusiastically. "Yes, that's another little chemical trick I learned some years back. A combination of sulfur and saltpeter and . . ." He hesitated. Proud or not, he wasn't willing to share all the details with them. "And a bit of this and that," he continued. "It creates a compound that burns fiercely or explodes if you contain it."

"It was very effective," Horace said, remembering how the red shape had swooped out of the sky, flashed across the clearing, then dissolved into a shower of flame and sparks in the treetops. "I think it was the final straw for MacHaddish."

"It nearly gave the game away," Malcolm replied. "As I said, it flew lower than we had expected and nearly hit me. That would have tangled me up in the wires and might well have set my cloak on fire. If MacHaddish had seen that happen, he would have seen through the whole thing."

"It's often the way," Will said. "Failure is just a few seconds away from success."

"That's true," Malcolm agreed.

Orman had listened patiently as they dissected the events of the previous night. Now, he thought, it was time for a few details.

"So what's the situation?" he asked.

"Not good," Horace said. "There's a war party of two hundred Scotti clansmen assembled on the other side of the border, and they'll be here in less than three weeks."

"So we have to take Macindaw before they get here," Will put in.

Orman, Xander and Malcolm all nodded. That much was obvious. It was Horace who added a jarring note to the conversation.

"And we're going to have to find an extra hundred men to do it," he said.

24

"WHAT ABOUT A NIGHT ATTACK?" WILL ASKED. "COULD WE GET away with fewer men that way?"

Horace shook his head. "We still need the numbers to keep the defenders guessing. Night or day, it doesn't make a difference. We need more men than they do."

They had been discussing the problem since the meeting in Malcolm's cottage had broken up early that morning. But so far, there was no sign of a solution. The two friends had decided to ride back through the forest to a point where they could study the castle, to see if there were any weak points in its defense.

They left their horses a few meters back from the forest edge and proceeded on foot. As Will had done when he had attempted to rescue Alyss, they approached from the eastern side, moving along the road where it passed through a slight depression—deep enough to conceal them from the castle ramparts. As the road angled up and reached a crest, they sank to their knees. The grim castle stood a little under two hundred meters away. Will was reminded of a crouching, waiting monster.

He picked sourly at a clump of dried, frozen grass thrusting up through the snow.

"Do you have to be so negative?" he said. "Sometimes it helps if you keep your thinking flexible."

Horace turned slowly toward him. It was a deliberate movement that was familiar to Will.

"I'm not negative, and I'm not inflexible," Horace said. "I'm just facing facts."

"Well, let's face some others," Will suggested.

"You can't ignore facts just because you don't like them, Will," Horace said, his irritation showing. "The fact is, siege work is a very precise, very ordered science. And there are rules and guidelines that have been laid down after years of trial and error and experience. If we are going to besiege a castle, we will need more men than the defenders. Not less. That's a fact, whether you like it or not."

"I know, I know," Will replied, irritated in his turn. "It's just I feel there must be more to it than merely saying we need three times as many men as the defenders."

"Four times," Horace put in.

Will gestured in annoyance. "Four times, then! And then we will win the battle. It leaves any innovative ideas or stratagems out of the equation and reduces it to numbers. What about ingenuity and imagination? They're part of a battle plan too, you know."

Horace shrugged. "Your area. Not mine."

And that was the problem, Will knew. People looked to Rangers for innovation and ingenuity when it came to planning a battle. But he had been wrestling with this problem since Horace had arrived from the south, and he was no closer to a solution. Some Ranger he'd turned out to be, he thought bitterly.

Perhaps the most infuriating part of it all was that he had a feeling that there was an idea floating around in his subconscious, hovering just out of reach. It had been triggered by something that he had seen or heard in the past few days, but for the life of him, he couldn't put a finger on it. It only made him feel more inadequate.

"Well, we know one thing," Horace said. "If we do attack them, it won't be from this side."

Will nodded. There was too much open ground to cross. Once their force broke cover from the forest edge, they would be in full view of the castle.

An attack from this side would have no element of surprise about it. By the time the attackers reached the walls, they could well have lost a third of their number to the defenders' crossbows.

Horace, as if reading his mind, took the opportunity to reinforce the point he had been making earlier.

"Another reason why we need to outnumber them," he said. "We could lose a lot of men attacking across open ground like this."

Will nodded gloomily.

"All right," he said. "Point made."

He looked up at Alyss's tower window, half closing his eyes in the effort to focus. The heavy tapestry that was used to keep out the wind had been drawn back, and the window formed a black rectangle in the gray stone of the wall. Then he thought he saw a flash of white, as if someone had just passed close to the window. It could only have been Alyss.

"Did you see that?" he asked. Horace, who had been studying the drawbridge and gatehouse, glanced at him curiously.

"See what?"

"I thought I saw something at Alyss's window," Will told him. "Just a flash of white, as if she'd passed by it," he added sadly.

Horace stared at the high window, but there was no further sign of movement. The window was a dark hole in the wall again. He shrugged.

"It was probably her," he said. He understood his friend's disappointment. It was galling to know that Alyss was barely two hundred meters away from them and they were powerless to help her. It must be worse for the Ranger, Horace realized, knowing that he had left her behind to face the danger alone.

"Pity I can't signal her," Will said. "Just to let her know we're here. It'd raise her spirits a little."

"Problem is, you'd let Keren know as well."

"I know," Will said disconsolately. "I'll send her a message tonight. Just to let her know we haven't forgotten her."

Horace decided it was time to distract his friend from these gloomy thoughts. He glanced around to the south, where more open country lay before the castle.

"Doesn't look any better that way," he said. "Any ideas?"

Remaining crouched, they squirmed backward until they were below the crest once more, then stood, dusting the damp snow from their knees and elbows. Will pointed to the west.

"The west side may be our best bet," he said. "The forest grows a lot closer on that side."

"Let's take a look, then," Horace said.

They made their way back to the tethered horses, mounted and rode north. They stayed inside the tree line, where the shadows would hide them from any watchers on the castle walls. Horace felt his spirits sinking as they rode. The castle seemed impregnable. Even with a larger force, it would be a tough nut to crack. With under thirty men, he could see no way they could accomplish it. Yet he didn't voice the thought because he knew how Will would react.

In addition, he sensed Will's underlying frustration. Horace had faith in Will's ability to overcome seemingly insurmountable problems. Will was a Ranger, after all, and he had been trained by Halt, recognized as the greatest of all Rangers. And Horace knew that Rangers had ideas—blindingly brilliant ideas that seemed to come out of nowhere. He had seen Will do it before, and he sensed, without really knowing how, that there was an idea building now, simply waiting for his friend to recognize and develop it.

If that were the case, it would not help matters if Horace were to tell him that he thought there was no chance of success.

Quite simply, they had to succeed, for Alyss's sake and for the sake of the Kingdom. When Caleb MacFrewin led his two hundred men through the trees in three weeks' time, he was going to have to find Castle Macindaw in the hands of a garrison who were determined to bar his way.

Then the Scotti would face similar problems to the one now confronting Horace and Will. They would have the numbers of men necessary for a siege. But they wouldn't have the supplies for a prolonged attack, nor the specialized siege machines and weapons. They didn't expect to have to take Macindaw. They assumed it would be in friendly hands when they arrived, leaving them free to range out into the Araluen lowlands and raid and pillage without the threat of a hostile castle at their backs.

Earlier that morning, Xander had left Grimsdell accompanied by one of Malcolm's people. They would travel across country on foot, planning to bypass Keren's road blocks. Once clear, they hoped to buy or, if necessary, steal horses from one of the farms in the area. Xander was carrying a written account of the situation at Macindaw, and the Scotti plans for invasion, to Castle Norgate. The report was signed by Orman and sealed with the signet ring of the Lord of Castle Macindaw. So in addition to Macindaw lying across their supply lines, and denying the Scotti a strongpoint, they would hopefully be faced with the prospect of a relieving force moving on them from the west. Speed was essential to the Scotti plans, and any delay in their scheme could be fatal for them.

Which brought Horace back to their present predicament. Finding a way to take Macindaw with less than thirty men. Once in possession of the castle, he had no doubt they could augment their current numbers by rehiring the members of the garrison Keren had forced out. They mightn't be willing to sign up for an attack on the castle, but once it was back in Orman's hands, word would go around the countryside, and Horace was confident most of the old garrison would return. After all, they were soldiers and there was precious little else for them to do in the dead of winter.

But it all had to be done within the next three weeks.

"This is the spot," Will said, interrupting his thoughts. They had ridden north toward the point where they had ambushed MacHaddish and his men, then turned west through the trees. Now, as they reached the western fringe of the forest, the going became more difficult. At this part of the forest, the trees grew together in a tangle that was almost impenetrable, so that they were forced to move out into the open ground.

On the western side, Horace saw, the forest reached up to within fifty meters of the castle. He could understand why the original builders had left it this way. Clearing the forest would have been a monumentally difficult task. And the very nature of the forest itself made it impassable for a large number of men laden with equipment, weapons and siege machinery.

Horace rubbed his jaw thoughtfully.

"Well, for once, our small numbers will be an advantage," he said, gesturing toward the thick undergrowth and close-growing trees. "I'd hate to try to move more than thirty men into position through all that."

Will nodded. "All we have to do is figure out a way to make Keren think we have another hundred men attacking from the east," he said.

Horace shrugged. "Or the south. Anything to get them off the west ramparts."

"Let me ask you something," Will said. The thoughtful tone in his voice made Horace look around at him quickly. Maybe the idea was coming after all.

"Go on," he prompted, and Will continued, choosing his words carefully.

"If we could distract them from this wall, could we manage with just one scaling ladder?"

"Just one?" Horace looked doubtful. "It's usually better to have as many as you can. That way you split the defenders' numbers."

"But if they're drawn to the south wall, say, and they don't see us coming until we're over the wall, then two of us could hold them off while the rest of our men come up the ladder, couldn't we?"

"Two of us?" Horace asked. "I assume you mean you and me?"

Will nodded. "I've been up there. The walkways on the ramparts are narrow," he said. "They could only come at us one at a time. I seem to recall you and I did a pretty good job holding off the Temujai at Hallasholm," he reminded Horace.

"True. But it all depends on our getting up and over the wall unseen. Even if we could distract most of the defenders with an attack on the south wall, they won't all go. Nobody's that stupid. And we'd have fifty meters to run, carrying a five-meter scaling ladder. We'd be spotted before we got a third of the way."

Will smiled. "Not if we're already there."

25

ORMAN, MALCOLM, GUNDAR AND HORACE SAT AROUND THE
table in Malcolm's cottage. Will was on his feet, pacing back and
forth in the small room as he explained his idea.

"Horace has told us that we need around one hundred men to
attack the castle—a force three times the size of the defenders."

The others nodded. It was logical.

"The idea is, we could get into the castle with thirty men if we
had another ninety to draw the defenders away from our real attack
point. Is that accurate?" He addressed the question to Horace. The
warrior nodded.

"That's pretty much the idea," he said.

"So with thirty men, we could pull off the actual attack?" Will
insisted.

The other three men watched the exchange with varying degrees
of understanding. It was a matter well outside Malcolm's area of experience. Orman was vaguely familiar with the theoretical problems
of besieging a castle. Gundar was fascinated to know how a force of
thirty men—the crew of a wolfship, for example—could force their
way into a fortified castle. It could prove to be very profitable knowledge in the future.

"Yes," Horace replied patiently. "But we still need those other ninety men to cause the diversion. And we haven't got them," he added, spreading his hands and looking sarcastically around the room as if ninety men might be concealed somewhere.

"Maybe we don't need them," Will said. "Maybe we only need one."

Gundar snorted with laughter. "He'd better be one hell of a warrior!"

Will smiled at the Skandian captain. "Oh, he is. He's a giant of a man. When I saw him, he was over ten meters tall," he said mildly.

Understanding dawned on Malcolm's face, although the other three remained puzzled.

"You mean the Night Warrior?" Malcolm said.

Will nodded and turned to Horace, who was looking thoughtful now that he'd caught on to the idea.

"It'll mean a night attack, but I assume there's no big problem in that?" Will asked.

Horace shrugged his shoulders. He was still considering what Will had said. If the Night Warrior loomed up in the sky outside Castle Macindaw, illusion or not, it might well provide the sort of diversion they needed.

Orman rubbed his chin thoughtfully. He had heard of the Night Warrior, of course, but he had never seen it.

"How big is he exactly?" Orman asked.

"He's massive," Malcolm replied. "As Will says, he can go up to ten meters tall, depending on the distance I have to throw the image. The farther I can project it, the higher he goes. But why stop at the Night Warrior? I could throw in some other shapes as well. The face of Serthrek'nish, for starters. And the odd dragon or troll, I suppose."

Orman looked around the table. "I seem to have missed out on something. Who or what is Serthrek'nish?"

"He's the Scotti demon we used to terrify MacHaddish," Malcolm explained.

Orman looked less than convinced. "He may have worked against MacHaddish," he said. "But Macindaw is manned by Araluens. They won't know Serker . . . Serkrenit . . . whoever he is . . . from a bowl of black pudding."

Horace grinned now. "Don't worry. You don't have to know his name to be terrified of him. He's a truly horrific sight, looming out of the mist like that."

"That's the only drawback to the idea," Malcolm now said, his face thoughtful. "I need fog or mist to project the shapes onto. That's why I chose the clearing the other night. A small rivulet runs through the north side, and that created the mist we needed. Same thing at the black mere," he added.

Will felt his whole idea collapsing like a house of cards. He'd been so wrapped up in it that he hadn't seen the basic flaw. No mist, no projected image. No image, no diversion.

Malcolm saw the disappointment on his face and smiled encouragingly. "It's not a big problem," he said. "We'll just have to place some perforated tubing through the point where we want the mist. Then we pump water through the tubes, along with a chemical or two to help the process along, and the mist will rise out of the perforations, as long as the weather is cold enough."

Will's spirits soared. His idea was back on track.

"How quickly could we put the tubing in place?" he asked.

Malcolm pursed his lips thoughtfully. "Maybe two nights," he said eventually. "We'll have to work after moonset, and we can't have too many people involved or we'll be spotted. Last thing we want is your friend Buttle sending a party out to investigate what we've been up to."

Gundar growled softly at the mention of Buttle's name. Will glanced sidelong at him. The huge Skandian reminded him of a bear—big, powerful and seemingly clumsy, but in actual fact fast and deadly. Then, he thought, smiling, that a lot of Skandians could be described that way. They were a very bearlike race. He thought he wouldn't want to get in Gundar's way when the time came to go up the scaling ladders. As that thought struck him, he realized that was another item they'd have to take care of.

"We'll need ladders," he said. "Can we get your people to work making them?" He addressed the remark to Malcolm, who nodded. Then he turned to Gundar. "Your men too, Gundar," he requested.

"I'll get them on it first thing tomorrow," the Skandian said. "How many do we need?"

Horace and Will exchanged a glance.

"You had some idea about using only one?" Horace reminded him. But Will shook his head.

"I'm still working on that. We'd better have backups. How many would you say?"

The young knight chewed a fingernail as he thought about it. The more the better, he knew. The more ladders there were, the quicker his men could be up on the ramparts and into the attack. But there were limitations.

"We'll have to manhandle them through that tangle of forest on the west side," he said. "That'll take a lot of time and effort. I'd say the most we could handle would be four. That makes about seven men to a ladder."

Will looked to Malcolm and Gundar, who both nodded agreement. "Four it is, then," Will said. "I doubt we'll have time to make more anyway. And as you say, it'll be a nightmare getting a five-meter ladder through that forest."

He addressed Malcolm again. "You know, it also occurred to me that we might be able to use something like that illuminated face that you had sailing across the clearing the other night?"

He phrased it as a question, but Malcolm was already shaking his head. "We needed overhead wires and cables for that. We can hardly rig that sort of thing on the open ground outside Macindaw without being seen."

"And if you are seen, the garrison will know it's all some kind of trick," Orman put in. "Then your whole plan collapses."

Will nodded, acknowledging the point. "I can see that," he said. "But I thought there might be some way to throw them high in the air, then have them explode the way that one did the other night. That was quite spectacular, believe me."

"Let me think on it," Malcolm said. "I can probably put together some kind of simple catapult to throw them. We could site that in the woods, after all. There's no reason why we couldn't do that from a concealed position."

"Exactly," Will said, his enthusiasm growing by the second. "The more diversions we have the better. And flying, glowing, exploding heads would make a great diversion."

He looked around the faces at the table, seeing enthusiasm and hope in all of them.

"Well," he said, "it's late and I still have to send a message to Alyss. I suggest we adjourn for the night and get to work in the morning. We have a lot to do."

There was a mumble of agreement from the others, and they all rose. Orman was still feeling left out of the full picture.

"Flying, exploding heads," he muttered to himself. "These Rangers really are peculiar folk."

26

ALYSS SMILED QUIETLY AS SHE READ THE CODED MESSAGE AGAIN. She had already read it the night before, when Will had sent it to her, of course. But she saved it to read one more time in the morning light before carefully placing it in the fire that burned in her grate.

She stooped before the fireplace now, watching the sheet of paper turn black and curl up in the flames. The paper might be gone, but the message of hope it contained remained clear in her heart. It was typical of Will, she thought, that he would take the trouble to travel miles through the grim trails that twisted through Grimsdell Wood in the middle of the night to send it to her.

It wasn't an urgent message. There were no important instructions to follow. It was simply designed to bolster her spirits and let her know she hadn't been forgotten.

There was a strange, veiled reference that had puzzled her. It read, *We have a guest from the land of Cobblenosskin.*

She frowned over that for several minutes. The name was vaguely familiar, and she searched through her memory for it. Then it came to her. Cobblenosskin had been a character in a fairy tale she and Will had been told when they were children in the Ward at Redmont. He was a mischievous gnome who lived in the wild mountains of Picta, far in the north. It was not a reference that would be immediately apparent to anyone unfamiliar with the old tale—Keren, for example. Will was obviously taking precautions against the possibility that the message might accidentally fall into his hands. But she took it to mean that, somehow, Will had captured someone from Picta—and the only possible candidate she could think of was the Scotti general who had visited Macindaw a few days previously.

At least, that's what she hoped it meant. "He's a talkative fellow," the message went on to say. If her suspicions were correct, it meant that Will and his allies had learned the details of Keren's plan.

And that was reason to smile indeed.

But even more so was the other obscure fact contained in the message. For the most part, it was a chatty, gossipy piece—as far as that was possible within the limitations of a brief coded message— designed to keep her spirits up and to remind her that she had friends close by. And now she knew that there was more than one old friend out there in the forest. Since she had assured Will that the stellatite was effective in countering Keren's mesmerism, he had felt it was safe to include another fact.

Love from Tug, the last line of the message read, *and from Kicker and his big friend.*

Kicker . . .

She had heard the name before. Obviously, Will thought it would mean something to her. Was it an animal of some kind? It sounded like an animal's name. A dog? Not with that name. Dogs didn't kick. Horses kicked. And then, once again, the meaning was clear. Kicker was the name of the battlehorse Horace rode. Horace was here!

She thought about it now, hugging the news to herself like a warm cloak. Will and Horace working together—Will with his wits and intuition and quicksilver mind, and Horace, dependable, determined, perhaps one of the most accomplished warriors Araluen had seen in years. She had no doubt at all that the two of them would manage to defeat Keren and any number of Scotti.

She almost felt sorry for the usurper. Almost. She smiled again, then heard the key turning in the lock.

She glanced quickly at the fireplace, reassuring herself that the page was completely burnt. She poked at the coals with a fire iron to crumble the blackened sheet to powder, then rose hurriedly, dusting her hands as the door opened.

It was Keren, of course, and her hands automatically went behind her back, her fingers searching for and finding the shining black pebble that permanently nestled in the cuff of her sleeve. But there was no sign of Keren's blue gem, and she relaxed. He had come for another one of his chats.

"You're looking cheerful this morning, my lady," Keren said. She realized she was still smiling, still feeling the warmth that the message had brought her. It would be a mistake to try to hide the fact now and adopt a hangdog, miserable air; Keren would be immediately suspicious. He would want to know what she had to be cheerful about in the first place. Instead, she widened her smile and gestured to the window.

"It's a beautiful day, Sir Keren. Even a captive can't help having her spirits lifted by such a sight."

And, indeed, she was right. The sky was a brilliant blue, shot with a piercing light and with not a cloud in sight. The frigid air had a clarity to it that brought the most distant objects into sharp focus. The wild beauty of the woods and the snow-covered fields that surrounded the castle seemed close enough to touch.

Keren smiled at her and moved to the window to study the view for himself. He put one foot up on the low windowsill. For a moment she had the awful fear that he might lean his weight on the bars that she was gradually weakening with the acid Will had left behind. But at the last minute, his hand went to the stonework surrounding the window.

"It is beautiful indeed," he said, his expression softening for a few seconds. "I think this is the loveliest time of all in this country."

There was that trace of sadness in his voice again, a tone she had become accustomed to in their recent meetings. She knew he was torn by his treachery. It couldn't be easy on one hand to love the country as much as he seemed to, and on the other, to be prepared to hand it over to its traditional enemies.

Of course, she knew, it made no difference to the land. It would be beautiful and wild and rugged, no matter who controlled it. Still, the emotional impact must be enormous, and Keren must know that somehow, things would never be the same again. But he had made his choice, and there was no point appealing to him now to turn back from the path he was following. She watched impassively as he straightened, taking his foot down from the sill, and turned to her. He made a visible effort to push the melancholy away, grinning at her again.

"You're an amazing girl, Alyss," he said. "You can remain positive and cheerful even when everything has gone against you."

She shrugged. "There's no point in worrying over things that can't be changed, Sir Keren."

He made a disclaiming gesture with his hand. "Please, let's not be formal. Call me Keren. We may be on opposite sides, but there's no reason why we can't be friends."

No reason, she thought, other than the fact that I'm a King's officer and you're a traitor to your country. But she didn't voice the thought. There was no sense in alienating Keren by slapping aside his overtures of friendship. Angering him would gain her nothing. Befriending him, on the other hand, might gain her a lot— particularly in terms of information. She smiled back at him.

"On such a beautiful day, how could I disagree?" she said, and his own smile widened in return. She thought she saw a sense of relief in him as well, as if he had been hoping that his offer of friendship would not be rejected out of hand.

"You know, I've been thinking," he said finally. "Have you considered what might happen to you when the Scotti arrive?"

Alyss shrugged. "I imagine I'll remain here in the tower," she said. "I assume that you weren't planning on handing me over to them?"

For a moment, she felt a cold chill of fear. Perhaps that was what Keren was planning. She hadn't really thought about what might happen to her. After all, she was assuming that Will—and now Horace with him—would effect a rescue and get her out of this place. Keren looked slightly wounded at the suggestion, and her fear was quickly allayed.

"Of course not!" he said with some vehemence. "There's no way I'd hand a lady of your quality over to those barbarians."

"Your allies," she reminded him dryly.

He shrugged the comment aside. "Perhaps. But only from necessity. Not choice."

"Do you think they speak of you in such glowing terms?" Alyss asked him.

He met her gaze frankly. "I'd be surprised if they didn't," he said. "There's no love lost between us. This is a practical arrangement only. I don't pretend it's any more than that. They need me, and they're willing to pay me well for my services. I'll get a share of all the booty they take out of Araluen."

"It must be daunting," she said, with a certain amount of genuine sympathy, "to view a future where you have no close friends, only companions created by necessity."

But her sympathy fell on deaf ears. Keren eyed her coldly, and she realized that he hadn't enjoyed having her spell out the future he faced.

"I won't be here forever," he said. "Once I've put enough money together, I'll be heading for Gallica, or Teutlandt, where I can buy a fief of my own. As a baron, I'll need no friends."

It was common practice, she knew, for the kings of Teutlandt and Gallica to sell baronies to the highest bidders. In Araluen, of course, advancement was dependent on performance and loyalty. But the underlying sadness in Keren's words led her, against her better judgment, to try one final appeal to him.

"Oh, Keren," she said, and once again her concern for him was genuine, "can't you see what your life will become? You're talking about loneliness and banishment—even if it is self-imposed."

He drew himself up a little straighter. "I know what I'm doing," he said stiffly.

"Do you? Do you really? Because it's not too late. The Scotti aren't here yet. You could send for help and hold the castle against them. Macindaw is a tough nut to crack, and they won't dare go farther into Araluen with this castle at their back."

"Are you forgetting the little matter of Syron's death?" he asked. She could say nothing to that, and he continued. "After all, I may not have intended it, but his death was a direct result of my plotting to betray my country. I doubt the King would look too kindly upon that."

"Perhaps he might be—" she began, but he stopped her with a raised hand.

"And then there's the small matter of my men. I've promised to pay them, and the money for that is coming from the Scotti. If I renege on the deal with them, how will I pay my men? And if I don't, how kindly do you think they'll take being cheated?"

Alyss knew he was right. She had known so before she spoke. His next words brought her back to reality. "But we began by discussing your future, not mine," he reminded her. "It may take me two or three years working with the Scotti to raise the money I need. But when I go, what do you think will become of you?"

She had no answer for him. She knew that if Will and Horace didn't manage to get her out of here, she would be facing years of imprisonment.

There would be no hope of ransom. Couriers, by dint of their occupation, were obliged to go into dangerous and uncertain situations. They lived by their wits, and they survived because of the respect given to their position—and the power of the Kingdom they served. But if Duncan were ever to pay ransom to have a Courier released, it would be a signal to every tin-pot rebel and minor princeling that there was a profit to be made by imprisoning Couriers and demanding money from Araluen.

All those in the Diplomatic Service went into the profession knowing full well that if they were captured, they could expect no help from the Kingdom.

Revenge, yes. If a Courier were harmed, King Duncan and his advisers could bring a terrible vengeance on the culprits. They had done so in the past on several occasions. That way, others would be discouraged from trying the same ploy.

Of course, if she were dead, she would gain little comfort from the fact that she had been avenged.

She realized that the silence following Keren's question had stretched too long.

"I imagine I'll cope, somehow," she said.

Keren shook his head. "Alyss, you might fool me with that attitude. But I doubt you're fooling yourself. You're too intelligent for that. As my prisoner, you enjoy certain privileges, but the Scotti won't see any reason to continue them. You'll become a slave. A drudge. Your only value to them will lie in the hard labor you can perform.

"They'll send you north across the border and sell you off. It's not a pleasant prospect, believe me. Scotti villages are primitive enough. Their slaves' quarters are almost unlivable."

Alyss stood up, drawing herself to her full height.

"How very kind of you to point all this out for me," she said icily. Keren shook his head, smiling at her, trying to placate her.

"I'm just pointing out the facts," he said. "Before I suggest an alternative. The only alternative, I think."

"Alternative?" she repeated. He had her attention now because for the life of her, she couldn't think what he was talking about. "What alternative?"

"You could become my wife," he said simply.

"Your wife?" she repeated, the rising pitch of her voice evidence of the shock she felt at the suggestion. "Why would I become your wife?"

He shrugged. The smile had faded from his face at her reply, but now it returned. She sensed that it was less than genuine, more an attempt to cajole her.

"It's not an altogether outrageous suggestion," he said. "As my wife, the Scotti would have to accord you the proper degree of respect. You would have the freedom of the castle." He stood and waved a hand at the surrounding countryside outside the window. "And the lands around here. You'd be free to come and go as you please."

"You'd trust me not to escape?" she said, still staggered by the enormity of the idea, and the arrogance behind it. He seemed not to notice the fact.

"Where to? We'd be surrounded by Scotti, remember. They're planning an invasion here, not just a simple raid. And besides, if you were to marry me, you would show a certain, shall we say . . . empathy . . . for my actions."

"You mean," she said coldly, "I would brand myself a traitor as well?"

He recoiled a little at the word. "Don't judge too harshly, Alyss. Remember, we wouldn't always remain here. In Gallica, you'd be a baroness with me."

She knew she shouldn't antagonize him, knew she should humor him. But his presumption was so enormous that she couldn't control her feelings.

"There is one small impediment," she said. "I don't love you. I don't even like you very much."

He spread his hands in a dismissive gesture. "Is that so important? How many marriages have you seen among people of our class that were based on love? In most cases, convenience is the deciding factor. And I'm not such a bad catch, after all, am I?" He added the last question in a lighthearted tone, still trying to jolly her into the idea.

"Our class?" she queried coldly. "Let me tell you what class I am. I'm an orphan. I have no family. I do have people to whom I owe allegiance and gratitude and even love. So, as a lower-class, lesser being than you, let me say that I do happen to believe that love is important in a marriage."

His face darkened with anger. "It's that Ranger you're thinking of, isn't it? I knew there was something between you."

Alyss had spent years training in diplomacy. But she also spent those years training to make her point quickly and succinctly. She forgot the diplomacy now.

"That is none of your business," she said. "The fact is, there are probably fifty people whom I would find easier to love than you. Knights. Rangers. Couriers. Scribes. Blacksmiths. Innkeepers. Stable boys. Because at the end of the day, they would all have one huge advantage over you. They would not be traitors."

She could see that her words cut him like a whip. He had been angry, but now he was furious. He turned stiffly and walked to the door. As he reached it, he looked back at her.

"Very well. But remember, when you're on your hands and knees in the freezing rain in a Scotti village, scrubbing out a privy or feeding the pigs, you could have been a baroness!"

He thought it would be the last word. But as he went to close the door behind him, she said softly, "The price would be too high."

He turned and their eyes met. There was no more cordiality between them. She had crossed a line in their relationship, and they would never go back.

"Damn you," he said quietly, and closed the door behind him.

27

Horace craned over Will's shoulder to look at the rough sketch his friend had completed.

He frowned. From where he stood, the device Will had designed looked like a handcart, except that the main body, where the load would be carried, appeared to be upside down.

"What do you think?" Will asked.

"I think if you try to carry anything in that cart, it'll all fall out straightaway."

"I'm not putting *anything* in it. I'm putting us in it," Will said.

"In which case, we'll fall out," Horace replied.

Will gave him a withering look and tapped the salient points on the drawing with his charcoal pencil as he explained. "It's quite simple, really. There are two wheels, shafts and a framework underneath and a sloping, planked roof on top. The whole thing rolls along with us walking along underneath it."

"Well, that'll stop us from falling out," Horace said. "But why are we under it in the first place?" Horace asked.

"Because if we weren't under it," Will said, with a hint of acid in his voice, "we'd be out in the open, where we could be hit by rocks and crossbow bolts and spears." He looked meaningfully at Horace to see if there was another question. But Horace's eyes were riveted on the drawing now, and a small furrow was forming between his eyebrows.

"The beauty of it is," Will continued, "we can disassemble it and reassemble it in a matter of minutes."

"Well, that's definitely an advantage," Horace replied. His tone of voice said that he thought it was anything but.

Will sat back in exasperation. "You enjoy being negative, is that it?" he asked.

Horace spread his hands wide in a helpless gesture.

"Will, I haven't the faintest idea what you've got in mind with this . . . thing. Bear in mind, I'm a simple warrior, the sort of person I've heard you and Halt refer to as a bash-and-whacker. Now you tell me you want us to walk around under a handcart that someone's built with the top where the bottom ought to be and expect me to get excited about it. And by the way," he added, "I've seen better drawings of wheels."

Will was looking critically at the drawing now, trying to see it through Horace's eyes. He thought that perhaps his friend was right. It did look rather strange. But he also thought Horace was being overcritical.

"The wheels aren't that bad," he said finally. Horace took the pencil from him and tapped the left-hand wheel on the drawing.

"This one is bigger than the other by at least a quarter," he said.

"That's perspective," Will replied stubbornly. "The left one is closer, so it looks bigger."

"If it's perspective, and it's that much bigger, your handcart would have to be about five meters wide," Horace told him. "Is that what you're planning?"

Again, Will studied the drawing critically.

"No. I thought maybe two meters. And three meters long." He quickly sketched in a smaller version of the left wheel, scrubbing over the first attempt as he did so. "Is that better?"

"Could be rounder," Horace said. "You'd never get a wheel that shape to roll. It's sort of pointy at one end."

Will's temper flared as he decided his friend was simply being obtuse for the sake of it. He slammed the charcoal down on the table.

"Well, you try drawing a perfect circle freehand!" he said angrily. "See how well you do! This is a concept drawing, that's all. It doesn't have to be perfect!"

Malcolm chose that moment to enter the room. He had been outside, checking on MacHaddish, making sure the general was still securely fastened to the massive log that held him prisoner. He glanced now at the sketch as he passed by the table.

"What's that?" he asked.

"It's a walking cart," Horace told him. "You get under it, so the spears won't hit you, and go for a walk."

Will glared at Horace and decided to ignore him. He turned his attention to Malcolm. "Do you think some of your people could build me something like this?" he asked.

The healer frowned thoughtfully. "Might be tricky," he said. "We've got a few cart wheels, but they're all the same size. Did you want this one so much bigger than the other?"

Now Will switched his glare to Malcolm. Horace put a hand up to his face to cover the grin that was breaking out there.

"It's perspective. Good artists draw using perspective," Will said, enunciating very clearly.

"Oh. Is it? Well, if you say so." Malcolm studied the sketch for a few more seconds. "And did you want them this squashed-up shape? Our wheels tend to be sort of round. I don't think these ones would roll too easily, if at all."

Truth be told, Malcolm had been listening outside the house for several minutes and knew what the two friends had been discussing. Horace gave vent to a huge, indelicate snort that set his nose running. His shoulders were shaking, and Malcolm couldn't maintain his own straight face any longer. He joined in, and the two of them laughed uncontrollably. Will eyed them coldly.

"Oh, yes. Extremely amusing," he said. "Highly entertaining. Why did I train to be a jongleur, I wonder, when we had two comedians like you available? Now I know," he added, with heavy emphasis, "why people call comedians fools."

Horace and Malcolm, with a supreme effort, managed to bring their snorting and laughing under control. Malcolm wiped his eyes.

"Aaah," he said to Horace, "it does you good to start the day with a laugh."

"It's late morning," Will pointed out.

"Better late than never," Malcolm replied.

Will seemed about to say something, but Horace thought it might be time to get to the business at hand.

"Will," he said, more seriously, "why don't you tell us what this thing is supposed to do?" Horace sensed that the idea would be sound, no matter how bad the drawing might be. He had never known his friend to have a bad idea.

"It's to get us closer to the west wall," Will said. "With our ladder."

Horace looked at the sketch again. "You plan to push this right up to the wall?" he said. "And this roofed-over section is to protect us from the defenders above, right?" He shook his head. "It'll take too long, Will. They'll have plenty of warning, and as soon as we come out from under the roof here, they'll be ready and waiting for us."

"I know that," Will said. "But as you pointed out, if we try to run from the tree line to the wall carrying a ladder, it'll take far too long—and they'll have time to get back on the wall again to fight us off."

"So? Wheeling this . . . thing . . . will take us twice as long. Sure, we'll be protected while we're on the way. But I still don't see—"

Will cut him off. "I plan to get us halfway to the wall," he said. "Then we'll rig it so that one of the wheels collapses."

"What's the point of that?" Malcolm asked.

"Let me take it from the beginning," Will said. "We assemble the cart at the tree line. We tie our ladder on top." Quickly, he sketched in a ladder on top of the roof. "Then, in the middle of the afternoon, Horace and I and, say, four of the Skandians get under it and start pushing it toward the wall."

"In the middle of the afternoon?" Horace said. "They're sure to see us! They'll be throwing spears and rocks at us—"

Will raised a hand for silence.

"We'll keep going till we're twenty meters from the wall, then we'll collapse the wheel here. The whole thing will sag over to the side. The defenders will think they hit something crucial or that the thing was badly built. In any event, they'll see we're stopped. Then the other four people run like hell back to the trees. We'll rig some kind of armor for them to protect them."

Malcolm nodded. "That sounds fair," he said.

But Horace had noticed an omission in Will's plan. "You said the other four run back. What about us?"

Will smiled at him. "We stay put, under the cart. They won't know we're there because they won't know how many people were hidden under it in the first place."

Understanding started to dawn in Horace's eyes now.

"So we'll be twenty meters from the wall . . . with a scaling ladder," he said softly.

Will nodded, his excitement evident. "All we have to do is sit quietly for a few hours. By that time, the wrecked cart and the ladder will have become part of the landscape. They'll be used to it, so they'll begin to ignore it. Then, when Malcolm starts his show to the south and everybody's attention is distracted, we break out and run for the wall with the ladder."

"We could make it before anyone notices," Horace said.

"That's the general idea," Will said, smiling.

28

HORACE CAME TO A HALT AND SET THE TIMBER BEAMS HE WAS carrying against a tree trunk. There were plenty of trunks to choose from. The path they were following twisted and turned among a tangle of trees and undergrowth. He wiped his brow with a scrap of cloth and sank to his haunches to rest.

"This is heavy going," he said to Will.

Will nodded. "It's slower than I thought it would be. These game trails are so bad they might as well not be here at all." He raised his voice and called to Trobar, who was still moving ahead of the rest of the party, clearing the worst of the undergrowth and vines from the long-disused track they were following. "Trobar! Take a break!"

The giant turned and waved an acknowledgment. He sat cross-legged in the middle of the track. Shadow, his ever-present companion, moved to sit beside him, eyes intent on him. Will smiled ruefully to himself. The name was appropriate, he thought. The dog had become like a second shadow to the huge figure.

Back along the track, the Skandians eased their burdens off their shoulders as well and sat on the ground. There was not enough clear ground for them all to gather around. They simply relaxed wherever they were on the track. Water skins were passed along the line, and the men drank as they eased their aching muscles. Low conversations broke out among the groups.

It was tough going, Will thought. He was used to moving through forests and among trees, and even he found this tangle of trees, vines, bushes and saplings almost impossible to negotiate. They were forced to follow whatever faint game trails they could find leading in the right general direction. But they were trails more in concept than in practice. Even with Trobar moving ahead with a large sickle, hacking away at the worst of the undergrowth, it was a struggle to make progress. The situation was aggravated by the fact that, at any given moment, nearly half their party was laden with the components for what had become known as the Upside-Down Cart. The framework timbers, the roofing planks, the shafts and the wheels had all been disassembled so they could move it through the forest to the western side of Macindaw.

Gundar made his way along the narrow track to where the two friends were resting. He was carrying half of one of the scaling ladders—they had three in all, each constructed in two pieces to make them easier to carry through the forest. He let it fall to one side as he reached them.

"Are we nearly there?" he asked cheerfully. He wiped his forehead with the back of his hand and took the water skin that Horace offered him.

"Just around the next corner," Horace lied, and the Skandian grinned at him.

"Now you can see why we prefer to do our traveling by ship," he said, and the two Araluens nodded agreement.

"In the future, I'm going to do the same," said Will. "This makes the Stormwhite Sea look easy. How are your men managing?"

Gundar regarded him with approval. A good leader was always concerned with his men's welfare.

"Oh, they're complaining, swearing and generally carrying on. In other words, they're fine. It's when Skandians don't complain that you know you've got trouble."

Horace stood up, stretching his back and neck muscles.

"We might as well take the opportunity to spell the carriers," he said. At any given time, only half of the Skandians had loads to carry—aside from their weapons and armor, of course. So at regular intervals, they would relieve the men carrying the cart components. Will noticed that Horace, however, hadn't asked for anyone to spell him so far. Gundar had obviously noticed the same thing.

"One of you lazy beggars back there come up and give the general a break!" he called out. It was the jocular term they had adopted for Horace. But while it was said jokingly, it also had a ring of respect to it.

A burly figure pushed his way along the narrow track to them. Even before he could make out the man's features, Will knew who it would be.

"Here, give them to me, General," said Nils Ropehander.

Skandians were a strange breed, Will thought. Since Horace had rammed Nils's helmet down on his head and broken his nose with a flat-hand punch, he had become one of the young knight's most enthusiastic followers.

"Can't say I'll be sorry to be rid of them," Horace said, passing the heavy hardwood planks to the Skandian. Nils swung them easily over his shoulder and turned to go back to his place in the line. Will, who had just risen to his feet, managed to dive sideways in time to avoid having his head knocked from his shoulders by the swinging planks. His startled cry puzzled Nils, who swung around to see what had caused it. As he did so, the planks clanged solidly against Gundar's helmet.

"For Loka's sake!" the wolfship captain snarled. "Watch what you're doing!"

Nils swung back, apologizing. Will saw it coming this time. He had been about to regain his feet, but he stayed in a crouch as the planks whipped through the air at head height above him. The situation could have gone on all day, but Horace, seeing his chance, stepped in close and grabbed the end of the planks, stopping Nils's back-and-forth movement.

"Just keep them still, all right?" he said.

Nils looked apologetic. "I don't know how that happened," he said.

Gundar was inspecting his helmet. There was a new dent there, he was sure of it. He looked accusingly at Nils. Like all Skandians, he was very fond of his helmet.

"When we get to Macindaw," he said, "let's just send him up the ladder with those planks. He'll clear the defenders out in no time."

"I'm sorry, Skirl," said Nils. "I didn't see you there. Didn't see the Ranger either."

"That's the point," Gundar told him. "Before you start swinging around like a demented milkmaid at a Spring Festival hop-dance, look over your damned shoulder!"

Nils nodded, looking suitably abashed.

"I'll go back to my place, then," he said. He seemed anxious to get away from their accusing glances. As he moved back down the track, they heard a series of thuds, cries of anger and apologies from Nils. Will grinned at the others.

"Time to go while we still have some men undamaged," he said. Raising his voice, he called, "Trobar! Let's move again, please!"

The giant nodded and rose to his feet, moving forward along the faintly defined trail, his sickle rising and falling regularly, widening the path for them. The dog slipped silently at his heels.

"Are we nearly there?" Gundar asked as they set out again. Horace turned back to him.

"Are you going to keep on saying that?" he asked.

Gundar smiled at him. "Oh, I haven't even started yet," he said.

It was late afternoon when they reached their destination. The men dropped the sections of the cart and the ladders to the ground, and they all moved forward to the edge of the trees to study the castle. This was as close as the Skandians had been to it so far.

"Keep back in the shadows," Will warned them. "We don't want them to see we're here."

There was no reply, but the warning was largely unnecessary. Over the years, the Skandians had done their share of attacking strongholds, and they knew the importance of surprise. Still, as they studied the castle, some of them looked dubious. None of them had ever attacked anything quite so substantial, certainly not with a single wolfship's crew. They might have stormed isolated towers and stockades. But Macindaw stood before them, bigger and more formidable than anything they had ever attempted.

"I hope your plan works," Gundar said. He was feeling the same doubts as his men.

"It'll work," Horace replied confidently.

I hope, Will added to himself. He glanced around at the men. "We might as well get some rest," he said. "Move back into the trees a little. I saw a clearing about twenty meters back. There's nothing for us to do at the moment. Malcolm and his team will be laying the last of the fog tubing tonight. Then we'll have all day tomorrow to reassemble the cart."

Gratefully, the group moved back to the clearing and settled down to rest. Will set a watch roster, arranging it so that he and Horace would be on watch during the early hours of the morning, when they could expect a signal from Malcolm to tell them that the preparations were all complete.

Hours later, they lay on their bellies on the damp ground at the trees' edge. Gundar had joined them. The castle, barely fifty meters away, was a dark, ominous bulk in the night.

They could see spills of light along the ramparts where torches were set in brackets, but there were vast areas of darkness as well. From time to time, sentries passed in front of the lighted patches.

"They're very casual," said Will. "I could have picked off half a dozen of them by now."

Horace glanced at him. "Maybe you should," he suggested, but Will shook his head.

"I don't want them to know we're here," he said. "Besides, if I shoot one, the others would stop parading in front of the light."

"Maybe," Horace agreed grudgingly. "But they didn't strike me as all that bright."

"There it goes!" Gundar interrupted.

From the far side of the castle, a kilometer to the south, a red light rose into the air, then burst in a shower of sparks. The three observers could hear a buzz of surprised conversation from the castle walls.

"Malcolm's ready," Will said. Horace nodded.

"So tomorrow night's the night."

"Are we nearly there?" Gundar asked, grinning.

29

THE SIGNAL ROCKET HAD BEEN SIGHTED ON THE WALLS OF Macindaw as well. Unfamiliar with the concept of explosive chemicals or fireworks, the sentries gripped their weapons more tightly, looking fearfully to the south and wondering what kind of sorcery was afoot.

Keren, summoned from a sound sleep, paced the ramparts uncertainly, peering into the night and waiting for the strange, soaring red light to be repeated. But as an hour passed with no further sign of activity, he eventually decided that it had been a false alarm, just one more example of the strange lights that could be seen near Grimsdell in the dark of night.

Before returning to his bed, he made a quick tour of the defenses, pausing at the west rampart, where the forest grew closest to the castle. John Buttle was already there.

"Anything stirring this side?" Keren asked. Buttle, like himself, had been roused from sleep by reports of the unearthly light in the sky. His nightshirt was tucked into his trousers, and he wore a hastily donned vest of chain mail over it. He shook his head, staring at the dark wall of the forest, barely fifty meters away.

"Nothing at all," he reported.

Keren drummed his fingers on the stone rampart. "This is the danger side," he said thoughtfully.

"You'd never get a large force through that tangle out there," Buttle replied. He had reconnoitered the surrounding land over the past weeks. "And if you did manage it, you could never form them up in time to attack without plenty of warning."

Keren was partly convinced. But only partly.

"Perhaps. But so long as nothing stirs out there, I'll stay suspicious. I don't know why Syron never had those trees cleared out."

"Because it would have taken years to do it," Buttle told him. "And you'd need hundreds of men as well. Trust me. Those trees are our best defense. It's a jungle in there."

"Hmm. Nevertheless, I want a close watch kept on this side for the rest of the night," Keren said. "You'll be here?"

Buttle yawned. "I'm going back to bed."

Keren's eyes hardened.

"That wasn't a question or a suggestion." His voice was cold.

Buttle stiffened angrily. "Very well, my lord," he replied. "I'll stay on duty till dawn."

"Good," said Keren, turning on his heel and heading for the stairway. Not for the first time, he wished that his second in command was a more congenial companion—someone more ready to take on some of the responsibility of leadership. He would have hoped that Buttle would offer to remain on duty to reassure his commander, rather than wait to be ordered to do so. He sighed heavily. He had calculated it would be almost two years before he could buy his barony in Gallica. He sensed that the time would lie heavy on his hands, and he cursed the elegant blond girl who had rejected his offer of marriage. At least she would have been suitable company.

Behind him on the rampart, Buttle's lips moved in a silent curse of his own. But his words were directed at his commander.

◆ ◆ ◆

Once Will and Horace had seen Malcolm's signal rocket, they spent a relaxed night. They were both young and used to spending time camping out of doors. They had pitched their little tents back from the tree line, and they crawled into them and slept till daylight.

They knew that no further action would take place that night. The signal flare had not been the prelude to an attack, so they could afford to relax. Over the coming day, their biggest enemies would be a strange mixture of boredom and anticipation. They were scheduled to perform their mock attack in the late afternoon and Will knew that, as the hours rolled by, the knot of tension in his stomach would tighten with each passing minute until he wished they could be on their way, doing something instead of waiting.

And so it proved to be. They assembled the cart and the ladder it was to carry and manhandled it through the bushes to the edge of the tree line, hacking away at undergrowth to clear a path for it. But, inevitably, they began their preparations too early so that, by the time they were ready, it was barely past midday, and they still had four hours to wait.

Will sat under a tree, pretending to doze, trying to calm himself, trying to ease that tight knot in his stomach. He glanced up at Horace, standing a few meters away, apparently unconcerned, chatting quietly to the four Skandians who would accompany them. Horace seemed to feel Will's eyes upon him. He looked across at his old friend and smiled, nodding reassurance.

Will wondered how Horace could be so calm. He was unaware that Horace was asking himself the same question about Will, feeling the same knotting of stomach muscles.

The day dragged on.

Will checked the cart for the tenth time, making sure that the left wheel was correctly rigged so that they could collapse it whenever they were ready, making it seem as if the cart had hit some obstruction. He inspected the roofing planks, making sure there were no gaps where a crossbow quarrel might slip through. And he questioned the four Skandians to make sure they understood their role.

"Look as if you're panicking," he told them. He was met with four blank stares. Panic was not an emotion the Skandians understood too readily. "Look scared," he amended, and saw the four pairs of eyes change from puzzled to hostile. "Pretend to look scared," he added, and, grudgingly, they nodded. He checked their shields as well. He had a small force at his disposal, and he couldn't afford to lose any of them in this preliminary skirmish. The shields were well oiled to prevent them drying out and becoming brittle. They were generously studded with brass plates and covered in hardened oxhide. The men would sling them on their backs as they ran back to the tree line from the ruined cart.

Their heads would be protected by their horned helmets. The only parts of their bodies that would be exposed were their legs. Still, thought the young Ranger, a leg wound could keep a man out of battle just as effectively as if he were killed.

"Don't run in a straight line," he warned them. "And don't bunch up. Head in different directions."

One of the Skandians drew breath, about to tell Will that he could stop mother-henning them. Then he realized that the young man was actually concerned about him and his three companions, and he felt a surge of warmth. Skandians weren't used to their commanders actually caring about them.

"Yes, Ranger," he said meekly.

Will nodded distractedly and moved away, his mind going over the actions they would have to carry out that afternoon.

Hours later, the sun was angling over the trees, casting long shadows toward the castle.

In the distance, they heard a hubbub of noise from the south. Will hitched his longbow over his shoulder, settled his quiver more comfortably and turned to Horace.

"Time to go," he said.

30

THE NOISE FROM THE SOUTH TOLD THEM THAT MALCOLM HAD begun the diversion they had planned. He had at least fifty of his people back in the trees—men, women and children—well out of sight from the castle but still within earshot. As he gave them the command, they began howling, yelling, chanting and banging bits of metal together—kitchen pots and pans, for the most part. It was a sobering thought for warriors like Horace and the Skandians to realize that the clash of sword on sword, glamorized in song over the years by bards and poets, sounded pretty much the same as the clash of serving ladle on saucepan.

Regardless of its origin, the noise served the purpose they had hoped for, drawing the attention of the defenders. They could see the men on the west wall running toward the south side as they tried to see if there was a major attack developing.

"Right!" Will called. "Let's go!"

Crouching, he moved under the shelter of the cart, followed by Horace and the four Skandians, who took their places at the shafts. He checked them quickly, making sure they all had their shields slung over their backs. The Skandians, glad that the waiting was finally at an end, grinned at him as he signaled them forward.

"Go!" he shouted, and they put their weight to the shafts of the cart. There was no need for Will and Horace to help with this task. The four burly Skandians could manage it easily, so the two Araluens positioned themselves at the front of the cart, where the head room was lowest. Since the Skandians were doing the hard work, it was only fair that they should be allowed the most room.

The cart started to roll, slowly at first as the Skandians forced it through the thin screen of remaining undergrowth. Will and Horace paced with it, crouching below the slanting roof. Then the cart burst through the last of the tangle and they were clear of the undergrowth. The Skandians fell into a jog, one of them calling the time for the others, and the cart, with the scaling ladder lashed to the top of it, began to roll at a brisk pace, lurching and jolting across the uneven ground toward the castle.

Even with Malcolm's diversion, they couldn't hope to remain unnoticed for long, and Will soon heard startled cries of alarm from the ramparts ahead of them. Almost immediately, there was a solid crack as a missile slammed into the planks of the roof above them. It was a crossbow bolt biting into the hard wood. That initial impact was followed in rapid succession by another three. Then there was a long gap and the pattern repeated.

So it seemed that there were only four crossbowmen on the western ramparts. The pattern of four strikes repeated itself after twenty or thirty seconds, about the time it would take to reload a standard crossbow. It was the main disadvantage of the weapon, particularly when compared to the blinding speed a skilled longbow archer like Will could achieve. The crossbow had a stirrup at the front. When the bolt was shot, the crossbowman had to lower the bow to the ground, place one foot in the stirrup and heave the string back with both hands, bending the heavy arms of the bow until the string engaged on the trigger mechanism. Only then could he load another missile, and only then could he bring the bow back to his shoulder and shoot again.

Will flinched as the final bolt in the second volley slammed into the woodwork only a few centimeters from his head. Then he peered through a carefully prepared peephole—big enough to see through but not big enough to admit a lucky shot from one of the crossbows.

"A few more meters!" he warned the Skandians. He wanted to be as close as possible so that he and Horace wouldn't have too much ground to cover when they mounted their real attack later in the night. But if he got too close, he would be exposing the Skandians to greater risk as they made their way back to the tree line. They were almost halfway. He gripped the cord that would release the left-hand wheel and waited another four paces before pulling.

The pin holding the wheel onto the axle came loose. The wheel continued turning for another meter or two, but as it did, it was working its way to the end of the axle until it finally spun clear altogether, letting the left side of the cart crash to the ground.

They heard the cheers from the ramparts quite clearly—cheers and cries of derision as the defenders saw the attack come to nothing. Two more bolts slammed into the cart as it stopped. Good, thought Will, that meant only two of the crossbows were loaded now.

"Get going!" he urged the Skandians.

They needed no further encouragement. Scrambling out from under the tilted cart, they broke into the clear, running for the shelter of the trees, spreading out as they went. More shouts from the ramparts, more jeers as the defenders saw their would-be attackers running ignominiously for their lives.

He saw another bolt smash into the shield protecting one of the Skandians. The force of the missile hitting his shield caused him to stumble. Will breathed a silent prayer of thanks that there were no archers with longbows or recurve bows on the castle walls.

The crossbow was easier to aim and fire than the longbow and required less training to develop the instinctive skill that he, and all Rangers, possessed. It was relatively simple to take an unskilled soldier and train him to use a crossbow in a matter of weeks. But you paid for that ease with a much slower rate of shots—and a reduced range.

He heaved a sigh of relief as the four men made it back to the trees unscathed. He settled down on the cold, damp ground under the tilted shelter of the cart and grinned at Horace.

"So far so good," he said quietly. "Might as well make yourself comfortable. Now we have to wait until dark."

Horace, crouched under the lowest part of the cart, rolled his eyes.

"My favorite pastime," he said. "Did you bring something to eat?"

As the afternoon wore on into early evening, the sight of the ruined cart gradually lost its novelty for the men on the ramparts.

Keren had been summoned to view the strange vehicle. He frowned at it and then shook his head.

"It's a diversion," he said. "They wouldn't attempt their main assault with just one ladder."

The more he thought about it, the more he became convinced that he was right. The west wall, where the trees were closest to the castle, was the obvious direction for an assault. And since it was the obvious one, it became less likely that the attackers would choose it. The attempt with the cart was a bluff—and not a very clever one, since it was easy to see that one cart and one ladder would be ineffective against the walls. Sieges like this were a game of guess and counter guess, bluff and counter bluff. His instincts told him that the strange cart was a diversion.

The more he waited, the more he became convinced that the attack would come from the south, or perhaps the east wall. They were the farthest points from the west wall, after all. But the south seemed the most likely. The enemy had already been active there, and he had a sense that they would try to lull him into a sense of false confidence with a few more demonstrations that came to nothing, then launch the real attack from that direction.

He jerked a thumb at the cart, lying tilted to one side a bare twenty meters from the castle.

"Set it on fire," he told the sergeant commanding the west wall. "And keep an eye on the trees. But I don't think this is where they're going to come at us. Be ready to shift your men to the south wall if we need you there."

In the confined, sloping space under the ruined cart, Horace wriggled to find a more comfortable position.

Will, watching him, shook his head in disapproval. "Try to keep still," he said. "If you keep jumping around like that, you'll tip the cart over."

Horace scowled at him. "It's all very well for you," he said. "You're trained to sit still for hours on end while ants crawl over you and your muscles cramp."

"If I can do it, you can do it," Will said unhelpfully. He craned to the peephole once more, studying the castle. He could make out three of the defenders peering in the direction of the cart, and he saw smoke rising from a brazier beside them.

Strange, he thought. The day was cold, but not so cold that they should need a fire on the ramparts to keep them warm, at least not until nightfall.

"What's happening?" asked Horace. He was bored and uncomfortable, and he wanted some form of distraction. Will waved him to silence. They were only twenty meters or so from the walls, and it was possible that they might be heard.

"Keep your voice down," he said. Horace rolled his eyes to heaven again and continued in a hoarse whisper.

"It's all right for you. You've got the peephole," he said. Will gave him another long-suffering look.

"It must be awful to be you," he said, "covered in ants, in agony from cramping muscles and not even a peephole to look through."

"Oh, shut up," said Horace. He couldn't think of a witty reply.

They were interrupted by the slamming impact of another bolt into the wood over their heads. Will frowned, wondering why the defenders should be wasting time and ammunition shooting at the stranded cart. The answer came to him a few seconds later.

Horace, who had flinched violently at the unexpected impact, sniffed the air. "I can smell smoke," he said.

Will craned once more to look through the peephole. He could see the ramparts, with the same group of men watching the cart intensely. Then he saw one of them raise a crossbow and shoot again.

"Here comes another," he warned his companion.

The bolt sped through the air toward them, trailing a thin ribbon of smoke behind it. Seconds later, there was another ringing thud as it struck the roof planks. Now the smell of smoke was stronger. Through the peephole, Will could see a lick of flame.

"They're shooting fire arrows," he said calmly. "Trying to set the cart alight."

"What?" Horace jerked upright, and his head thudded against one of the support frames on the cart. "We'd better get out of here!"

"Relax," Will told him. "I had the planks soaked with water before we started."

Horace sat back doubtfully. He remembered now that for ten minutes before they had left the shelter of the trees, the Skandians had poured water and melting snow over the planks.

"Besides," Will continued, "have you ever tried to set a piece of hardwood on fire by dropping a burning stick on top of it? The odds are the arrows will scorch the wood a little, but they'll burn out before the fire can really take hold."

"The odds are?" Horace repeated. "What odds might they be?"

Will regarded him patiently. "What do you want to do, Horace, jump out and put out the arrows and then wave to the men on the ramparts?"

Horace looked uncomfortable, realizing he might have been premature in his reaction.

"Well, no," he said. "But I certainly don't want to be caught under a burning cart either."

"The cart won't burn. Trust me." Will told him. Then, seeing that the last two words had absolutely no effect on Horace, he continued, "And even if it does, we'll have plenty of time to get out of here. But there's no point running for it now. How will we feel if we give our plan away and then sit back in the trees and watch the fire go out?"

"Well, maybe . . . ," Horace said, a little mollified by Will's logic—and by the fact that the smell of smoke hadn't grown any stronger. He put his hand against the planks, beneath the spot where one of the bolts had struck it. The wood didn't feel any warmer there than in other parts of the roof.

Another two burning bolts hit the cart in the next few minutes. But, like the first two, they soon burned out, causing nothing but surface scorching. Eventually, seeing that the fire arrows weren't working, the defenders on the ramparts gave up the attempt.

◆   ◆   ◆

The afternoon wore on, and the light began to fade as the watery winter sun sank below the level of the trees. Horace pulled his cloak tighter about him. It was cold sitting here immobile for hours on end.

"What time is it?" Horace asked.

"About five minutes later than the last time you asked," Will told him. "You're getting as bad as Gundar, with his constant 'Are we nearly there?'"

"I can't help it," Horace grumbled. "I don't like just sitting around doing nothing."

"Try composing a poem," Will said sarcastically, wishing his friend would shut up.

"What sort of poem?" Horace asked.

"A limerick," Will told him, through gritted teeth. "That would seem to be about your speed."

"Yeah. Good idea," Horace said, brightening a little. "That'll take my mind off things." He frowned thoughtfully, looking to the heavens for inspiration. His lips moved silently for several minutes, then the frown deepened.

"I don't have anything to write it down with," he said.

Will, who had managed to doze off in the silence, jerked awake. "What?" he snapped, crankily. "Write what down?"

"My limerick. If I don't write it down, I might forget it."

"Have you thought it up yet?"

"Well, I've got the first line," Horace said defensively. Limerick writing was proving to be harder than he'd expected. "There once was a castle called Macindaw . . . ," he declaimed. "That's the first line," he added.

"Surely you can remember that?" Will said.

Horace nodded reluctant agreement. "Well, yes. But when I get two or three or four lines worked out, it'll get harder. Maybe I could tell them to you and you could remember them?" he suggested.

"Please don't," Will said, biting off the words.

Horace shrugged. "Well, fine. If you choose not to help."

"I do."

Will's replies, Horace noted, were becoming shorter and shorter. "All right then," he said, a little huffily. His lips moved again, stopped, restarted. He closed his eyes to concentrate. This went on for some five minutes, and the more Will tried to ignore him, the more he was drawn to Horace's facial contortions. Finally, the broad-shouldered warrior realized his friend was watching him.

"What rhymes with Macindaw?" he said.

31

As the afternoon lengthened into evening and then into night, Horace became increasingly restless and bored. He shifted position continually and sighed repeatedly. Will steadfastly ignored him. This annoyed Horace, who knew his friend was intentionally taking no notice of him.

Eventually, after a particularly extended sigh, followed by a prolonged shifting of position and shuffling of shoulders and buttocks, Will could no longer pretend not to notice.

"It's a pity you didn't bring a trumpet," he said. "That way you could make a bit more noise."

Horace, pleased that he had finally provoked the beginning of a conversation, answered immediately. "What I don't get," he said, "is why we didn't run the cart out here now, instead of doing it hours ago? We could have waited comfortably in the trees until nightfall, then run out, lost the wheel and had only an hour or so to wait for Malcolm's monsters. It would have been much less boring than crouching here all afternoon and into the night."

"It's supposed to be boring," Will snapped. "That's the idea."

"You wanted to be bored?" Horace asked.

"No." Will spoke very patiently. He adopted the tone an adult might use talking to a very young child. It had been some time since he'd done that with Horace, and the warrior found that he didn't like it any more now than he had previously.

"I wanted the sentries to be bored. I wanted them so used to the sight of this cart that it became part of the scenery. I wanted them to look at it for hours and hours with absolutely nothing happening so that they eventually believed that nothing is *going* to happen. If we'd only come out of the trees now, they'd still be suspicious when the time comes, and they'd possibly still have their eyes on us. This way, they've seen the cart clearly, in full daylight, and they think they have nothing to fear from it. They're bored with it, in fact."

"Well . . . maybe . . . ," Horace said reluctantly. Actually, what Will said made sense. But still, he was bored. And cold too. They were sitting on a mixture of melted snow and saturated grass. And the earth itself still held the bone-numbing chill of winter. As he had the thought, Horace felt an overwhelming need to sneeze. He tried to smother the sound, but only succeeded in making it louder.

Will looked up angrily, shaking his head in disbelief. "Will you shut up?" he said tautly.

Horace shrugged in apology. "I'm sorry," he said. "I sneezed. A person can't help it when they sneeze."

"Perhaps not. But you could try to make it sound a little less like an elephant trumpeting in agony," Will told him.

Horace wasn't prepared to take that lying down. Crouching down, perhaps. But lying down, never.

"And of course, you'd know what an elephant sounds like! Have you ever heard an elephant?" he challenged.

But Will was unabashed by his logic. "No," he said. "But I'm sure it couldn't be any louder than that sneeze."

Horace sniffed disdainfully. Then wished he hadn't. Sniffing

only created the urge to sneeze again, and he fought against it val-
iantly, finally quelling it. He sensed Will was right. The sneeze had
been particularly loud.

On the ramparts, the corporal in command looked at one of the
soldiers standing by him.

"Did you hear that?" he asked.

From the soldier's reaction and the way he was staring into the
darkness, it was obvious that he had. "It sounded like an animal," he
said uncertainly. "In pain."

"A big animal," the corporal agreed uneasily. They peered into the
night together. Fortunately, neither of them connected the strange
sound with the ruined cart. Will had proven to be right. The sentries
barely noticed the dark shape anymore. "God knows what goes on in
that forest," the corporal said eventually.

"Whatever it was, it seems to have gone now," said the other man.
He hoped he was right.

Twenty meters away, under the cart, Horace had his cloak doubled over his head and his fist rammed up tight under the soft carti-
lage between his nostrils to prevent another sneeze. The following
day, he would find a bruise and wonder how it got there.

When the urge eventually subsided, he sagged against the cart,
his eyes streaming.

Will, who had seen the immense effort he had gone to, patted his
shoulder. "Good work," he said sympathetically.

Horace nodded, too exhausted for further comment.

The moon rose, passed over them, flooding the land around them
with pale light, then sank below the tops of the trees in the west.
Will felt his heart rate begin to accelerate. The time of waiting was
nearly over. He looked at Horace and realized his friend knew it

too. He was no longer shifting and twitching. Instead, he was slowly and carefully stretching his cramped arm and leg muscles, easing out the kinks caused by long hours of inactivity. Carefully, the tall warrior unfastened his round buckler from where it was tied to the side of the cart.

Will watched as he removed the thick white canvas covering the front of his shield to reveal the glossy white-enamel surface, with its gleaming green oakleaf symbol in the center. "Good to see you'll be fighting under your true colors." He smiled.

Horace smiled briefly in return. He was becoming focused now. Will could see that this was a different person from the fidgeting, complaining Horace who had sheltered under the cart for the past eight hours. This was a very deadly, very serious Horace, a master of his craft, and Will was glad he was here. Once they hit the top of the ramparts, he knew it would be Horace who would bear the brunt of the fighting until the Skandians could make their way up the ladder to join them. He couldn't think of anyone he would rather have by his side.

He realized that he had preparations of his own to make. He checked that his quiver, with its twenty-four gray-shafted arrows, was firmly in position. His longbow was tied to the underside of the cart, and he untied it now. It was unstrung, of course. There was no point leaving it under tension for the hours they had spent waiting. He checked that the string was in position, without any tangles or loops. The bow had a draw weight of eighty-five pounds, and it would be virtually impossible to string it in the cramped position under the cart. He'd do it as soon as they moved out from under the shelter of the sloped roof. He checked the big saxe knife at his belt and touched his hand to the throwing knife in the hidden sheath at the back of his collar. The sheath's position was a little awkward, and he remembered how he had been unable to reach it quickly during the fight with MacHaddish. He made a mental note to tell Halt and Crowley that the collar sheaths were a bad idea.

In the distance, from beyond the far side of the castle, they heard the drawn-out moan of a ram's horn—one long note that went on and on, finally fading away.

"Start counting," Will told Horace. The arrangement with Malcolm was that the huge image of the Night Warrior would be projected twenty seconds after the horn stopped.

As Horace counted, Will slipped out from under the cart, staying behind it so he was still shielded from the ramparts as he set the string on his longbow. He felt Horace begin to stir under the cart.

"Come on out," he said, "but stay down."

Horace crawled into the open, half straightening behind the cover of the cart.

They both peered into the dark sky above the castle. They wouldn't see the projection from here, but they might see the reflection of the light in the low clouds, Will thought.

"There it is!" whispered Horace. There was a brief flash of light in the sky. Then they saw the next demonstration as a ball of fire rose into the night, hissing and trailing a banner of sparks behind it before exploding high above the ground in a shower of red embers.

Then the flash repeated itself, just for a few brief seconds.

It was important, Malcolm had told them, not to leave a projection in place for more than a second or two. Any longer and the eye could focus clearly on it and realize that it was a crude outline that didn't move. Flashing it on and off like this, with other lights to distract the watchers' eyes, created a sensation of movement and uncertainty.

"Let them think what they see, rather than really see it," Malcolm had said.

They could hear voices shouting on the ramparts now as men reacted to the terrifying images shimmering in the fog.

"Let's go!" Will said. He drew his saxe and slashed the bindings that held the ladder on top of the cart's roof.

Horace threw it easily over his shoulder, his shield slung over his back, and together they ran for the castle wall. Keren was in the main hall of the keep when he heard the shouting and the bang of the first rocket exploding. He was already armed and wearing chain mail, and he dashed into the courtyard, climbing the stairs to the south ramparts two and three at a time. The shouting was coming from that side, and he realized he had been right. This was where the attack was coming.

He reached the ramparts and found the sentries gathered in a small knot, staring fearfully into the darkness. Their voices formed an incomprehensible babble as they all talked at once.

"Silence!" he yelled, and as they obeyed, he singled out the sergeant in charge. "Sergeant, what's going—"

He got no further. Suddenly, in the dark night sky, some two hundred meters from the castle's south wall, a gigantic shadow figure loomed against the mist. Huge, evil, terrifying.

And gone, almost as soon as it appeared.

Keren actually staggered back at the sight of it. But then a demonic red face began to rise from the ground, soaring into the air and exploding into darkness. And even as it did, another massive shape loomed in the mist—the black shadowed outline of a dragon that seemed to quiver and shake and then disappear.

A strange, hollow voice could be heard, laughing hysterically. The sound chilled Keren. The men around him shouted in fear. Several dropped to their knees, doubled over as if to hide from the horrible sights before them. He kicked savagely at the nearest man.

"Get up, you yellow-skinned coward!" he cursed. But his voice was hoarse, and his throat was dry. He could feel the skin on his arms prickling and dimpling, and the hairs on the back of his neck rising in fear. Then, fifty meters from where they had first seen it, the giant warrior flickered on and off again. A series of colored lights flashed across the ground at the height of a man's head, and the laughter was back, more bone-chilling than before.

Buttle appeared beside Keren, his face haggard with fear. He pointed wordlessly into the night as the dragon reappeared, then a huge lion, then the warrior again, all interspersed with images of that demonic face soaring into the air and disappearing.

"It's sorcery!" he cried. "You said there was no sorcerer! Look at this, you fool!"

"Get hold of yourself!" Keren snarled at him. "It's a trick! It's nothing but a trick!"

"A trick?" Buttle answered. "I know sorcery when I see it!"

Keren grabbed the man and shook him. "Get hold of yourself!" he said savagely. "Can't you see? This is what Barton wants! They'll be coming at us any minute, so get the men to the ramparts!" He gestured at the cowering sentries, grouped together in fear and backing as far away from the wall as they could.

More and more men had run from the east and west walls to view the terrifying scene outside the castle. As Buttle hesitated, half accepting that Keren might be right, they heard a voice shouting:

"Here they come!"

32

HORACE HAD GONE UP THE LADDER AT A RUN, WHILE WILL KEPT up a constant stream of arrows, picking off any defender who showed himself over the ramparts. Nearing the top, the warrior paused for a second, then hurled himself upward, rolling into a ball and somersaulting high into the air so that he sailed over the top of the ramparts and the two defenders who crouched there, waiting for him.

He landed lightly on his feet, turning and drawing his sword in the same motion. The two startled defenders recovered their wits and began to move toward him. He cut the first man down with ease. As the second came at him, Horace deflected his halberd thrust, seized his collar and propelled him over the inner edge of the walkway. The man's startled cry cut off abruptly with a heavy thud as he hit the flagstones of the courtyard.

More defenders were moving toward him, coming from the north wall. He turned to face them.

"Will! Up here! Now!" he yelled.

The warning cry of "Here they come!" caused immediate panic among the men on the south wall. Thinking that the terrifying apparitions were now attacking the castle, three of them broke and ran for the stairs. Keren moved too late to stop them. But the next man who tried to follow them met the point of his sword.

"Get back to your position!" Keren told him, and the man backed away.

Keren felt the bitterness of despair. Deep down, he had known that he couldn't count on men like these in a real battle.

"They're coming!" the voice cried again, and this time Keren realized it was from the west wall, now dangerously short of defenders. In the dim light, he could see a tall figure, his sword rising and falling as the few men left tried to stop him. As he watched, a smaller figure appeared over the top of the ramparts. He balanced on the battlements themselves, and unslung a longbow from his shoulder.

With a sick feeling, Keren realized he had been deceived. Worse, he had deceived himself. The real attack was on the west wall and it was happening now. He grabbed Buttle's arm and pointed.

"I told you it was a trick! That's where the real attack is coming from!" he yelled. "Get the men over there and hold the west wall! I'm going to call out the rest of the garrison! I'll bring them up the northwest tower stairs and we'll catch them between us!"

Buttle, seeing a human enemy he could attack, nodded briefly. He turned and bellowed orders to the men on the south wall and then led them at a run along the walkway to the southwest corner.

Quickly, Will took stock of the situation. Horace was holding his own with the defenders from the north wall and needed no immediate help. But then the door to the southwest tower banged open and a group of armed men emerged. Will's first arrow was on its way almost immediately and the soldier leading the charge went down. Then another behind him fell silently and a third staggered, screaming, as an arrow appeared in his thigh.

Three men dead or wounded in a matter of seconds. Those behind them suddenly lost their enthusiasm for the battle. Perhaps the
strange monsters in the sky might be preferable to this deadly rain of
arrows. They faded back to the shelter of the southwest tower. As the
door slammed behind them, they heard two more arrows thud into
the hard wood.

Keren had bolted down the stairs to the courtyard. He ran toward
the garrison dormitory in the southeast tower. Men were spilling out
the door, confused and disorganized, still fastening their armor and
buckling on their weapons. They saw their commander and hesitated, waiting for orders. Keren gestured to the west wall.

"They're on the west wall!" he said. "Go up the northwest tower
and flank them!"

Still the men hesitated, and he stepped toward them, threatening
them with his raised sword.

"Get moving!" he yelled and, reluctantly at first, then with
growing conviction, they began to run across the flagstones of the
courtyard to the northwest tower. Keren started after them, then
paused. He knew their resolve wouldn't last long once they faced
the Ranger's arrows. Coming to a decision, he stepped forward and
held out his arm to stop the last three men.

"You three come with me," he ordered them. Then he turned
toward the keep—and the tower above it.

The Skandians were swarming over the rampart now. Will wasn't
surprised to see that Nils Ropehander was in the lead. The man had
become Horace's shadow.

"Help the general!" Will said, pointing.

Nils nodded and rushed to support Horace. his battleax already
whirring in a giant arc.

The soldiers engaged with Horace, already hard pressed, were horrified by the sight of the huge, yelling Skandian charging at them, grotesque in his fur vest and massively horned helmet. They began to back away, trying to force their way through the men behind them.

Nils hit them like a one-man battering ram, scattering them in all directions. Their cautious backpedaling became a panicked rush to get back to the shelter of the northwest tower.

Will was directing traffic, sending a few more men to reinforce Horace and Nils, then setting up a defensive screen to engage the men from the southwest tower whenever they decided to renew their attack.

Satisfied that they had a secure foothold on the west wall, Will now cast around anxiously for Keren or Buttle.

They were the two danger men, and Will knew it was vital to find them quickly and deal with them.

In the southwest tower, Buttle peered through a spyhole set into the oak door. He could see the Skandians on the ramparts and he knew that it was vital that they be driven back now. In a few more minutes, their position would be unassailable.

He had a dozen men with him and he drove them toward the door, threatening, cursing, hitting with the flat of his sword.

"If they get any further, we're all dead men!" he yelled as he drove his reluctant warriors out onto the ramparts ahead of him. They charged the Skandian line with the courage of desperation. The Skandians saw them coming and smiled.

Behind them, Buttle quietly closed the door and ran down the stairs to ground level.

He had recognized the tall warrior fighting the men from the far tower. They had met some weeks before, by Tumbledown Creek, and the freelance knight had been arrogant and dismissive of Buttle's authority. That was a score to be settled, he thought. There was a trapdoor in the walkway just behind Horace's position, with a stairway leading up to it from the courtyard below. Buttle headed for it now.

In the forest to the west, someone else was remembering events from the past few weeks.

Some days prior to the attack, Trobar had been quietly patting Shadow when he felt the ridge of a massive scar under her soft fur. He parted the black hair gently and saw the livid sign of a recently healed wound there. He shuddered at the size of it. It was a miracle the dog had survived such an injury. When he had asked Will about it, the Ranger had related the story of how he found the dog, severely wounded and close to death, by the roadside in Seacliff Fief. Buttle, the dog's original owner, had tried to kill her when she rebelled against his brutal treatment. Will had nursed her back to health.

Trobar knew Buttle. He had watched him from the forest when the dark-bearded murderer had ridden through the countryside, recruiting new troops for the castle.

Now, Trobar thought, Buttle would pay for the injury he had done to Shadow. The huge man was normally a gentle, peaceful soul. But the thought of his friend's agony, and the savagery of the man who had caused it, hardened his heart. As the sounds of battle raged on the castle ramparts, Trobar retrieved a massive club he had fashioned from a tree branch earlier in the day and loped quietly across the open space to the now-empty ladders at the foot of Macindaw's west wall.

♦ ♦ ♦

Horace stepped aside as Nils led a group of twelve Skandians in a wild charge at the men who had emerged from the southwest tower. Nils could handle that situation, he thought, as Buttle's men fell back before the Skandians' terrible axes. At the other end of the rampart, Gundar and the rest of his men had the upper hand over the defenders Keren had sent to the northwest tower. The Skandians could manage without him for a few minutes. He'd suffered a dagger slash on the wrist of his sword hand and he took the opportunity to bind it with a clean cloth. He leaned his sword against the battlements as he concentrated on winding the cloth around the wound, stemming the blood that ran down over his sword hand.

"Horace!"

He looked up. Will was at the edge of the ramparts, pointing to the courtyard below. Horace moved a few paces from the wall for a better view. He could see nothing to explain Will's interest. He looked up inquiringly.

"It was Keren!" Will explained. "I saw him go into the keep."

With the battle raging on the walls, there was only one possible reason why the renegade would head for the keep—and the tower above it. Instinctively, Will knew what it was.

"He's going after Alyss!"

Horace thought quickly. Will wasn't needed here anymore—the situation was well under control.

"Go after him!" he called back. "I'll take care of things here."

Will nodded and looked around. There was a derrick close by, with a rope dangling from it down to the courtyard. He leaped for the rope, grabbing it and wrapping his legs around it to slow his descent.

Horace gave his attention back to the rough bandage. Holding one end with his teeth, he tied a clumsy knot with his left hand. He inspected the result. It would do for the moment. And besides, the fighting was almost over.

Almost.

Horace's fighting instincts were finely tuned. Any foreign, unexplained sound was a potential threat, and he heard one now behind him—a slight grating noise as seldom-used hinges were forced to turn against the light rust that had coated them.

He turned toward the sound in time to see John Buttle emerging from a trapdoor in the walkway.

33

WILL STOPPED INSIDE THE DOOR TO THE KEEP AND LOOKED warily around him.

The entrance hall and the dining hall beyond it were deserted. The garrison must all be on the ramparts, he realized, and the servants were probably cowering somewhere below, in the cellars and the kitchen.

Keren, he assumed, would have headed for the top of the tower. Will ran to the stairway now, set in the center of the keep hall. The keep at the lower levels was an expansive building, with the dining hall, sleeping quarters and administrative offices taking up the first three floors. Above this, it narrowed to the tower that Will had climbed, set back in line with the north wall and wide enough for only one or two rooms on each floor.

At the lower levels, centrally located, was a broad stone stairway that would be difficult to defend. Once he reached the tower itself, however, that stairway would be a narrow spiral, set to the left-hand side and twisting to the right as it ascended. In that way, a right-handed swordsman climbing the stairs would be at a disadvantage to a right-handed defender. An attacker would have to expose all of his body in order to use his sword, while the defender could strike

with only his right side exposed. It was standard design for a castle
tower.

He pounded up the first four floors, then swung left toward the
spiral stairs, slowing down as he went. He couldn't see what lay in
wait around the curved stone walls and it was only prudent to assume that Keren could have left men to delay any pursuers. One
man could hold the stairway indefinitely, as attackers could only approach one at a time.

Will considered the bow in his hand and decided it was not the
right weapon to use in this restricted space. He slung it over his
shoulder and drew his saxe knife instead. Heavy enough to deflect a
sword stroke, it was also short enough to swing easily in the confined
space.

He paused at the entrance to the stairwell, letting his breathing
settle. Silent movement would be his main advantage in this situation and it was hard to remain silent when your breath was coming
in ragged gasps. He started up the stairs, moving carefully, his soft
boots making no sound on the stones. He was grateful that it was a
stone staircase. In some castles, the designers used wooden stairs,
loosely fastened so that they squeaked in protest underfoot.

Carefully, he stole his way upward. The stairway was lit at intervals by torches in brackets. They created another problem for him.
As he passed the first, his shadow loomed onto the wall above and
in front of him, giving ample warning that he was approaching. If he
were defending these stairs, he thought, he would wait beyond one
of the torches, looking for the approaching shadow of an attacker
moving upward so that he could . . .

A sword blade glittered bloodred in the torchlight as it flashed
down at him from above!

He leapt back, managing somehow to retain his feet, as the blade
struck sparks off the wall and steps. His heart raced. Apparently,

the unseen defender agreed with him on the best place to wait for an attacker. He paused, waiting to see if the swordsman on the stairs above would show himself. But there was nothing. He heard a faint chink of metal on stone—possibly the man's mail shirt brushing against the wall as he changed position.

Seconds passed. Will frowned as he contemplated the situation. All the advantages lay with the man above. He could remain unseen. The shadows thrown by the torchlight would warn him of Will's approach . . .

The torchlight! That was the answer.

He retreated a few paces down the stairs until he reached the torch in its wall bracket. Tugging it free, he started up the stairs once more, saxe knife in his right hand, torch in his left, held out as far as he could reach.

Stopping just short of the spot where the sudden attack had come out of the darkness, he tossed the torch underhand, up the staircase. It hit the outer wall and rebounded into the center of the stairs, its flickering, uncertain light now behind where the defender waited.

A giant shadow loomed in the stairway as the man above moved to retrieve the torch and throw it back down again. Will darted up the stairs, taking advantage of the momentary distraction. He had time to hope there wasn't more than one man waiting above him. There was a dark shape on the stairs, bent over to reach for the torch, blocking its light. The man saw him too late and swung an awkward, off-balance overhead cut with his sword.

Will deflected it easily, the sword blade shrieking off the stones, then he continued his upward movement and lunged, feeling the saxe knife bite into flesh. The man cried out in pain and stumbled forward. He crashed into Will, and the Ranger grabbed him with his left hand, just in time. There was a second man waiting, and he leapt forward now, cutting at Will with his sword. But the stroke was blocked by the body of his own comrade, slumped against Will. The first defender screamed again as the sword took him across the back, shearing through his mail shirt. Desperately, Will shoved him away and bounded back down the stairs, leaving the body between him and the second defender.

The wounded man lay moaning and Will saw another shadow moving, heard hard-shod feet on the stairs as the second defender retreated upward, placing the light between himself and Will once more.

The light on the stairs was dark and uncertain, with the torch lying on the steps, rather than placed high on the wall in its bracket. Will moved carefully upward once more, using the tip of his saxe to flick the fallen man's sword back down the stairs. It rang loudly on the stones as it bounced. He started forward again, moving infinitely slowly to avoid the slightest noise, his own ears searching the silence for the sound of any movement.

Then he heard it. Breathing. It was barely perceptible but it was there—the in and out breathing of a man whose adrenaline is running at full charge through his veins. He couldn't be more than a few meters away. Will paused, seething with impatience. Somewhere above him, Keren had Alyss and was doing god knows what with her while Will wasted his time playing tag on the stairs. He searched for an idea but none came.

Suddenly, he darted forward four paces, then quickly reversed direction and sprang back as another sword, wielded by an unseen defender, rang off the stones. The man was there. He was ready and waiting. He was alert. He was just around the next bend in the stairs.

An idea started to form.

Will estimated the man's position, his eyes measuring the curvature of the outer wall of the stairway. The defender would be just beyond that bend in the wall . . . so if Will moved backward a little, he could find a point midway between him and the unseen defender.

Silently, he descended three steps. Then a fourth.

He sheathed the saxe knife and unslung the longbow from his shoulder. Carefully nocking an arrow, he studied the wall, picking a point that would be halfway between his position and that of the man who waited for him. He raised the bow and drew, aiming at the stone wall above him, pausing to estimate the right position.

Then he released.

And, in the rapid succession that only a Ranger could achieve, within a few heartbeats, he sent another three arrows after the first, all aimed at the curved wall, allowing a slight variation with each. The arrows struck and ricocheted violently from the stone, striking sparks as they went, flying around the curve in the wall in a sudden volley.

Above him, he heard a surprised cry, then a muffled curse and a clang of metal on stone as at least one of the arrows found a mark. But he was already bounding up the stairs, catching the startled defender by surprise.

The man, unprepared by the sudden volley of ricocheting shots, had dropped his sword as he tried to free an arrow from a painful wound in his side. He looked up in fright as Will appeared, then glanced to where his sword lay on the stones. It was that moment of delay that brought about his downfall—literally. Will grabbed his shirt front and heaved him down the stairs, sending him crashing into the outer wall, then tumbling head over heels down the staircase. The man shrieked in pain as the arrow in his side was driven deeper. Then he was silent, the only sound his inert body sliding a few meters farther down the stairs.

Will retrieved his other three arrows and inspected them briefly. The heads were slightly bent where they had skated off the stone wall, but they would serve for the same purpose again. In fact, he thought wryly, they might even be better suited to the task now. He continued up silently, alert for another sudden attack.

But there would be none. Keren's third man had listened as his two companions had been overcome by their mysterious pursuer. He had seen nothing. But he had heard the screech and clanging of swords and arrows on stone, then the ominous sounds of falling bodies on the steps. He waited at one curve until he saw the elongated shadow of whoever it was who had disabled his comrades, saw it moving toward him as the attacker moved upward.

And his nerve went. He could hear the cries of the Skandians in the courtyard. He knew the battle was over. He had seen the monstrous shadows in the night sky. Now he saw this other shadow coming after him—silently. He turned and ran up the stairs to the next landing, where a tower room offered him shelter. He plunged inside and slammed the door behind him, shooting the bolt across to keep intruders out.

Will heard the running footsteps. Heard the door slam shut. Throwing caution to the winds, he went up the stairs like one of Malcolm's rockets, taking them two and three at a time to get to Alyss before Keren could harm her.

34

As he emerged from the trapdoor, Buttle saw that Horace was unarmed, and his face split in a wolflike grin. He had his heavy spear in one hand and a sword in the other. Horace had nothing but the round buckler slung at his back.

Horace's eyes darted to the sword leaning against the wall a few meters away. Almost as soon as he looked, he began to move, but Buttle was wickedly fast. He jerked back his right arm and hurled the spear, aiming it to intersect Horace's path to the sword. Even as he moved, sensing the danger, Horace twisted away to his right, falling to the wooden walkway and rolling desperately to regain his feet.

He was only just in time. Buttle had followed up with the speed of a snake, and his sword blade bit into the planking beside Horace's elbow. Horace kicked out sideways, catching Buttle in the back of the knee and sending him staggering. In the few seconds that he gained, he scrambled to his feet and shrugged off the shield's sling, gripping it by the edges in both hands, holding it in front of him.

He parried Buttle's next two strokes with the shield. Then, unexpectedly, he released his left-hand grip and swung the shield back-handed in a flat arc at Buttle's head, the heavy steel circle suddenly turning from a purely defensive piece into a weapon of attack.

Buttle tried to deflect it with his sword blade, then realized almost instantly that the shield was too heavy and leapt backward. Horace followed up his advantage, sweeping the shield in wide, flat arcs, swinging high and low, trying to catch Buttle in the legs, the body or the head.

But he was only buying time, and he knew it. Once Buttle overcame his initial surprise, he could use the sword's greater mobility and expose the shield's clumsiness as a weapon. He lunged at Horace's body, and the warrior was forced to revert to his double-handed grip on the shield as Buttle drove forward, lunging and cutting, looking for an opening in Horace's defense.

In Horace's position, most warriors would have given in or run. But Horace never accepted defeat. It was one of the traits that made him the great warrior that he was.

As he parried Buttle's sword strokes, his mind worked overtime, trying to find a way to defeat the bearded man before him.

If he could remount the shield on his left arm once more and draw his dagger, he could . . . but he knew Buttle would never give him the time he needed for that.

He considered throwing the shield, spinning it like a huge discus at Buttle and following up with the dagger as his opponent tried to avoid it. But Buttle was fast—as fast as any adversary Horace had ever faced—and an attempt like that would definitely be last ditch.

He parried two more sword cuts and deflected a thrust. Buttle may have been fast, but he was not a particularly skillful or inventive swordsman, Horace realized. He could probably parry Buttle's strokes for some time. But he couldn't simply continue to fight defensively. One mistake on his part and the battle would be over.

They faced each other, circling slowly, sword and shield moving together. Action. Reaction.

And then, in an instant, the impasse was broken.

In his peripheral vision, Horace saw a huge figure looming over the wall at the head of one of the scaling ladders. Trobar. He towered above them for a second, saw Buttle and dropped to the walkway, a huge wooden club in his hands.

Without hesitation, he charged at the man who had tried to kill Shadow, swinging the club in huge, murderous arcs.

Buttle retreated desperately, ducking and swaying to avoid the monstrous club. Trobar shambled after him, off balance and awkward yet moving with surprising speed. The club thundered against the stone walls and wooden flooring. A twenty-centimeter piece broke off and went spinning away into the darkness below as he struck the walkway on one follow-through. Trobar grunted with the effort, his eyes fixed on the man who had hurt Shadow.

Yet courage and the desire for revenge were not going to be enough. Buttle was too fast and despite his fearsome appearance, Trobar was totally unskilled in weapons and combat. His clumsy, crushing blows with the club were a primitive, instinctive reaction to his anger. He soon tired, his strokes becoming wilder and increasingly off-target.

Horace saw Buttle's confidence growing and knew how the fight would end. He dashed desperately back to where his own sword still leaned against the wall. As his fingers closed around the familiar grip, he heard a startled cry of pain behind him. Looking back, he saw the club fall from Trobar's nerveless fingers as Buttle withdrew the sword from a thrust in the giant's side.

Trobar clutched at the sudden fierce pain, feeling his own hot blood course over his fingers. Only his massive strength kept him standing for a few seconds. He looked, uncomprehendingly, down to his side, where the sword had cut into him. This was how Shadow must have felt, he thought vaguely. He saw that Buttle was about to thrust at him again and, hopelessly, threw up his arm to ward off the sword.

The point of the blade thrust into his massive forearm, sliding through muscle and flesh, jarring off the bone. Trobar whimpered in pain once more as Buttle angrily withdrew the sword. He had aimed for the giant's heart, but Trobar's last-minute reaction had thwarted him.

This time, he thought.

But there was to be no second time. As the blade darted forward again, Horace's sword flicked it to one side. And now John Buttle learned what swordsmanship was really about.

He staggered back desperately under Horace's lightning-fast and constantly varying attack, never knowing where the next strike was going to be aimed, never knowing from which direction it might come. Horace's sword was a glittering wheel of light in the flare of the torches, a nonstop onslaught that left Buttle no time to plan his own counterattack, and barely time to defend himself.

He was holding the sword in both hands now, horrified by the crushing force behind each of Horace's single-handed strokes— seemingly delivered without the slightest effort. Every one jarred his hands, wrists and arms. He knew he could never hope to defeat this man, and so he took the only way he could think of.

He leapt back and dropped his sword, hearing it clatter on the walkway timbers.

Then he dropped to his knees, hands held out wide.

"Mercy!" he shouted hoarsely. "Please! I surrender! Mercy, I beg you!"

Horace's downstroke had already started, and his eyes flinched with the effort of stopping. Buttle saw the stroke begin and cowered, turning his face away from death. Then, as the sudden pain didn't come, he looked up, fearfully, to see Horace standing over him, a disgusted look on his face.

"You really are a gutless piece of scum, aren't you?" Horace said. He looked back to where the huge figure of Trobar had sunk to the planking, blood soaking the walkway around him. Then he looked at Buttle again, remembering all that Gundar and Will had told him. In one smooth movement, he sheathed his sword. He saw a light of hope kindle in the kneeling man's eyes, hope overlaid with a crafty, self-serving expression.

Cowards and bullies, they were all the same, thought Horace. His thoughts went back to the past again, to his confrontation with the three bullies who made his life a living hell in his first year as an apprentice.

In a sudden blind flare of rage, he grabbed Buttle by the front of his shirt and heaved him to his feet. As part of the same movement, Horace hit him with a short, savage right cross, perfectly timed, perfectly weighted, perfectly executed, with no wasted motion.

Buttle screamed as he felt his jaw dislocate. His vision went black, and his knees turned to jelly. Horace let go of his shirt front and allowed the insensible figure to crash to the planks, bouncing off the stone wall as he went. Horace shook his head, then turned and hurried back to Trobar.

The giant was alive, but he had lost a massive amount of blood. Horace rolled him over carefully. Long and bitter experience had taught him to carry a basic first-aid pack whenever he went into battle. It was in a pouch on the back of his belt, and he found a clean bandage there. He held it against the sword wound in Trobar's side, binding it in place with the giant's own belt. The bandage was instantly soaked with blood, but at least it stanched the flow.

Trobar's eyes were open, and he looked at Horace, uncomprehending. Horace forced a smile onto his face.

"You'll be fine," he said. Trobar's lips moved, and Horace shushed him.

"Don't try to talk. Rest. Malcolm will fix you up," he said. He hoped the doubt that he felt didn't show in his eyes. The wound was a serious one, and even Malcolm's skill would be tested by it.

Trobar tried again. This time, he managed a vague croak. Horace saw the fear in the giant's eyes. And as he saw it, he realized that Trobar wasn't looking at him. He was looking behind him.

He swung around. Buttle, his face swollen and distorted, blood running down from his mouth, stood above him, his sword raised in a double-handed grip high over his head. There was hatred in his eyes. Hatred and triumph. In another second, Horace would be dead.

But there wasn't another second. Gundar Hardstriker's ax came spinning out of the night, rotating end over end with a peculiar *whoomp-whoomp-whoomp* sound.

Eight kilograms of solid wood and heavy iron, it struck Buttle in the back. He grunted in pain, his eyes glazed in surprise and shock. The sword fell to the ground behind him as he staggered under the impact. He tried feebly to reach behind him to pluck the massive weapon free, but he lacked the strength and the purpose. He took a pace to the left, lurched, reeled.

And fell into the dark courtyard below them with a resounding thud.

Horace came wearily to his feet as Gundar joined them.

"Nice throw," he said.

The Skandian nodded. "All I could do," he said. "I knew I couldn't reach you in time."

He peered anxiously over the edge of the walkway, down at the crumpled figure on the flagstones below. Horace moved beside him and dropped a hand on his shoulder.

"Don't worry about him. He's finished," he said.

Gundar looked at him dismissively. "To hell with him. I hope my ax is all right."

35

By now, the defenders at either end of the west rampart had retreated into the two corner towers. Horace inspected the solid oak door of the southwest tower and frowned. It would take a small battering ram to break through. And he assumed the northwest tower door would be no easier. Below, he heard shouting voices and the sound of running feet. Peering over the edge of the walkway, he saw members of the garrison streaming out of the towers into the courtyard. They were heading for the main gateway, where the fortified gatehouse would give them shelter from the attackers.

The way down through the two towers was blocked. But Buttle himself had shown them another route to the courtyard. Horace gathered the Skandians around him. Several had been wounded during the fighting, and he left two of them to look after Trobar. The others were still fit for battle. He led them down the narrow steps beneath the trapdoor that Buttle had used. As they reached the courtyard, he knew their tendency would be to stream after the retreating garrison in an undisciplined throng.

He restrained them by sheer force of will until all of them were down the stairs. Then, forming them into an arrowhead formation, with himself at the tip and Gundar and Nils to his left and right, he led them at a steady, disciplined jog toward the fleeing defenders, currently jostling each other to get through the narrow entrance to the gatehouse.

Hearing the battle chant of the Skandians as they approached, those inside the gatehouse slammed the ironbound oak door shut, leaving nearly twenty of their comrades locked out, backs to the wall, facing their attackers. When there was less than ten meters between the two groups, Horace raised his right hand and called the order to halt. He had the natural gift of command, and it never occurred to the Skandians to ignore him.

"Form a line," he told them, and the arrowhead formation spread out into one line, facing the terrified enemy.

"I'll give you one opportunity to surrender," he told the members of the garrison. "That opportunity is now."

Keren's men eyed the Skandians fearfully. In normal circumstances, they would have surrendered readily enough, but this battle was far from normal. They knew these savage sea wolves were in league with supernatural forces. They had all seen the terrifying apparitions that had risen from the mist in the south. If they surrendered, they had no idea what would become of them. Perhaps they would be sacrificed to the huge warrior they had seen, or the red-faced demons who had soared into the night sky. This was more than a normal battle. They were pitted against the forces of the underworld, the black evil of sorcery, and no sane man would willingly surrender himself to such an enemy.

A long silence greeted Horace's challenge. None of the garrison would take the responsibility. None wanted to single himself out. Finally, Horace shrugged.

"I gave them a chance," he said softly. Then he turned to the wolfship skirl. "Gundar, can you take care of this?"

Gundar, who had recovered his ax and was anxious to use it

again, snorted in derision. "This ragtag bunch?" he said. "Nils and I could do it on our own. You go and help the Ranger, General."

Horace nodded. He slid his sword back into its scabbard and stepped out of the line.

Gundar waited until one of the other Skandians moved into the space Horace had vacated, then he raised his battleax and roared out the time-honored Skandian battle command.

"Follow me, boys!"

There was a roar from twenty-three throats, and the battle line surged forward. They hit the defenders with a crash of steel, driving the terrified castle garrison back against the stone walls of the gatehouse. Horace watched for a second or two, then turned to run toward the keep tower.

36

IN THE TOWER, HIGH ABOVE THE COURTYARD, ALYSS HAD HEARD
the first shouts from the sentries on the south wall and moved to the
window in time to see the enormous images Malcolm was projecting
into the night sky. She recognized the giant, shadowy warrior as the
apparition that Will had described to her. Then the other images
appeared, followed by the amazing sight of the demon's head rockets
soaring into the sky and exploding. She quickly realized that such an
elaborate display must have a definite purpose behind it, other than
being designed to simply terrify the castle's garrison.

The attack on the castle was under way.

Alyss had a shrewd idea as to how the images were generated,
and she knew that they were harmless. The cries and shouts that
drifted up to the tower window told her that the men on the ramparts were well and truly alarmed by the mysterious sights they were
seeing.

Alarmed and distracted.

The tower window faced to the south, and she looked down to
the south wall below her, quelling the misgivings she felt as she
peered down from such a great height. She could see the two end
towers on the wall, and as she watched, she saw men moving from

the west wall to the south wall, where Malcolm's light show seemed to pose a visible threat. But she realized that all this light and sound was a diversion. The real attack would come on the west or north or east wall.

And it would come soon.

She looked around the room, wondering what she could do to prepare for the attack. Will would come for her, she knew that much. But which way? The tower stairs would be easily defended by a few men. That left the outside. He had come that way once before, scaling the wall in an unsuccessful rescue attempt when she had first been imprisoned in the tower. Then, her fear of heights had triggered her refusal to climb back down with him, and her stomach tightened at the thought that this time, it might be the only way out of the tower. Then she set her jaw firmly. If Will asked her, she would do it—fear of heights or no fear of heights.

She examined the two center bars on the window, tugging at them gently. They were held by the barest thread of metal now. The acid she had been pouring onto the bars each night had corroded the iron so that now it was nearly eaten away. The acid flask, hidden on the deep lintel above the window, was still a quarter full—more than enough to finish the job.

She heard renewed shouting and she peered down at the walls, moving to the side of the window to try to see more of the west wall, where the sounds seemed to be coming from. As she watched, a group of men began running along the wall to the southwest tower. Now she heard the distinctive sound of weapons—swords clashing on swords, axes slamming into shields. Her heart soared as she realized that there were attackers on the west wall. She shifted from one foot to the other in an agony of frustration, wishing she could see farther along the west wall to where the fighting was taking place. But the southern aspect of her window defeated her. She could only see the southwest tower and the first few meters of the walkway. She would have to simply wait to see what transpired.

She walked quietly to the chair by the table. Deliberately pulling it out, she sat, hands in her lap, feet together, breathing deeply to calm herself. She closed her eyes and felt herself relax. She must put her trust in Will. She knew he would never let harm come to her.

Just as her accelerated heart rate started to return to normal, the door to the room slammed back on its hinges and Keren dashed in, sword in hand.

Now, in the confusion of the moment, with his castle under attack and his men folding before the assault, there was no sign of the charming, easygoing persona he had assumed over the past weeks.

She stood up quickly, the chair going over backward behind her. As they faced each other for a second or so, her hands went behind her back, her fingers seeking the reassurance of the stellatite pebble in her cuff. But Keren was across the room in a flash, grabbing her arm and dragging her toward him. As he pulled her right arm and hand from behind her back, he dislodged the tiny star stone pebble from its hiding place, and it clattered to the floor, bouncing toward the table. Keren glanced around at the tiny rattling sound but saw nothing. Alyss let out a little cry of alarm and tried to go after the stone, but Keren was too strong for her. Swinging her by the arm, he half dragged, half threw her into a corner of the room.

"Get over there, damn you!" he said. He was fiddling with the hilt of his sword, and her eyes dropped to it to see what he was doing. There was a soft leather cover over the pommel, held in place by a leather thong. He was scrabbling at the knot, undoing it. Alyss drew herself up to her full height, her chin high and her back straight. She smiled at the renegade. All his easy self-assurance was gone. He could feel the hangman's noose around his neck—the reward for treason.

"It's over, Keren," she said calmly. "Any moment now, Will is going to walk through that door, and your little plan will be finished."

He looked up at her, and she could see the hatred in his eyes. Hatred for her personally, because she had rejected him, and hatred for her position, as a representative of the country and King he had betrayed.

"Not quite," he said. He had finally undone the knot and he removed the cover from his sword hilt. She let out a gasp of fear as she saw it.

The pommel of the sword was the blue gemstone he had used to mesmerize her. He thrust the sword toward her, hilt first, the glowing blue stone raised to eye height.

"Just relax, Alyss," he said soothingly. "Just let yourself go and give in to the beautiful blue."

In spite of herself, she could feel the stone taking control of her, feel the sense of warmth and well-being that it generated. She tried to see Will's face, but there was only the blue stone . . . the beautiful blue . . . the blue of the ocean . . . the . . . no! Ignore the stone, she thought. Think of Will!

But the blue is so gentle . . . think of when we were children and we . . . the stone really was beautiful . . . Beautiful, blue, pulsing light and peace and quiet and relaxation and . . . Will! Where are you? Forget Will, the stone whispered. Will is gone. I am here. The blue is here.

A little flame of resistance in her mind, a flame that fought desperately against the soporific effect of the blue stone, slowly flickered and died. The stone had her. Completely.

"Take the sword," Keren told her, and she did. She held it upright, like a cross, her hands on the blade a few centimeters below the crosspiece. The pommel was level with her eyes, and she gazed into the depths of the blue stone, seeing other shimmering dimensions. Seeing a flow of movement and color that amazed her and warmed her and enveloped her.

"You're going to help me get out of here," he told her.

Very slowly, she nodded. "I am," she agreed.

The stone was closer to her than it had ever been before. Holding it like this, she could peer into its depths, admiring the way the light swam and shifted as she moved the stone slightly from side to side. She wondered how she had ever lived without this wonderful blue in her life. She loved it. She smiled at it.

She was still smiling when Will quietly entered the room.

He felt a surge of relief as he saw her unharmed and apparently unconcerned. As he had made his way up the staircase, keyed up and ready at any time for a further attack, he had been terrified at the thought of what he might find. Keren, knowing his rebellion was over, might well have killed her as a last gesture of hatred and spite. And the thought of a world without Alyss in it left an enormous black hole in Will's heart. He knew if it came down to it, he would allow Keren to escape if it would keep Alyss safe. His gaze swept the room, and he saw the renegade knight backed into a corner. Somehow, Alyss had contrived to take his sword away from him. Although now she was holding it in a strange position, blade down and the hilt at eye height, the way a knight might hold his sword if he were about to swear an oath on it.

He felt the first twinge of uneasiness. Something was wrong. Keren was smiling too.

"Alyss?" Will said softly. There was no response. She seemed fascinated by the sword.

"Alyss!" His voice was louder, sharper this time. Still there was no response. He saw Keren moving, glanced at him as the knight drew a broad-bladed dagger from the sheath on the right side of his sword belt.

Will had entered the room with his bow ready, an arrow nocked on the string. He brought it up now, coming back to half draw, a heartbeat away from drawing and loosing.

"That's enough," he said, his voice harsh. He wasn't sure what was happening here, but he knew something was very, very wrong.

Keren's smile widened, and he allowed the dagger to slide back into its sheath, showing his open palms to the Ranger. This was working out very well. He knew that if he had tried to use Alyss as a shield, threatening her with the dagger, Will could have picked him off with consummate ease. Keren was well aware of the skills that all Rangers possessed with the longbow.

This way, however, he could nullify Will's ability without any risk to himself. Will would undoubtedly be willing to shoot him. He would never be able to shoot Alyss.

"Alyss?" Keren said pleasantly.

Her eyes flicked away from the stone for a second as she answered, then returned to it.

"Yes, Keren?"

"Will is here," he said.

For a moment, it seemed that the name meant something to her. She frowned thoughtfully. Then she seemed to shrug.

"Will who?"

And the smile on Keren's face widened as he faced Will. The blue stone was so close to her and its hold was so strong that it had finally defeated the image and the thought she had used to fight its influence.

"Apparently, she doesn't know you," he said pleasantly.

Will looked at Alyss again. She seemed quite normal, except that her attention was fixed on that blue pommel stone. . . . His heart sank as he realized what had happened. It was the blue gem-stone she had spoken about, the focus for Keren's control over her mind.

But what about the stellatite? She had told him that it had been effective in countering the blue stone's powers.

For a moment, he had the wild hope that she was foxing, pretending to be mesmerized to lull Keren into a false sense of security.

His gaze darted around the room and he saw a tiny, glittering black stone on the floor by the table—the stellatite. His momentary hope faded, and he knew she was entrapped. He turned back to Keren.

"It's over, Keren," he said. "You've lost. That rabble of yours won't stand up to thirty-odd Skandians."

Keren shrugged. "I'm afraid you're right," he said. "But where on earth did you find Skandians to help you?"

"Ask your friend Buttle. In a way, he's the one who brought them here. Now, why don't you just surrender and make things easy for all of us?"

Keren laughed. "Believe it or not, I'm not interested in making things easy for you! I think I'd rather just walk away."

"You're not walking anywhere. You have two choices: You can surrender now, or I can put this arrow through you. Frankly, I don't care which way we do it."

"Surrender? And then what?"

Will shrugged. "I can't promise anything other than a fair trial."

"After which I'll be hanged," Keren said.

Will felt another worm of doubt. Keren was more relaxed than he ought to be. Or he was an expert actor.

"You know," the renegade continued, in a chatty tone, "there's an interesting thing about that blue stone and its effect. When Alyss comes out of the trance, she won't remember anything that was said or done while she was in it."

"That won't be any consolation to you if you're dead," Will replied.

Keren held up an admonishing finger. "Aaah, you see, that's the thing. I'm not sure if my death would break the trance . . . or make it permanent."

Will smiled, trying to look more confident than he felt. "I think it's a safe bet to say the trance would be broken."

"Perhaps." Keren paused, looking thoughtful. "But assuming you're right, how would she react to the thought that she had murdered her best friend?"

Will frowned. "What are you talking about, Keren?"

The knight shrugged. "Well, she'd know she'd done it. She'd be standing over you with her sword covered with blood and you dead at her feet. I wonder how she'd cope with that?"

"All right, this has gone far enough. You have five seconds to surrender. Or five seconds to die. You choose."

The bow came up. The arrow slid back to full draw, and Will centered his aiming picture on Keren's chest. At this range, with the bow's full draw weight behind it, the arrow would slice through his chain mail like butter.

"Alyss?" said Keren.

"Yes, Keren?" she replied.

"Kill the Ranger," Keren told her.

37

ALYSS LOOKED AWAY FROM THE BLUE STONE FOR A SECOND, gazing steadily at Keren as she considered his command.

"Of course," she said simply. Her tone was so matter of fact, so unconcerned, that Will's heart missed a beat. Quickly, she reversed her grip on the sword, spinning it in a half circle so that the blade was uppermost and she held the hilt in a two-handed grip. In that position, the blue stone was still well within her field of view, although she was focused on Will. There was no sign of recognition in her eyes, nothing but a casual acceptance of Keren's command. She took a pace toward Will, the sword rising higher for a more powerful downward stroke at him.

Will brought the bow up, the arrow coming back to full draw almost instantly, aiming at Alyss's heart. He saw a slight frown cross her face as she recognized the threat.

"That's far enough, Alyss," he said. Even mesmerized as she was, she wouldn't blindly obey a command that would lead to her own death. Would she?

She stopped, looked to Keren for advice. He smiled encouragingly at her.

"He's bluffing," the renegade said. "He would never hurt you. Go ahead and kill him."

And Will realized that Keren was speaking the truth. He couldn't harm her. He thought for a moment that he could shoot to disable her, to put an arrow through her wrist or her arm and force her to drop the sword. But he pictured the cruel broadhead slicing through her flesh, tearing tendons and muscles, perhaps leaving her permanently crippled, and he knew that he couldn't bring himself to cause her that sort of pain. Not Alyss, of all people. He just couldn't.

"Alyss . . . please," he said, hoping that he might reach her somehow.

"Go on," Keren prompted her. "I told you he wouldn't harm you."

"Yes. So you did," Alyss replied. Will was appalled by the fact that her behavior continued to seem so normal. She didn't appear to be in a trance of any kind. She wasn't speaking slowly or in a monotone. She actually smiled at Keren as she spoke. She seemed interested in the fact that Will would threaten her but then refuse to carry through the threat. But it was a detached interest, rather as she might comment on an unexpected change in the weather. She started toward him once more.

But there was a threat that Will was more than willing to carry through. He swung the arrow back to Keren, this time centering his aiming picture on the renegade's throat above the chain mail, just to make sure it would be a killing shot.

"If she takes one more step, Keren, you're a dead man. Tell her."

There was a momentary flash of concern in Keren's eyes. Then it disappeared as he assessed the threat posed by the gleaming arrowhead.

"Just wait a moment there, Alyss," he said.

She stopped again. She looked at Keren, expecting more instructions, her eyebrows raised in a question.

Will couldn't help a grim smile twisting his lips.

"We seem to have an impasse," he said. "Now snap her out of this, and you can go."

He'd made the decision as he spoke. He could always hunt Keren down later, if necessary, and, besides, the way out of the castle was probably well and truly blocked by Horace and the Skandians. But the longer this dangerous situation was maintained, the greater the chance that something would go terribly wrong. He saw Keren's shoulders slump fractionally as he realized Will had won.

"Go?" the renegade asked him. "Go where?"

Will shrugged. "Anywhere you choose. I'm giving you a chance."

"And you're also planning to come after me," Keren said. It wasn't a question. Will felt he didn't need to answer.

"Keren?" Alyss said. "I'm getting a little tired here." She still had the sword raised above her head. Keren smiled at her.

"It won't be long now, Alyss." Then he turned back to Will. "You know, as I said, the interesting thing here is that when Alyss comes out of the trance, she won't remember anything that she has said, or heard, or done. It will all be a blank to her."

"Fascinating," said Will, his voice a little tighter than he wanted it to be. "Now bring her out of it."

"Yes, perhaps I should do something," Keren agreed. "Alyss?"

"Yes, Keren?"

"You know you must do anything I say, don't you?"

"Well, of course I know that, Keren." She turned to face him.

"Good. Then listen to me carefully. If the Ranger harms me in any way, kill him."

Alyss nodded, then turned back to Will. She could see the arrow was now aimed at Keren, and she knew that if the slightly built figure released that arrow, she would still have to go ahead and kill him. Yet it seemed a pity. He looked like a nice enough young man, the kind of person she could really like.

She hesitated, a small frown creasing her forehead. Somewhere, deep within her mind, a memory was stirring. Just the very ghost of a memory. A faint consciousness that perhaps she knew this person. Yet if she knew him, why would Keren want her to kill him? It was tempting to let go of the thought and just sink back into the oblivion that the blue stone would provide. But years of training and discipline asserted themselves. Alyss had always prided herself on her ability to solve problems, and here was one to be solved.

"What was your name again?" she asked.

Keren's eyes, up to this moment fixed on Will, snapped around to her as he sensed a change in her attitude. She shouldn't be asking questions. She should be obeying without any hesitation.

"His name doesn't matter!" he snapped at her. "Do as I tell you!"

Alyss shook her head as if to clear her thoughts. "Yes. Of course. Sorry," she said. Yet, even as she agreed, there was a note of uncertainty in her voice.

Will glanced at her, seeing the torment in her eyes. He was resigned to the fact that he must kill Keren and that, if he did, Alyss would kill him. And he knew that if that happened, Alyss would be tortured by the fact for the rest of her life. As Keren had said, she would regain consciousness and find herself standing over the dead body of her friend, a bloodstained sword in her hand. And there would be nobody left alive to tell her how it had all come about.

He simply couldn't leave her with that burden. Keren, sensing that his hold over Alyss's will was somehow slipping, decided to wait no longer.

"Kill him! Kill him now!" His voice cracked as he screamed the order at her.

"Of course," Alyss said. There was the faintest hint of reluctance, but she stepped forward, the sword going up to full stretch as she measured the distance to Will. And in that instant, he had to leave her some vestige of memory or forgiveness for what she was about to do.

"Alyss," he said quietly, "I love you. I always have."

He saw it in her eyes. A moment of confusion. A flash of conflicting emotions. Then a sudden blinding clarity and an overwhelming sense of horror. She looked up at the sword, high above her head, and a scream was torn from her as she realized what she was about to do.

She threw the sword away from her and collapsed to the floor, sobbing uncontrollably. Her shoulders heaved as the sobs racked her entire body.

Will dropped the bow, all thoughts of Keren forgotten as he moved to her. Oh, god, he thought, let her be all right!

He had no idea what harm the sudden shock of realization might have done to her mind. He dropped to his knees beside her, trying to reach down and embrace her, trying to lift her from the floor. Anything to quell that awful sobbing, the sound of a tortured mind. But she huddled in a ball, defying his efforts to get his arms around her and lift her.

"Alyss, it's all right! It's all right! You're fine now!" he crooned to her. But it was all too clear that she wasn't, and she remained oblivious to his words and his touch.

"Damn you to the deepest corner of hell."

He looked up. It was Keren, moving toward him, the sword discarded by Alyss in his hand.

"Maybe she couldn't kill you. But I can!"

Galvanized into movement, Will sprang away from Alyss's huddled form. Keren followed, sweeping the sword through the air in a succession of wild cuts. It was this that saved Will's life—for the moment. There was no science or skill in Keren's strokes, just the raw emotion of wild hatred and unreasoning revenge guiding the sword.

Will regained his feet, the saxe knife sliding from its scabbard just in time to parry a side cut. He reached behind his neck for the hidden throwing knife, but once more he was impeded by the cloak and the collar of his jacket. This concealed sheath really was a bad idea, he thought bitterly. He parried another cut from Keren, but without the added leverage of the standard two-knife defense, he was at a disadvantage against the longer weapon. All he could hope to do was avoid that sword for as long as possible.

Gradually, he saw the rage in Keren's eyes subsiding. He reached for his collar again, trying for the throwing knife. But Keren saw the movement and leapt forward, lunging so that Will only barely avoided the darting point of the sword, then Keren spun the sword in his hand to deliver a high overhead back cut, almost as part of the same motion.

Will felt a cold hand around his heart as he realized that Keren was an expert swordsman and his training was beginning to reassert itself over his initial blind rage. Will couldn't hope to win this one-sided battle. He retreated before another thrust, felt the wall at his back and knew he'd made a mistake. He slid sideways from the next cut, the sword striking sparks from the stones in the wall. Keren pursued him as he slid along the wall, a series of blindingly fast strokes and thrusts giving him no chance to retaliate.

It was the sound that roused Alyss. The grating screech of the sword skipping off stone. She looked up to see Will retreating desperately before Keren's clinical attack, warding off the sword with a totally inadequate knife.

She rose to her knees, then to her feet, shaking her head to clear it. Somehow, she knew, this was all her fault. She'd placed Will in this danger. Now she must save him. She needed a weapon . . . any weapon. She swayed on her feet, then her senses cleared and she knew where to find one. Two quick steps took her to the window. She seized the weapon and moved to where Keren had trapped Will in a corner. The point of the sword was now leveled at Will's throat. The saxe knife lay on the floor between them, finally smashed from Will's grip by the massive force of a two-handed overhead stroke.

Will faced Keren calmly, waiting for death. Then he saw Alyss moving behind the renegade.

"Alyss! Run!" he yelled. "Get Horace!"

It was only natural that Keren, poised to thrust the sword into Will's throat, should turn as the Ranger called to her. As he did, she flung the contents of the leather-covered bottle into his face.

His scream was terrible as the acid burned into his skin and eyes. The pain was excruciating, and he dropped the sword, clawing at his face, trying to ease the dreadful burning. He stumbled in wild circles around the room, screaming all the while. Alyss watched in horror as Keren reeled blindly, trying in vain to find some respite from the agony. She backed away, felt Will's arm go around her.

They both became aware of a stench of burning flesh.

Keren's movements became wilder and more erratic. His throat was hoarse from the nonstop screaming, and he stumbled and whirled in uncontrolled circles, one moment throwing his arms out to regain balance, the next clutching his hands to his ravaged face once more. He staggered into a wall, rebounded, lurched a few paces, then lost balance and reeled backward.

Toward the window.

His back and shoulders struck the bars, and for a moment they supported him. Then the thin threads of metal that held the two center bars in place gave way, opening a wide gap behind him. He teetered backward for a second, but the low sill of the window caught him just behind his knees.

His scream was long and drawn out—a mixture of pain and blind fear. It hung in the night above his falling body, like a long ribbon trailing behind him.

Then, abruptly, it stopped.

Alyss turned to Will, her face troubled.

"Will, what happened here?" she asked. She surveyed the wrecked room, chairs and table upended during Will's desperate fight with Keren, the sword discarded again on the floor, the empty bottle lying beside it where she had dropped it. Her mind seethed with images, but they seemed so bizarre and unlikely that she knew they couldn't be true.

Will smiled, his arm still around her shoulder. He pulled her to him and let her rest her head on his shoulder.

"What happened," he told her, "is that you just saved my life—twice."

He kissed her forehead gently to calm her. He sensed the confused tangle of thoughts in her mind. But she pushed back a little from him, searching his face with her eyes.

"Twice?" she asked. "When was the first time?"

Will smiled at her. "Never mind."

38

WILL TAPPED GENTLY ON THE INFIRMARY DOOR, HEARD Malcolm's call of "come in" and entered.

The healer was bent over Trobar, who was stretched out on four mattresses set on the floor in a corner. There was no bed large enough in the castle to accommodate him, so he had to remain on the floor until he was strong enough to make his way back to Healer's Clearing. Malcolm turned as Will entered and smiled a greeting.

"Good morning," he said.

"Morning. How's the patient doing?"

Malcolm pursed his lips before answering. "Far better than he should be. He'd lost enough blood to kill two normal men by the time I got to him. Lord knows how he survived."

"I suppose he started out with enough blood in him for three men," Will said. "He's certainly big enough." He smiled at Trobar. The giant looked weak, and far paler than normal. But he was smiling at Will's joke, and his eyes were clear and alert—far better than the glazed, feverish look he had about him when he had first been brought down from the ramparts after the battle.

Will heard a familiar *thump-thump* on the floor. He turned to see

Shadow lying on her belly in the far corner. Her chin was on her forepaws, but her eyes never stopped moving as they took in everything in the room.

"Morning, Shadow," he said. *Thump-thump* went the heavy tail. He glanced at Malcolm. "Is it acceptable to have a dog in the sickroom?" he asked.

The healer allowed himself a thin smile.

"I'd say it's essential," he said. "Both of them drove me mad until I let her in here."

"Hmm," said Will noncommittally. He was going to have to address this situation when he headed south, he thought. And it was going to be difficult. Then he pushed the awkward thought aside. He'd be here for some time still. He'd face it later.

"I thought I'd drop in on Alyss, if you think that's a good idea," he said.

Malcolm nodded. "I think it's an excellent idea. It's time she had some company."

It was two days since the battle. Keren's men, already defeated, had surrendered immediately when they learned of their leader's death. They were now confined in the castle's dungeons.

Alyss had spent the time in a state of bewildered shock. Malcolm said it was almost certainly the result of her being snapped out of Keren's mesmeric trance and finding herself with a sword raised, only a second away from murdering Will. It was similar, he said, to the way sleepwalkers could be sent into shock if they were roused suddenly from sleep.

The healer had given her a sleeping potion and had put her to bed.

"Rest will be the best thing for her," he said. "She's a strong-willed girl, and she'll heal herself, eventually. But she'll do it sooner if she's rested and strong."

Now, apparently, he thought that process was far enough along to allow her a visitor.

Will mounted the keep stairs. Alyss had been returned to her comfortable rooms on the fourth floor. He had looked in on her several times, but had hesitated to wake her as she had been sleeping. He'd hesitated over something else as well. In the tower, he had told Alyss he loved her, and he realized that he had spoken the truth. In a way, he had always loved her, he knew. She was his oldest and dearest friend in the world. But there was an even stronger bond between them now that they had grown up. Somewhere along the way, that friendship and that long history of companionship had turned to love.

Or at least, it had as far as he was concerned. He wasn't sure if she felt the same way.

Keren had said she would remember nothing that was said or done while her mind was under his control. But Will's declaration had broken that control, and he suspected that, since that was the case, she might have some memory of what he had said. He had asked Malcolm about this, not telling the healer what he had actually said to the girl. Malcolm had been uncertain in his answer.

"Perhaps she will remember," he replied. "Perhaps not." He saw the frustration on the young man's face and added, apologetically, "We just don't know enough about the workings of the mind for me to give you a straight answer. What might be true for one person might be utterly false for another."

The only way, Will decided, would be to see if Alyss raised the matter herself. If she didn't, it would mean that she was embarrassed and awkward because she didn't feel the same way about him, or that his words had not had sufficient impact to remain in her memory—which, to his way of thinking, amounted to the same thing.

Will had spent the previous five years almost exclusively in Halt's company, and he was not really equipped to deal with a social situation like this. Now that he had admitted the depth of his feelings for Alyss, he dreaded the thought that she might not return them—that she might reply with the statement that, over the years, has proved the death knell for so many relationships: Can't we just stay as friends?

He'd discussed it, in the strictest confidence, with Horace. Horace, after all, was a knight who moved in the highest social circles at Castle Araluen and was far more used to spending time in female company.

The tall warrior had claimed to be completely unsurprised when Will confessed how he felt.

"Of course you love her!" he'd replied. "She's been your best friend since you both could walk, and now she's grown up to be beautiful, talented, intelligent and witty. What's not to love about all that?"

Horace's solution to the problem was typical. Just come right out and tell her. But then, as a warrior, he always favored the direct approach. Rangers, Will told him, were more inclined to look for the subtle nuances of a person's behavior to determine their true feelings.

"You're more inclined to be devious, you mean," Horace had said, dismissing the statement as pretentious balderdash.

Will couldn't find a suitable reply to that, so they dropped the subject.

Altogether, it was a confusing and awkward situation for the young Ranger. He paused now outside Alyss's door, wondering if he should wait another day. Then he decided that he was only trying to postpone the inevitable, and he rapped on the door, a little more sharply than he had intended.

"Come in."

He felt a surge of nervousness at the sound of her voice, then he opened the door and went in.

Alyss was sitting up in her bed, close to the window, where she could look out over the surrounding countryside. The last of the snow clung stubbornly to the treetops and gleamed in the sunshine. She turned from the view and smiled at him.

"Will," she said. "How lovely to see you."

She wore her pale blond hair down, brushed till it seemed to shine. She looked tired, but pleased to see him. He moved to the side of the bed. There was a straight-backed chair there, and he sat down. She reached out and took his hands. It was a natural, unaffected movement. A gesture between friends, he thought.

"How are you feeling?" he asked her. His throat was dry, and the banal words seemed to stick in it as he spoke them.

"I'm fine. A little tired is all."

He nodded. He couldn't think of what to say next.

"I've got a million questions to ask," she said. "I've been having the wildest dreams." She rolled her eyes dramatically. "I've been wanting to ask you about everything that happened in the tower the other night."

He watched her carefully. "You don't remember anything?" And he thought he saw a momentary flicker of hesitation in her eyes. It was only there for a fraction of a second, but he was sure it was there.

"Not really," she said, and he knew he'd been right about the hesitation. She did remember—but didn't want to admit it.

Truth be told, Alyss was feeling every bit as confused as Will. She had indeed been having dreams. She dreamed that they were back in the tower and she was about to hurt him in some terrible way when suddenly, out of the blue, he was telling her that he loved her—words she had been hoping to hear from him for longer than she could remember.

But she didn't know if the dream reflected what had really happened or something she wanted to have happened. They looked at each other, both uncertain, both unwilling to declare themselves.

He shrugged.

"Perhaps we should leave it until you're stronger," he said.

She studied him carefully. "Was it really that awful?" she asked.

A dark look entered his eyes as he remembered those grim moments.

"Yes. It was, Alyss. But as I told you on the night, you saved my life. And that's the important thing."

There was a long silence.

"Any sign of the relief column from Norgate?" she asked. She sensed that he was relieved to hear the conversation move on to a safer, more general, topic.

"Our scouts say they're ten days away."

"What about the Scotti?" she asked. After all, they were an immediate threat, and they were closer than the Norgate forces. But Will shrugged.

"I doubt they'll be coming. You knew we let MacHaddish go, didn't you?"

She sat up straighter at that news. "Let him go? Whose idea was that?"

"Mine, actually. And everyone else reacted pretty much the way you just did when I suggested it."

"Well, then—" she began, but he cut her off.

"We brought him here first and showed him that the castle was fully garrisoned by wild Skandians. Plus some of Orman's original men have begun to filter back in. So we showed him around, told him the relief force from Norgate was due any day, then turned him loose to report back to his commander."

He didn't mention that he had also taken MacHaddish to one side and made him a personal promise: If your army comes back here, you will be the first one I look for. The Scotti general hadn't been frightened by the threat. But he knew it was genuine, and he respected it.

"So," Alyss said thoughtfully, "he'll report that Macindaw is back in enemy hands, and probably a tougher nut to crack than it was before."

"Exactly. Skandians will be much harder opponents than your average provincial soldier. They're professionals, after all." There was a note of pride in his voice, and she couldn't help smiling at him.

"You really like them, don't you?"

"Skandians?" he said. "Yes, I do. Once they give you their word, they will never go back on it. They're terrible enemies, but they make the best allies you could ask for. Horace says if he had an army of them, he could conquer the world."

"Does he want to conquer the world?"

He smiled. "Not really. It's just the sort of thing warriors say."

"And what about you? Any dreams of world domination for you?"

He shook his head. "I just want to get back to my peaceful cabin at Seacliff Fief."

"I seem to recall there was a pretty little innkeeper's daughter back there?" she said. Her tone was light and teasing, but there was a purpose behind the question. Will shrugged.

"Oh, I'm sure she's forgotten all about me by now."

"I doubt it. You're not an easy person to forget."

He said nothing. He didn't know how to answer that, and the silence between them grew longer. Abruptly, he became aware that he was still holding both her hands. He released them and stood, sending the chair skating back on the floorboards.

"I'd . . . better be going," he said. "Malcolm told me not to tire you out."

She forced a yawn in reply to make things easier for him. She was, after all, a trained diplomat.

"I am a little sleepy," she said. "Come by tomorrow and see me again?"

"Of course." He made his way to the door, unwilling to turn his back on her, and sidled out, half waving, half saluting as he went. "Well, I'll see you then, then." He realized how stupid that phrasing sounded.

She waved, just fluttering her fingers at him, and smiled good-bye. He groped for the door handle, got it open somehow and went out, closing the door behind him.

In the anteroom, he paused, leaning his forehead against the rough stone of the wall.

"Oh, damn it all," he said quietly.

In the bedchamber, Alyss was saying exactly the same thing.

39

THE RELIEF FORCE FROM NORGATE CLATTERED ACROSS Macindaw's lowered drawbridge and filed through the gatehouse into the courtyard.

There were twenty mounted knights and a hundred marching men-at-arms, and all of them stared around curiously at the grinning Skandians who manned the battlements. Sir Doric, the Battlemaster of Norgate, who was leading the force, saw the small welcoming group waiting in front of the keep and turned his horse toward them. Will noted that there was a Ranger riding beside him. That would be Meralon, he thought, the Ranger assigned to Norgate Fief. He knew little about the other man, but he had heard that he was in-clined to be stuffy and a little set in his ways.

Orman, wearing a heavy gold chain from which hung the official seal that marked him as chatelain, stepped forward to meet the two riders. Will, Horace and Malcolm stayed back, in deference to Orman's reinstated authority.

Sir Doric raised his hand and called the order for his men to halt and stand at ease. He and Meralon continued to walk their horses forward. It was a formal moment, but the formality was shattered when a figure burst from the second rank of mounted men. He was riding a horse much smaller than the battlehorses who surrounded him, and up until now, he hadn't been visible. Now, however, he slid out of the saddle and raced across the intervening space, falling to his knees before Orman.

"My lord!" said Xander. "We're here at last. I'm sorry it took so long! I did all I could!"

Will, watching Sir Doric, saw a frown of disapproval cross his features. There was a certain protocol that should be followed at moments like this, and the Battlemaster seemed to feel the secretary should know that.

Sir Doric, it should be noted, was something of a snob.

"That's all right, Xander," Orman told him. Then, in a lowered tone, he added, "Do stand up, there's a good fellow. The leader of the relief force wants to tell us that we're safe."

Xander took up his position behind Orman. Doric and Meralon brought their horses to a standstill, and both men dismounted. It was Will's turn to frown. Politeness dictated that they should have waited until Orman invited them to step down. If Orman was offended, however, he showed no sign of it.

"Welcome to Castle Macindaw. Sir Doric of Norgate Fief, isn't it?" he said. "I'm Orman, castle lord."

Sir Doric slapped his gauntlets on his thigh once or twice. He looked around the courtyard before answering brusquely, and a little distractedly, "Mmmm? Yes. Yes. What the devil are all these Skandians doing here?"

A tiny frown creased Orman's forehead. In the weeks since he had been forced to flee his own castle and hide in the forest, he had lost much of the sardonic behavior and superior attitude that Will had first noticed in him. It was remarkable what a few weeks spent roughing it in the forest could do for a man, Will thought.

"They appear to be defending the castle," Orman said quietly. "Surely Xander told you they were helping us?"

But Doric's eyes were still roving the battlements. "Mmm? Yes. Your man said something about mercenaries. But I thought you would have got rid of them by now. Not safe to have them inside the castle, what?"

"Some of their friends died getting in here," Orman told him. "I thought it would be churlish to ask them to leave straightaway."

Doric made a shooing gesture with the back of his right hand, rather as if he were brushing flies away. "No. Get rid of them. My men are here now. You don't need these damned Skandians!"

"They can't be trusted, after all." That was the Ranger, Meralon, adding his contribution.

Will felt a slow heat rising in his face and started forward. A hand gripped his forearm and stopped him. He looked up at Horace, who mouthed the words, "Easy now." He nodded. His friend was right. He reined in his temper, then stepped to Orman's side.

"I trust them," he said.

The two pairs of eyes swung to him, assessing him. Doric frowned. The cloak was definitely the same cut as a Ranger's cloak, but it was patterned in black and white. Will ignored the Battlemaster and addressed Meralon.

"Will. Ranger fifty," he said. The other Ranger nodded.

"Meralon. Twenty-seven." He put a little stress on the number, to imply that he was senior to Will. In fact, he wasn't. Aside from Crowley and a select command group of senior Rangers, all members of the Corps were equal in rank. Their numbers were assigned as they became available, when other Rangers retired or died. It was sheer chance that Will, as the newest recruit to the Corps, had received the number fifty. "You're Halt's apprentice, aren't you?" Meralon added disparagingly.

"I was," Will replied.

Meralon nodded once or twice, then continued in a patronizing tone, "Yes, well, as you grow a little older, Will, you'll learn that Skandians aren't to be trusted. They're a treacherous race."

Will forced himself to take a deep breath before he answered. There weren't many fools in the Ranger Corps, but he realized he'd just met one. He doubted the man had any personal experience of Skandians.

"You're wrong," he said firmly. "I trust them, and we need a garrison here."

Doric interrupted, waving toward the ranks of men in the courtyard. "We can supply that. I'll leave fifty men here."

"And you'll leave Norgate weakened if you do. You must have stripped the garrison to put this force together."

Doric hesitated. The young Ranger was right. It was all very well to put together an expeditionary force for an emergency rescue. But to leave a large number of them here would weaken Norgate seriously.

Before the Battlemaster could answer, Will added, "And there's a Scotti army just across the border who might well decide to attack Norgate if they see its garrison is under strength."

He was right again, Doric realized. The fact did nothing to soften his brisk manner. He turned on Orman.

"What happened to your normal garrison?" he demanded, an accusing note in his voice.

"The usurper, Keren, got rid of them. They're scattered all over the countryside. It'll take months to get word to them and get them back here."

"Well, you've made a right mess of things, haven't you?" Doric burst out.

For a moment, Orman flushed angrily. This was a delicate situation. As chatelain, he was equal in rank to the fief's Battlemaster. Both of them answered to the Baron at Norgate, and it was difficult to know who had the final say in matters here. It was a situation that called for large amounts of tact and diplomacy, qualities that Sir Doric seemed to have left behind at Castle Norgate.

"And we remedied the situation, thanks to the Skandians," Orman said smoothly. "Without their help, the castle would be in Scotti hands by now. So we've made an arrangement with them to stay on as garrison until I can recruit enough local men."

"An arrangement?" Meralon said incredulously. "Who exactly made this arrangement?"

"I did," Will replied.

Meralon nodded again. He was still fuming over Will's blunt statement that he was wrong. "Yes, I might have known. Everyone says you and Halt have a blind spot where these pirates are concerned."

Still controlling his anger, Will replied, "The Skandians need a place and materials to build a ship. We've agreed to give them that. In return, they'll garrison the castle as long as necessary. We need them. They need us. It's a good arrangement all around."

"But it's not up to you to make arrangements, is it? This is not your fief. I am the Ranger here, not you. And I don't approve of the deal you've made with these pirates."

Meralon was slightly taller than Will, and he leaned down to bring their faces level. Will was tempted to step backward, but he realized this would be a mistake. He held his ground. He drew breath to answer, but Horace stepped forward and fore-stalled him.

"Two things," the young knight said, deciding it was time he took a part in this discussion. "First, I'd like everyone to stop referring to the Skandians as treacherous pirates. They're friends of mine."

His voice was quiet and calm. He spoke deliberately. But there was no mistaking the underlying threat in his words. He studied the Norgate Ranger. Like Will, Horace had been briefed by Halt and Crowley before he came north. He had asked the same question: Why couldn't the local Ranger take care of the problem? They had told him that the mission was secret and the local man would be recognized. He realized now that their reasoning went deeper. The job required energy and imagination and the ability to improvise. Meralon simply wasn't up to the task.

He saw he had everyone's attention, so he addressed Meralon directly.

"And if you're in charge here, as you claim, where the devil were you when you were needed?"

Meralon opened his mouth to reply, but Horace waved his words aside. "I don't recall seeing you coming up with a plan to take the castle. I'm sure you didn't provide a force to do it with. And I certainly didn't see you storming the battlements with me."

There was a moment's silence. Horace reflected that he had never had the nerve to speak to a Ranger this way. He respected and admired the Corps too much for that. And as he had that thought, another realization struck him.

"In fact, if you're the local Ranger, how did you let this situation develop in the first place? I thought you people were supposed to keep an ear to the ground?" He waved his arm around the castle courtyard. "All this should never have happened. And that's what I'll be saying in my report."

Meralon spluttered, too furious to speak. Sir Doric took up the challenge for him.

"And who the devil might you be?"

Horace looked at him and smiled, but without the slightest trace of humor. He was a self-deprecating person and he usually eschewed titles. But he felt it was time for a little rank-pulling. He folded his arms across his chest.

"I am Sir Horace, knight chevalier of the Oak Leaf, B company commander, Araluen Royal Guard and Appointed Champion to Cassandra, the Princess Royal."

Now, that really did stop the conversation. Words like *Royal Guard* and *Princess Cassandra* gave Horace considerable cachet. He was a man who had access to the highest authority in the land, and he was planning a report—a report that said he found arrangements here unsatisfactory.

Doric allowed himself one bitter sidelong glace at Meralon. Why did you let this happen? it said. Then he addressed Orman in a more placatory tone.

"Lord Orman, perhaps I spoke in some haste. Forgive me if I've caused offense. After all, it's been a long, hard ride to get here—"

"And of course, you and your men are tired and need rest," Orman took the proffered olive branch smoothly. Will was impressed by the chatelain's tact. Orman had no wish to score points or gloat. All he wanted was an amicable solution to the situation. "Perhaps my people could show your men to their quarters?"

"I'd be grateful, sir," Doric said, with a slight bow.

Orman turned to his secretary. "Xander, take care of it, please." Then, turning back to Doric, he said, "And perhaps we could continue this discussion over luncheon, after you've had a chance to rest and bathe and change?"

Doric's bow was more evident this time. "Again, sir, you're too kind. We could use a rest, eh, Meralon?"

Meralon, tight-lipped, muttered agreement. Rangers, of course, enjoyed the highest level of independence, being answerable only to the King. But Horace's royal connections had trumped that ace very neatly. Besides, Meralon knew that Will's actions, while unorthodox, had been successful. And success tended to make the unorthodox acceptable. Brushing past Will, he followed Doric and Orman into the keep, leaving Will, Horace and Malcolm to bring up the rear.

"Since when have you been Evanlyn's champion?" Will asked in an aside. Horace grinned at him.

"Well, I'm not, actually. But I'm sure it's just a matter of time."

40

Farewells were the hardest part of life as a Ranger, Will thought as he led Tug out of the castle stable, Shadow following at his heels. He had hoped that perhaps he and Horace and Alyss might be able to slip quietly away, but, of course, that was impossible. They had made friends here over the past months, and those friends wanted the chance to say good-bye.

The situation at Macindaw was virtually back to normal. Sir Doric and Meralon had led the relief column north, to the border with Picta, to ensure that the Scotti army had actually withdrawn. Doric and his troops would remain on patrol in the immediate area until he was sure the local situation had stabilized. As time passed, his force would be progressively reduced, but he planned to maintain a strong presence in the area for at least the next few months.

The Skandians continued to man the walls as a temporary garrison. Those who weren't on duty were busy at a small creek a kilometer away—a tributary that ran down to a larger river that in turn led to the sea. The skeleton of their new wolfship was already laid out on the bank.

Will stopped. Horace and Alyss, leading their horses behind him, followed suit. Orman, Xander and Malcolm stood waiting for him. Behind them, he could see the bulky forms of Gundar and Nils Ropehander. And behind them, the even larger form of Trobar, now sufficiently recovered to leave the infirmary and limp painfully down the stairs to bid his own good-byes. Will thought he knew whom the giant wished to farewell.

Orman spoke first, as was only fitting.

"Will, Horace—and Lady Alyss, of course—I owe you far too much to ever try to repay you. Please accept my gratitude and my friendship as a totally inadequate reward for your services."

Horace and Will shuffled awkwardly and mumbled their inarticulate replies. Alyss, naturally, took the lead.

"Lord Orman, it has been our privilege to serve you. You've proved yourself a loyal servant of the King."

Orman bowed. "You're too kind, Lady Alyss," he said. Then he turned to Will. "It occurs to me, Will, that I made some unkind remarks about your musical ability when you first arrived. I shouldn't have done that."

Will shook his head ruefully. "I think your comments were pretty accurate, Lord Orman." When Will had first arrived at Macindaw, posing as a jongleur, Orman had made scathing comments about his lack of classical training and the fact that he sang "country ditties and doggerel."

The ghost of a smile touched Orman's mouth. "Oh, I know they were accurate. I just shouldn't have made them." He became serious for a moment. "I'm sorry you lost your mandola, by the way."

Will shrugged. Buttle had smashed the mandola in a rage after Will, Orman and Xander had escaped from the castle.

"It may be a blessing in disguise, my lord," he said, and the smile returned to Orman's face.

"Best if I don't comment on that. But Xander has something to say," he prompted.

The little secretary stepped out from behind his master. He bowed his head briefly to Will.

"My gratitude, Ranger," he said. "You saved my master's life, and you saved the castle." He looked at Horace. "Gratitude to you as well, Sir Horace."

Horace bowed.

Will couldn't resist a final dig at the secretary.

"Have you forgiven me for overpaying the Skandians, Xander?" he asked.

Humor was not the secretary's strong suit. His air of gratitude was instantly replaced by the harried manner he usually assumed. "Well, you know, I'm sure we could have got them for much less. You really should have consulted me before you—"

"Xander?" It was Orman.

The secretary stopped in midflow and looked up at his master.

"Drop it."

"Yes, my lord." Xander hung his head. "Sorry," he mumbled to Will.

Will shook his head. The man was irrepressible. "Don't ever change, Xander," he said.

"He won't," Orman told him with some feeling.

Then it was time to grasp Malcolm's hand. The thin, birdlike little man smiled at him.

"You did well here, Will Treaty," he said. "I think all of us will be safer in the future. We understand one another a little better."

Will knew that Orman had offered Malcolm a position in the castle. He hadn't heard if the healer had accepted.

"Are you going to move your people into Macindaw?" he asked.

Malcolm shook his head. "They're shy. They don't like being in the public view. I'll stay in the forest with them. If Orman needs a healer, I'll be available."

"But no more Night Warrior? No more lights and noises in the forest?"

The little man tipped his head thoughtfully to one side. "Oh, I don't know about that. Orman has agreed to keep our secret, and the Skandians will move on eventually. I think I'd prefer it if the locals still regarded Grimsdell as a place not to go."

"You're probably right," Will agreed. "That reminds me. This is yours."

He fumbled in a pocket and produced the black stellatite stone. The day after the battle, he had returned to the tower room and searched the floor until he found it.

The healer smiled. "Oh, that? Keep it if you like. It's just a pebble."

"But . . . it's stellatite. It's invaluable! You said—"

"I'm afraid I wasn't completely honest with you," Malcolm said, not the least contrite. "I told you mesmerism was a matter of focus. This gave Alyss something to focus on, and that broke the power of the blue stone."

Alyss and Will exchanged puzzled looks. Then Will turned back to the healer.

"It's worthless?"

"Not completely. The fact that you both believed in it made it valuable. As I said, mesmerism is a matter of belief. You believed this river pebble was a star stone, so it became one."

Will shook his head in disbelief and slipped the pebble back into his pocket. "I'll keep it as a memento," he said, "of a very devious healer. Good-bye, Malcolm. Take care."

"Godspeed to you, Will." Malcolm smiled. "And you, Horace.

Maybe with you two gone, I'll be able to get a cup of coffee for myself."

Will turned to shake hands with Gundar. He should have known he'd never get away with such a formal gesture. The Skandian seized him in a massive bear hug, lifting him from the ground, squeezing him so that he could hardly talk.

"Good fight, Ranger! Good battle! I'll be sad to see you go!"

"Pu' me dow'...," Will managed to gasp, and the Skandian set him back on his feet again. He checked his ribs to make sure they were intact.

"Drop in and see me at Seacliff Fief someday, Gundar," he said.

The skirl roared with laughter. "We'll come for dinner!" he bellowed, delighted at his own joke.

"Just make sure you let us know you're coming," Will warned him. This time, Nils joined in the laughter.

Alyss and Horace were making their own good-byes. As Will waited for them to finish, he caught Trobar's eye. The giant looked away sadly, and Will walked to where he stood behind the assembled group. Shadow followed, of course. She looked up at Will as he stopped a few paces short of Trobar. She was too well trained to leave his side without permission.

"Go on," he told her quietly, and she went to Trobar, her tail wagging in that slow, heavy rhythm of border shepherds.

The gigantic man knelt to farewell her, fondling her ears, rubbing under her chin in the way she loved. Her eyes closed with pleasure at his gentle touch. Will felt a sudden heaviness in his heart. He dropped to one knee beside them.

"Trobar," he said quietly, "look at me, please."

The giant raised his eyes to Will. The Ranger could see the tears freely running down the big face.

"I think a dog belongs with the person who names her," Will

said, his voice a little unsteady. "Shadow needs you more than she needs me. She's yours."

He saw the disbelief in Trobar's eyes. The giant couldn't speak. He pointed numbly to his own chest, and Will nodded. "Look after her. If she ever has pups, I'll come and take the pick of the litter."

He held out his hand to Shadow, palm facing her, in the motion that told her to stay.

"Stay, Shadow," he said, then he ruffled her head one last time. "Good-bye, girl," he choked, then, unable to bear it any longer, he rose and walked quickly to where Tug waited for him. His vision was blurred, and he fumbled with the reins as he prepared to mount.

The little horse turned his head and looked steadily at his master. I'll make it up to you, the look said.

Will swung into the saddle, and Tug's hooves clattered on the flagstones as he trotted toward the drawbridge. Alyss and Horace, caught by surprise at his sudden exit, hurried to complete their farewells and follow him.

They were half a kilometer down the track before Horace noticed something was missing. He looked around them, his eyes seeking a familiar black-and-white form.

"Where's the dog?" he asked finally.

Will kept looking straight ahead. "I gave her to Trobar," he said.

Then he touched Tug with his heels and cantered on ahead of his friends. He didn't want to discuss it just now.

41

WINTER WAS ON ITS LAST FRIGID BREATHS AS THE THREE OLD friends rode southward. With each passing day, the snow receded further, going from a complete ground cover to isolated patches of melting snow until, eventually, it disappeared completely, and the wet, brown grass was showing the first tinges of green. Will realized with surprise that it would soon be spring.

He and Alyss maintained a façade of friendship, but there was a subtle undercurrent of tension between them. Neither of them realized, however, that the other felt it. Will thought that the slight awkwardness between them was caused by his own reluctance to bring things to a head. He had no idea that Alyss felt exactly the same way.

A perplexed Horace watched his friends as they tiptoed around the subject of the mutual affection they both stubbornly refused to admit.

They're supposed to be the smart ones, he thought, while I'm just a dumb warrior. So if I can see what's going on, why can't they? Sometimes, he reflected, people can be too intelligent for their own good. Too much thinking could confuse things. He felt tempted to knock their heads together, but Horace was not the type to intrude in such a delicate area.

Added to that was the fact that he wasn't completely sure about his own motivation. Recently, he had been seeing more of Evanlyn—as he and Will still thought of Princess Cassandra. In fact, she seemed to be seeking him out more often as a companion. Much as he enjoyed her company, he couldn't help feeling a little awkward about it—as if he were somehow taking advantage of his position to go behind Will's back. He knew that Evanlyn and Will had always had a special relationship and regard for each other. In fact, he sometimes suspected that Evanlyn might enjoy spending time with him because it reminded her of the times when Will was around.

If Will were to develop a strong relationship with someone else—Alyss, for example—it might well clarify his own position with Evanlyn. As a consequence, Horace couldn't be sure that he wouldn't be serving his own interests by intervening between Alyss and Will.

So he kept silent.

Inevitably, the little party came to the point where their paths must diverge. Alyss would head southwest to Castle Redmont. Horace's path lay to the east and Castle Araluen, while Will had received messages from Halt and Crowley that directed him southeast to the Gathering Ground for a debriefing.

More farewells, Will thought gloomily as they stood in a silent group by the triple fork in the road. Alyss's small escort of men-at-arms, released from Macindaw's dungeons when the castle had been retaken, stood a respectful distance apart as the three old friends bade each other farewell.

Will and Horace shook hands, nodded to each other, shuffled

their feet, muttered a few unintelligible words and slapped each other awkwardly on the back several times.

Then they stepped apart. A typical farewell between two young males.

Alyss embraced Horace and kissed him on the cheek.

"Thanks again, Horace." She smiled. "It was getting very boring in that tower. I know if it weren't for you, I'd still be there."

Horace grinned at her. He felt no awkwardness being around the tall, elegant Courier.

"Aaah, you'd have talked your way out of it before too long," he said. They smiled, and she kissed his cheek again.

Then she turned to Will. She looked deep into his eyes, then finally said, "Thank you, Will. Thank you for everything."

He shook his head. "It's me who should thank you, Alyss. You saved my life, after all."

They paused, then she leaned forward, rested her hands lightly on his shoulders and kissed him. But this kiss was not on the cheek. Once, long ago, he had marveled at the softness of her lips. He remembered that time now.

She stepped back, and again they looked into each other's eyes. Then, impulsively, she embraced him, and felt his arms go around her in return. They held each other for a long, long time.

"Write to me, Will," she whispered, and she felt his head nod.

Finally, he got control of his voice and managed to say, "I will. You too."

Then he stepped back, suddenly breaking the contact between them. He nodded to her and to Horace and said in a rushed, unsteady voice, "Good-bye, both of you. I'll miss you both so much. . . ."

He paused, and for a moment Alyss thought he was going to say more. She actually took a half pace toward him. But he finished abruptly, "Damn! I hate farewells!"

He swung up into the saddle and, in the same movement, turned Tug's head to the southeast road. Horace and Alyss watched the horse and rider grow smaller and listened as the sound of hoofbeats faded. Once, Will held up a hand in farewell. But he didn't look back.

He never did.

42

At the Gathering Ground, Halt and Crowley listened to Will's report. He had already sent a written account ahead by messenger, but the two senior Rangers wanted a report in person. So much could be left out of a written report. They nodded as he described events over the evening meal. Crowley was particularly interested in his description of Malcolm's skill as a healer—as well as his ability to create illusions and images and his knowledge of arcane chemicals.

"He could be a handy person to have on call," he said. "Do you think he might be willing to work with us from time to time?"

Will considered the question. "I think he might. So long as we guaranteed to safeguard his privacy. His first priority is to protect the people who have come to him for help."

The Commandant nodded several times. "We'll talk about that later. Right now, I'd better get started on my report for the King."

Halt stood and caught Will's eye.

"Let's take a turn around the Ground," he suggested. "I can't stand to hear Crowley grumbling and groaning as he tries to write reports." Will grinned and rose to join him.

They left Crowley chewing the end of a pencil and muttering to himself and walked in silence for some time. They stopped under a giant spreading oak that marked the end of the Gathering Ground. Instinctively, they sought the concealment of the shadows, avoiding the open ground around them. Part of being a Ranger, Will thought.

"You did well," Halt said finally. "I'm proud of you."

Will looked at his old teacher. The simple words meant more to Will than any number of awards or decorations or promotions. As on so many previous occasions, Halt's face was concealed in the shadow of his cowl.

"Thanks, Halt," he said.

Halt turned to look at him in his turn. Will's features were shadowed too, but Halt was a student of body language, and he saw the boy's shoulders were slumped a little. He'd felt an air of sadness surrounding Will since he had arrived.

"Everything all right?" he asked. He saw the slight shrugging movement of Will's shoulders under the cloak.

"Yes . . . well, no . . . oh, I suppose so."

"Well, there are three answers to choose from," Halt said, not unkindly. He waited, but Will didn't seem about to say anything further. They started walking again. They were silent, but the silence was a companionable one. It took them both back to old times, and they felt a warmth at the memory.

"Halt," said Will eventually, "can I ask you a question?"

"I think you just did," Halt replied, with the faintest hint of a smile in his voice. It was an old formula between the two of them. Will grinned, then sighed and became serious.

"Does life always get harder when you get older?"

"You're not exactly ancient," Halt said gently. "But things have a way of turning out, you know. Just give them time."

Will made a frustrated little gesture with his hands. "I know . . . it's just, I mean . . . oh, I don't know what I mean!" he finished.

Halt eyed him carefully. "Pauline said to thank you for rescuing her assistant," he said. This time, he was sure he saw a reaction. So that was it.

"I was glad to do it," Will replied eventually, his voice neutral. "I think I'll turn in. Good night, Halt."

"Good night, son," Halt said. He chose the last word intentionally. He watched as the dim figure strode away toward the fire, seeing the shoulders straighten as he went. Sometimes, life threw up problems that even the wisest, most trusted mentor couldn't solve for you. It was part of the pain of growing up.

And having to stand by and watch was part of the pain of being a mentor.

43

THERE WAS A SENSE OF DÉJÀ VU ABOUT ARRIVING BACK AT Seacliff Fief. Very little seemed to have changed in his absence. The shadows were lengthening in the late afternoon. The trees that had lost their leaves during the winter were busy regaining them now. There was a feeling of peace and safety about the gentle woods and fields that was in distinct contrast to the past few months.

The ferry was drawn up on the far side of the narrow strip of water that separated Seacliff from the mainland. After he rang the gong, Will waited patiently as the ferryman cast off the mooring ropes and hauled the flat-bottomed boat back across the river.

"No charge for you, Ranger," the man said automatically as Will urged Tug forward, and the little horse's hooves clattered on the ferry's deck. Will allowed himself a wry smile. Halt had taught him to always pay his way. He took out a royal and handed it down to the man.

"One person. One animal. I make that a royal."

The ferryman showed mild interest, glancing around.

"No dog this time?" he asked. Of course, Shadow had been with him when he first arrived at Seacliff, badly injured and riding on the back of his pack pony.

"That's right," Will said, and his tone told the man he didn't wish to discuss the matter. The ferryman shrugged. He was happy not to get into a conversation with a Ranger.

Will dismounted and leaned on the rope rail at the bow of the ferry as the cumbersome boat began to slide across the narrow waterway to the island. The ferryman's comment had highlighted his sense of aloneness. After weeks spent in the company of Horace, Alyss, Gundar and Malcolm, he felt the solitude all the more keenly. Even the comfort of the dog's company was denied him now.

A shaggy head butted him, and he looked around into Tug's eyes.

I'm still here.

He smiled again, then rubbed the rough muzzle and scratched behind the horse's ears.

"You're right, boy," he said. "I've still got you, and thank god for it."

Tug shook his mane in that violent, vibrating way that horses have. It seemed an affirmation of Will's statement. Will glanced around and saw that the ferryman was watching him suspiciously. He had spoken in a low tone, so there was no way the man could have heard what he said, and for that he was grateful. It wouldn't do to have it known that a grim-faced, taciturn Ranger could actually be moping from loneliness. But the fact that he was talking to the horse confirmed the ferryman's superstitious belief that Rangers were black magicians. He turned away and made the warding sign against sorcery. The sooner this one was off his ferry, the better.

The blunt prow grated into the beach. The ferryman tossed a hawser around a pole sunk deep in the sand, hauled it tight and secured it with a quick series of half hitches. Then he unfastened the bow rail, allowing Will to ride off onto dry land.

"Thank you," Will said.

The man didn't reply. He watched as the cloaked and hooded figure disappeared into the first of the trees, made the warding sign again and then settled down to await his next customer.

The stag's head banner still floated above the castle as Will rode out of the trees at the top of the winding path. The village seemed unchanged, and he experienced the same looks as he rode through— a mixture of wariness and interest. Some of the villagers wondered where the young Ranger had been, what he had been doing. Others were more than content not to know anything at all about his movements.

He rode past the inn. Alyss had joked about the pretty innkeeper's daughter who lived here. When Will had first arrived in Seacliff, he had enjoyed the girl's company. Delia was her name, he remembered. But there was no sign of her and he felt vaguely disappointed. He could have done with the sight of a friendly face.

As he rode up to his little cabin in the trees, there was no welcoming curl of smoke from the chimney. Not surprising, he thought. Delia's mother, Edwina, the woman engaged as caretaker, would have had no warning of his imminent return. He unsaddled Tug, rubbed him down and fed and watered him. Then he carried his saddlebags inside.

At least the cabin was clean and tidy. Edwina had obviously dusted while he had been gone. There was no musty, confined smell either, telling him she must have aired the place regularly. He dropped his saddlebags across his bed and returned to the larger room, his footsteps sounding loud in the empty cabin. He glanced down, saw the dog's water and food bowls ranged neatly beside the fireplace. He shrugged sadly, picked them up and took them outside, setting them down on the small veranda, against the wall of the cabin. He didn't want to sit around staring at them through the night.

Oh, for god's sake, snap out of it! he told himself. So you're on your own. That's the way you chose to be. You chose it when you chose to be a Ranger. You chose it again when you wouldn't take the risk of telling Alyss how you felt about her. So stop moping and get on with life. Do something useful. Light a fire and make dinner.

Moving more briskly, he went back inside and began setting kindling in the potbellied stove that stood in the center of the living room. As the tiny yellow flames licked around the wood and grew brighter and fiercer, he felt a strengthening of his resolve. He'd warm the cabin up, light a few lamps and drive the gathering darkness back a little. Then, he decided, he wouldn't make his own meal. He'd wander over to the inn and have dinner. And Delia might be there.

Yes, he thought. That's what he needed. A good dinner, and a pleasant time with an attractive girl. He'd report to the castle tomorrow. But tonight it was time for him to cheer himself up!

He turned as he heard a footstep behind him. For a moment, since Delia was on his mind, he thought that the figure framed in the doorway was her. Then his eyes adjusted and he recognized her mother, Edwina.

"Sir, you're back. I'm sorry, I had no idea you were—"

He waved her apology aside. "Not your fault, Edwina," he told her. "I should have sent word ahead that I was on my way. But I see you've taken care of things while I've been gone."

"Oh, yes, sir. I made sure I opened the place up every few days to let the air in. Place gets musty and moldy else."

She was looking around curiously, and he saw her gaze light on the two bowls that he'd placed outside the front door. He forestalled the next question.

"I left the dog with a friend," he said, and she nodded, not sure whether he thought that was a good or bad thing.

"I'm sure you did, sir. Well, I'll be happy to bring your dinner over directly. Are you hungry, sir?"

Will smiled. "I'm starved—and looking forward to your cooking. But I think I'll eat at the inn. Save a place for me, would you? I'll be over in an hour or so."

"Indeed, sir. We'll be honored to have you. And welcome home." She gave a hint of a curtsy and turned away. Will's spirits rose a little. Amazing what the sight of a friendly face and a few words of welcome could do, he thought.

"Edwina?" he called, and she paused at the edge of the porch, turning back to him.

"Yes, sir?"

"Your daughter, Delia, I trust she's well?" He made sure his voice sounded casual. Her face lit up in a smile of motherly pride.

"Oh, indeed she is, sir! You've heard, have you?"

"Heard? Heard what?"

"Why, the happy news, sir! She was married, not two weeks ago. To Steven, the ferryman's boy."

Will nodded, a smile frozen on his face. At least, he hoped it looked like a smile.

"Excellent," he said. It was an easy word to say with his teeth clenched. "I'm delighted for her."

Some things had changed in Seacliff, he was glad to see. Over the next few weeks, as he settled back into the daily routine of the quiet little fief, he saw a new sense of application and professionalism in the Battleschool. Discipline had been tightened. The drills for apprentices were being properly conducted, and all around there was a greater sense of sharpness. Baron Ergell and his Battlemaster,

Norris, had learned their lesson when they had nearly lost the fief to Gundar's marauding Skandians, he thought.

Of course, when he first reported in on his return, Ergell and Norris had both quizzed him eagerly over the reason for his sudden departure some months earlier. But he told them nothing, politely averting their questions.

"Just a little trouble up north" was all he would say. There was no need for them to know details about the actions of the Ranger Corps. They accepted his reticence as the natural secrecy people associated with Rangers.

He did offer to invite Horace to spend some time at Seacliff, to give tuition on sword drill. The Oakleaf Knight was recognized as one of the Kingdom's best swordsmen, and Will knew he regularly visited Redmont to conduct classes. Norris seized on the idea eagerly.

"I'll write to him," Will promised. In fact, the prospect of having his best friend visit from time to time was a decidedly pleasant one.

Before he had a chance to write the letter, however, he received some interesting items of mail himself. Prominent among several envelopes was a large parcel, carefully wrapped in oilcloth and padded with wool clippings to protect it on its long journey. He looked curiously at the place of origin and was interested to see it came from Castle Macindaw, Norgate Fief.

He unwrapped it eagerly. Inside a case of shaped leather lay a beautifully formed, gleaming mandola. There was a brief note as well.

I felt I owed you this. Perhaps a better instrument will improve your technique. My thanks once more.

Orman.

He inspected the beautiful instrument, his hands running over it reverently. On the head stock was a single word in elegant script: *Gilet.*

Gilet, he thought, the master luthier renowned for creating some of the finest instruments in the Kingdom. Quickly, he tuned it and played a few notes, marveling at the richness of its tone and the silky smoothness of its touch. But, much as he admired the instrument, he felt little desire for music in his life these days. Somewhat sadly, he set the mandola to one side.

There was a letter from Crowley, a general dispatch alerting Corps members to a self-proclaimed prophet and his followers who were working their way through the Kingdom—and bilking people of their savings. In addition, there was a note from Gundar. The skirl had paid a professional scribe to write it for him. The new ship was nearly ready, he said. They had decided to call it *Wolfwill.*

Will smiled to himself. Doubtless one of the Skandians would carve a suitably horrific figurehead for the ship. He hoped Gundar would honor the joking promise he'd made at their parting and come visit one day. He began to tidy away the oilcloth and torn envelopes and found another letter that had been concealed when he tossed the mandola's wrapping aside. He ripped it open without looking to see the sender's name.

His heart lurched as he read the first few words. It was from Alyss.

Dearest Will,

I trust this letter finds you well and happy.

Lady Pauline is keeping me busy, but she gave me some time off to entertain Horace last week. He was visiting for one of his swordsmanship classes. He said to give you his best wishes. While he was here, I told him about a strange dream I keep having. We're back in the tower, and I have Keren's sword in my hand, and he's telling me to hurt you, and I can't refuse him. But then you say the most amazing and wonderful thing, and it completely breaks his hold over me.

    Horace says it might not be a dream. He believes it's a memory. I wish with all my heart that he's right, and that you did say what I think you said. He also told me that people like you and me spend too much time thinking things over and not enough time just coming out and saying them. I think he's right. Write to me please and tell me what you did say. In the meantime, I'll take Horace's advice and just say it myself.

    I love you.

    Alyss.

He dropped the letter on the table, staring at it. He could write to her. A letter would take a week to reach Castle Redmont. But Tug was outside, saddled and ready, and he could be there in less than three days. He dashed to the bedroom and began cramming spare clothes into his saddlebags. He'd leave a message at the inn, telling Baron Ergell he'd be gone for a few days.

Or a week.

His boots rang on the floorboards as he made his way to the door, stepped down from the veranda and slung the saddlebags over Tug's back. The little horse looked up in surprise. There was an energy and a purpose about his master that he hadn't seen for some time. Will was about to mount, then he hesitated. He ran back inside and picked up the Gilet in its case, slinging it over one shoulder. Suddenly there was room for music in his life after all.

Making his way outside again, he paused for a second as he locked the cabin door behind him. He was conscious of an unfamiliar sensation, something he hadn't felt for some time. Then he realized what it was and smiled quietly.

It was happiness.